A SEED MUST FALL

By

Roy Melton

ISBN: 1-4033-1108-0

This book is printed on acid free paper.

1st Books - rev. 05/31/02

Dedication

This book is dedicated to
The Copilot,
My abiding joy.

Introduction

The ancient Greeks embodied the best informed and freest society of their age. They sought truth constantly, diligently, and fearlessly. It was said that they became the world's first true tourists, going to the "earth's edge" for no other reason than simply to see what was there.

Many, disillusioned with their own plethora of deities, searched everywhere for a more sound theology. They were called "god seekers."

Chapter I

In their search for worshipers of the great Celtic god, Wodan, Philo and Biocles had come upon a clearing in the forests populated by the central Germanic tribes. They lay quiet and hidden in a slight swale behind a fallen tree because the activity of the red-bearded men indicated that something important was about to happen. Huge oak logs were stacked in what appeared to be a giant funeral pyre, and before it was prepared a rustic altar of hewn timber.

Philo and Biocles had known each other from childhood. Both were descended from old Greek aristocracy and had been trained in the martial arts as well as the athletic ones. They were in their mid-twenties, full of health and strength. Philo's frame was a slim six feet. He was faster and quicker than Biocles, and he possessed a deep sense of spirituality that fastened Biocles allegiance.

Once when Philo's mother was grieving over her barrenness, Biocles saw Philo prostrate himself before the statue of Artemis and pray. His face shone even though it seemed that his jet black hair, brows, and beard would have shaded it. He had prayed with his dark blue eyes wide open staring into space as though he saw something no one else saw. Within less than a year, Philo's mother had a daughter. They had called her Dorea, the gift.

Biocles was shorter and more muscular. He had a round face, thick locks of curly brown hair and warm brown eyes.

They had left Athens to find what Philo had called "a god greater than Zeus," not gold, not jewels, not women, not fame, but another god. Philo had explained that there must be a more genuine god. Socrates, Plato, and Aristotle had belittled the Greek gods. The whole theological system, they said, was little more than personifying, then deifying, both natural things and natural passions. But, creating this theological void, they had left nothing to fill it. Were better gods to be found? Not many Greeks seemed to care, but to Philo the question screamed for an answer.

As twilight fell, the logs were set afire. Flames shot ten meters into the sky and threw shadows into the forest beyond. Rustic people dressed in coarse cloth and skins drifted into the clearing a few at a time. They were humming low pitched, mesmerizing music and swaying with the sound of it.

As the flames caught hold of more logs, Philo thought this would be a pyre befitting Caesar himself. Some of the smaller logs crumbled and, when they fell into the midst of the inferno, they threw sparks into the air draft that floated first directly up, then out onto a gentle south wind. If these people had not chosen an evening after an April afternoon shower, this would have started a forest fire that would have spread all the way to the Oder River.

Caesar obviously knew nothing of this or he would have dispatched troops for its dispersal. Rome had long since banned such paganism, but Pax Romana had yet to transform the Baltic hinterlands.

Over three hundred people gathered. Amidst their humming and swaying and between the immense fire and the altar, the Druid priests appeared chanting liturgies that Philo and Biocles did not comprehend. They were dressed in drab robes with hoods, universal apparel of the devout.

The fire rose higher, grew hotter, and roared louder.

Biocles lay close to Philo in the moist leaves behind the fallen tree. Now, at last Philo thought, he will see what we have come over a thousand kilometers to see. He knew Biocles had come mostly because he had come.

Biocles looked first at the pagan rites taking place before him, then into the blue eyes of Philo. They were the eyes of a lesser god as far as Biocles was concerned, eyes that conveyed a spirit he hadn't known in any other man, intense, sincere, searching.

They did not speak for a long time as the rites began to take on a heavier tone. Repeatedly they heard Wodan, Wodan, Wodan.

The figure of the subgod, Cernunnon, emerged from the shadows and stood before the altar. He was the essence of fertility to these people. Save for a loin cloth, his only raiment was a deer skin draped over him. Deer antlers were mounted on his head, and his face was painted white as snow except his nose which was a musty brown. He did a pantomime of sowing and reaping, of catching fish, of sun and rain, of hunting experiences and finally of animal propagation. This was done as the robed priests sang the hymns of the great god, Wodan.

The fire rose higher, grew hotter, and roared louder.

Abruptly, the singing stopped and Cernunnon stood still. From behind the fire, away from Philo and Biocles' hiding place at the edge of the forest, came two Druid monks leading a beautiful boy whose hands were bound. The lad was about eleven years old. He wore only a small, white loin cloth. His pale, white skin and blonde hair contrasted with everything around him so that his small figure stood rightly for purity in the midst of evil. He looked terrified. It seemed as though he wanted to cry out, but had found his vocal cords paralyzed.

Biocles thought, surely this isn't going to be what it looks like. No more did he look at Philo.

The monks grasped the child by the shoulders and feet and forced him upon the altar. While they held him, others came and tied the child down with leather tethers. Then they backed away, and the high priest appeared before the altar. He was a tall, lank figure with a shaven face, a large nose and bloodshot eyes. His complexion was ashen and a scowl was fixed upon his countenance. He wore a metal helmet with ox horns protruding from its sides and a black robe with the figure of a snarling red bear sewn across the chest.

All was silent as the high priest closed his eyes and tilted his face to the stars. He began to chant, and as he did, the people also closed their eyes and began to hum, creating a resonance like the inside of a hive of a thousand bees.

On and on this chanting and humming went until the entire clan was in a trance, their spirits given over to a power outside themselves, supposedly Wodan.

The fire rose higher, grew hotter, and roared louder. It reached a roaring crescendo of burning fury. Huge logs glowed cherry red. Millions of skittering, glittering sparks sputtered and swirled in the inferno. Monstrous, angry tongues of red, yellow, and orange lashed at the heavens. The roar was like a hundred mighty winds and the heat, even several steps away, would have been unbearable for him had not the high priest been of such a single mind. Sweat soaked his garments; it dripped from his ears and nose; it ran down his arms and legs.

None of this, however, affected his performance. He drew a dagger from his robe and grasped the haft with both hands. With his arms extended completely, holding the dagger high above his head, he launched into the final rites of human sacrifice.

The child's larynx thawed for an instant. He screamed a high note of agony that pierced the dense forest in every direction. It seemed that this was expected. It didn't break the spell cast on the clan.

Through the shouting, unintelligible chant of the priest, Biocles discerned a faint smile. "Meet me at the boat," he whispered to Philo. Then he sprang to his feet and dashed to the altar while priest and clan stood with closed eyes praying. He knelt before the opposite side of the altar from the priest, drew his knife, and went to work on the leather bindings. The lad looked at him, and he held a finger over his lips asking him to be quiet.

Philo prayed, "Oh, Apollo, god of the pure in heart, give Biocles dexterity and speed."

An enormous log burned in two and fell rumbling from the crest of the fire. It hit with an awesome crash. Simultaneously, the priest's dagger descended in a swift and deadly arc. It struck with a loud thud, and all the people screamed with the pain of sacrifice.

CHAPTER II

When the clan opened their eyes, they gave another scream for they found the dagger had not sunk into young and pliable flesh but into the surface of the wooden altar. They caught a glimpse of a strange figure clad in tailored leather running effortlessly with the weight of the lad into the dark forest, and they beheld a befuddled priest waving his arms and shouting.

A roar erupted from the crowd. The high priest stood ranting about the great displeasure of Wodan. Then a hundred torches lit the edge of the woods and a wild chase was on.

Biocles charged straight for the river until he was almost winded. He curled to his left until he felt he was on the flank of the oncoming mob. There he hid himself and the child in bushes near a small opening in the forest.

Philo thought he would never fully understand Biocles. As he circled away from the mob, he thought of all the times he had seen Biocles throw himself in harm's way with complete abandon. It were as if this was what he was happiest at; this was what he lived for.

Philo crept along through the trees being careful not to expose himself to any of the clan that might not have gone after Biocles. Every sense he possessed was honed for detecting danger, so it was a startling contradiction for him to come upon a vision of Athena, herself. She stood half hidden beside the black trunk of a giant oak tree, but a ray of firelight caught her golden hair and shining face.

Instinctively, Philo knelt before her for a blessing. To his surprise, she reached out to him cautiously and looked directly at him with tear-filled eyes of light violet amethyst that pled for help. As Philo had expected, he saw a face more beautiful than anything he had ever beheld, delicate, but well framed bones, straight teeth, full lips, long thick eye lashes.

Marlena recognized that this man was like the one who carried her brother away. He wore similar clothing, and was clean shaven, and too, he had the look of compassion she had seen on the face of her brother's abductor, for she had not closed her eyes as the others had.

She placed her hand on Philo's shoulder and began to beg him to take her to her small brother. When Philo looked at her without comprehending, she held a hand horizontally at her waist to indicate "short." Then she pointed to herself and by motions such as these convinced Philo that the lad belonged to her.

At first, Philo could not believe that this Athena was human. Now it seemed that not only was she human, but she was asking for his help. But, he asked himself, how could this be the mother of the lad? She was not old enough. Surely she could not be more than nineteen. Maybe, in the darkness, he had misjudged the child's age. Then it occurred to him that this could be a sister. There was no doubt that she wanted to be with the boy. He took her hand and energy exploded in his body. It was wonderful that she, indeed, was not a goddess.

Biocles placed a hand gently over the lad's mouth and placed the index finger of his other hand across his own lips. He put his arm around him and held his trembling body close. The red bearded men of the clan were coming with their torches and shouting.

As Biocles expected he had placed himself away from the center of the mob. But as he and the lad lay silently, a single Celt approached the small thicket. He drew near and thrust his torch in their direction. Closer and closer he came until Biocles knew he and the lad would be discovered.

Biocles picked up a rotted limb and hurled it beyond the Celt. It fell crashing into the brush, and the Celt heard this noise behind him. He turned away for an instant and Biocles was upon him before he could cry out.

The Celt was prone upon the ground with Biocles' knee in his back and both arms around his neck. He turned the Celt's head farther than its normal limit and heard the cervical vertebrae snap. Then he dragged him to the bushes and covered his body with leaves.

Biocles had an inborn sense of justice that he never questioned. He had not stopped to think of the ethical problem of exchanging the boy's life and perhaps his own for that of the strong Celtic man with the red beard. He had not reasoned that the Celt was doing what he perceived to be the right thing. He had not come to Germania to fight. He certainly had not come to kill, but he had taken up the boy's cause and that was that. Now all his faculties, mind and strength, were about saving the boy's life.

The hundred torch bearers went far into the woods, circled and returned. Some came close to Biocles' hiding place as they returned to their village, but none looked directly into the thicket as their unfortunate countryman had. When they were safely by, Biocles took the lad's hand and led him through the forest.

Philo and Biocles had purchased the small boat from tribesmen down river. When they had approached the area of the Wodan worshipers, they had hidden this craft in tall reeds on the river bank next to a large outcropping of boulders that could be located in dim light if necessary. It was this precaution that probably saved their lives.

As Biocles and the boy approached the area of the boulders, they moved cautiously. Two or three steps then listen; two or three steps then listen. It was a beautiful, clear night. A half moon shone almost directly overhead. The soft breeze moved newly forming leaves and grass. Frogs croaked along the river's edge and crickets sang in the grass. Occasionally, an owl hooted or a night hawk screeched.

Biocles separated all these sounds from the ones he wanted to hear. Had the Celts sent some of their men ahead this far? Had Philo gotten here before he did? He was about to decide to stop and wait when a low whisper came from the reeds nearby, "Minotaur."

It was Philo. He had given Biocles the nickname after the battle at Corinth when Biocles, in a losing cause, had destroyed a whole squad of Roman soldiers. Minotaur was the mythical monster of Crete, half man, half bull. Philo appeared to have thought it was fitting. Biocles thought it unbecoming to his "gentle" nature, but accepted it knowing the term was bestowed in admiration. No one but Philo ever addressed him so.

"Phil," whispered Biocles. Phil was not only short for Philo, but also was the beginning of "phileo," brotherly love. Then both showed themselves. Their wards threw themselves at one another.

"Marlena," cried the lad.

"Arn," said the beautiful blonde goddess. They buried themselves in each other's embrace.

"Looks like they're already acquainted," said the startled Biocles. "Where did you find her?"

"As near as I can tell she's his sister," explained Philo.

"Have you seen her in the light? Is she as pretty as I think she is?"

"She is as beautiful as Athena herself. In fact, at first I thought she was Athena."

"Ah, Phil, always finding the ladies, even in far away places. I don't know how you do it."

"Don't make light. Believe me, this lady is very special."

"Then I take it you want to take her with us."

"She would most likely be killed as the next reasonable substitute for her brother if she returned to her people. They believe in sacrificing the best."

"Do you think the boat will float with the four of us?"

"It will have to," said Philo. "You got us into this by grabbing that boy. Now you must say a prayer to Poseidon that he will keep this small craft afloat."

"Oh mighty Poseidon, god of all waters …"

"Say it to yourself, we have to leave this place."

"Now, in the dark?"

"It's the only lead we'll have on those barbarians, my Minotaur. You must say a special prayer for the rapids. In the dark they'll be close to impossible."

There in the soft moonlight each of the four introduced himself by pointing a finger into his chest and saying his own name.

"Philo."

"Biocles."

"Marlena."

"Arn."

These four crammed into the boat just big enough to hold them. Biocles opened a small pack he had in the corner of the boat and removed his extra tunic. Then he helped Arn put it on. Arn fit like a pea in a pumpkin shell, but at least he was warm. They pushed through the reeds at the river's edge and headed downstream. Philo and Biocles paddled quietly.

They were young men but they were accustomed to danger. In their youth, they had wrestled one another at the palaestra where Biocles had prevailed more often than not. Then as Ephebes, they trained at the Academy. It was in those days while training as soldiers that Biocles first discerned the depth of Philo's soul for he never seemed pleased at besting another man in a sword fight or beating him in a race. At his best, he had surpassed them all, but there was never an inkling of pride that showed in it.

Then the prayer about the baby sister had happened and Biocles began to regard his friend as one having his own private audience before the gods. Time and again, upon beholding the acts of Philo, Biocles had repeated to himself a line from Aristophanes, "Where he sets his altar, there the gods alight."

Philo knew nothing of this. He would have been appalled. He did often wonder how Biocles seemed confident in the midst of danger while he was much more nervous than he revealed. Many times in battle, he had felt the impulse to retreat only to have Biocles plunge into the fray with abandon.

Philo and Biocles knew the power of moving water. They had seen comrades torn limb from limb in rapids such as those they faced.

They thanked Apollo for the light of the moon as they came to the end of the mirror surfaced deep pool and heard the roar ahead.

"Can you see the vee?" yelled Philo.

"There to the left," shouted Biocles.

With their rustic paddles, they swung the boat left and headed into what experience had told them was the deepest part of the rough water ahead. Beyond the v-shaped smoothness, however, were only boulders and whitewater.

When it came to the whitewater, the little boat began to bounce. Philo and Biocles fought to keep the tiny craft straight. If it should get turned sideways amidst these swells and boulders, they would surely capsize. The roar was so great that they had to shout as loud as possible to be heard. Arn hid himself in his sister's arms as spray wet them all. The boat dipped time after time and took on water. In spite of the strong Biocles and the agile Philo with their paddles, the awesome power of the water current took control. The boat swirled and hit a boulder. Marlena and Arn clung to the boat with all their strength. Biocles used all his effort to keep the boat from striking the boulder solidly. When he pushed away with his paddle, it snapped and Biocles was thrown overboard. Beneath the churning waters, he fought to resurface.

The tough leather clothes he wore were both a blessing and a curse. They saved his body from laceration on the rocks, but the weight of them, being water soaked, was like an anchor pulling his tired body relentlessly toward the bottom of the river. Fortunately, the water was not deep. When his lungs, then, were about to explode, he did indeed bump the bottom. Inverting his body, he bent his legs and used them to spring upwards. Almost immediately he popped into fresh air. Disoriented, he had been struggling to the side and even downward beneath the water. Now he opened his mouth wide and inhaled with a gasp.

When he surfaced, he didn't see the boat. All he could do was try to stay alive by floating with the current and avoid getting smashed into the rocks.

Philo was shouting for Biocles, trying to locate him in the churning waters. Arn had released the embrace of his sister and he, too, was looking for Biocles.

They hit another rock and Arn tumbled over the side. His cry of surprise was drowned by the water. Marlena screamed like a wounded animal. She grabbed his arm and held on.

Philo was fighting the water with his paddle and shouting for Biocles. Then he saw the small body of Arn hanging from the boat. Marlena clung to him with both hands and screamed for help. The current tugged at Arn, but Marlena clutched him tight. She turned her face to Philo, and the moonlight shone directly upon it. Her teeth were clenched and the determination of an Olympic wrestler was in her eyes. Wet hair strung down her cheeks and onto her shoulders. Her body trembled from the effort she exerted. Arn gripped her arm so hard that he brought blood where his fingers dug in.

Philo knew he couldn't spring directly for the lad or he would capsize the boat. He spread his body along the bottom of the craft, distributing his weight. The boat hit a huge swell, and Arn's body jerked.

Philo could see Marlena's grip tighten. She seemed to hold Arn with more than physical strength. It were as though all she had was in peril. It were as though her own life hung there from the side of the boat with Arn. If Arn were to be swallowed up into the waters, then so would she.

Philo brought his chest into Marlena's face and reached for Arn. He grabbed one wrist and Arn's hair, then he pulled with Marlena. Arn kicked the water, and his little body popped back into the boat.

The three lay tangled in an exhausted mass on the bottom of the little boat. They hardly noticed that they were spinning into calmer water.

A hundred meters downstream Philo recovered and screamed for Biocles. He guided the boat to the safety of a small gravel bar as the waters calmed. Then he jumped from the boat and beached it. It was about to sink from the water they had taken. The three fugitives fell exhausted upon the smooth gravel. Philo prayed to Zeus. Marlena and Arn turned their heads to stare at him blankly. Then, they gave weak smiles to one another. They were not consoled by prayer, but they were glad to be alive.

Philo looked at their drenched bodies and wondered how much emotional shock the young lad could absorb. Arn had had enough in one evening to last a lifetime. But will for survival is very strong in the young, and Arn, even in his youth, appeared to possess a stout heart.

"Phil," came a weak voice from the water.

Philo looked toward the sound and saw an extra large knot on a log drifting downstream. The knot slowly took the form of Biocles' head. Again came the soft voice, "Phil."

"Hang on old friend," shouted Philo. He waded into the river and pulled Biocles safely ashore. "You're in league with Poseidon, Minotaur. A little rapids 'll never get you."

Biocles could not answer.

CHAPTER III

No adult in the village of Kresboden slept that night. In the log meeting lodge on the east side of the central clearing, Daga, the priest of Wodan, organized a search party.

The place was lit with small oil lamps scattered along the walls. The crude windows of the lodge were closed and in the giant stone hearth a small fire was lit to ease the bite of the spring chill. The aromas of wood and oil smoke blended with that of the moist earthen floor. Most of the clan sat on wooden benches. Some, however, too excited to rest, milled along the side and back walls. No one there could remember such a crass, sacrilegious, insolent thing ever happening at Kresboden. Curses and whispers of astonishment were being exchanged.

So distracted was the entire group that no one took notice of the quiet red giant, Otto. Unlike the rest, he sat stroking his flaming, bushy beard with a puzzled, but not totally displeased, look on his ruddy face.

Daga, still dressed in his ritual costume, stood in the front of the lodge before the hearth and spoke with more control than he had the moments immediately after the theft of the sacrificial child. Still intense anger seethed from his dark countenance.

"We have learned that Marlena, Arn's sister, has disappeared. She will slow the progress of the stranger who took the child if she is with him. Perhaps she has hired this scoundrel to do this dirty work. It will make no difference. We'll catch them all, and Wodan will have a greater offering than we had anticipated."

Cheers arose. The clansmen stomped their feet and beat on the wooden benches.

"There's no doubt that these infidels have gone east through the forest. In the dark night since the moon has set, we have not been able to track them. In the morning you men will divide into three groups and fan out toward the east. One group will find the tracks. Now, Karl, you will take the first group directly east. Herman, you will take a group southeast, and Otto, will take a group northeast. You will take provisions for three days in case you are delayed. You'll leave at first light. Don't wander unnecessarily and smudge the tracks. Once tracks are found, you must move rapidly. Do you have questions?"

Otto stood. He was a giant, standing six and one half feet with a chest like a bear's and arms and legs like huge tree limbs. His red curly hair came to his shoulders and a bushy beard covered most of his face. Green eyes flashed from deep sockets. Otto was the tribe's most respected warrior. He had killed so many men that he had quit counting. He did not feel dependent upon Wodan, but he knew that worship was important to clan life so he never overstepped religious boundaries.

"Revered one, shall we kill the intruder or must we bring him back?"

"Arn and Marlena must be returned. The intruder must be killed for his sacrilege. If he is trouble you may kill him on the trail, but you must return evidence. Bring his head to us. It will go into the fire to quench the wrath of Wodan."

Otto took his seat to calls of approval.

"Now, O, protector of our fatherland," the Priest began to pray, "have mercy on us for letting your offering slip away. Show us the way the infidel escapes and give us wisdom to capture him and appease thy wrath."

And so the evening slipped away. The men chosen to find Biocles rested until dawn, then they gathered a few provisions and left.

Dawn found the fugitives except for Philo still asleep on the gravel bar. He had imposed watch duty upon himself and stayed alert most of the night. When the mist on the river turned from midnight blue to pale gray, he had his first daylight view of the sleeping face of Marlena. She, as did Arn and Biocles, dozed on willow branches Philo had cut hastily the evening before. Her flaxen locks moved gently in the morning breeze and brushed the velvet of her cheek. All night long Philo had anticipated the sight. He was not disappointed. How, he thought, could such pristine beauty rise from such a backward people. He stared for long minutes until he was captivated completely. The goddess in repose, the essence of sweetness, the essence of beauty, perhaps the essence of love, what would Pindar have said? No matter, it was moments like this that made poets of clods. One didn't need words to know he was experiencing living poetry.

A fish splashed in the river nearby. A morning lark sang. The gray mist began to take on a cast of yellow, and Philo knew they must go. He shook Biocles.

"Awaken mighty warrior. Your work has just begun if you plan to truly rescue these heathen siblings."

"Oh no. Every bone in my body hurts. I think I must have bounced off every rock in that cursed river."

"Don't condemn the river. If we get out of here, it's the only way we can make it."

"I suppose you're right," said Biocles, then more awake. He went to the river's edge and threw water in his face. He drew the small boat completely ashore and turned it over to empty the water they had taken the night before.

Philo took his ax and chopped a sturdy tree limb to replace the paddle Biocles had destroyed on the boulder. He mumbled to himself, "The Minotaur has saved my life again. How many times has it happened! Now he has saved the lives of these too, and it is as though he has done nothing at all."

"We must go," Biocles was speaking gently to Arn and Marlena.

Philo and Biocles had studied some of the language of these people as they had proceeded north. They dared not try their tongues at it the night before when they might have been misunderstood, but now Biocles found his simple words were perceived.

Arn began to pour forth phrases by the dozen.

"That's what I was afraid of," he said to Philo. "Now he thinks I know the whole language."

"Don't worry, he'll soon know better," said Philo with the first laugh he had in two days. They both began to laugh. They put their arms around one another's shoulders and began to sing a song of Greek victory.

For their part, Arn and Marlena thought they had surely been rescued by forest nymphs. As children they were told stories about them. These friendly creatures showed themselves only to the pure of heart and only when there was a desperate need. Marlena had not believed the stories until now.

The boat trip that day was more pleasant than the one the night before. Philo, however, would not let them stop until dusk. He wanted as much distance as possible between them and their pursuers. The spring sun warmed them as Philo and Biocles guided their little craft steadily down stream.

Marlena pointed out landmarks along the way and repeated their Germanic names. There were steep rock cliffs, single huge boulders, marshes, brooks coming into the main stream from this side and that, huge trees that seemed to stand alone above the others, and springs that flowed from the cliffs to form small waterfalls.

She described these with expressions of simplicity and motions of grace. Her eyes alternately widened with wonder then narrowed with fear. She gestured, arms extended or wide open. She craned her slender neck to see further like a child beholding these sights for the first time.

All of this Marlena performed without the slightest pretense, totally unaware of her beauty. Biocles listened with interest. Philo was enchanted.

It is a friendly stream that has gravel bars because the smooth pebbles of these places, washed frequently by high-water, are always clean and provide good camp sites. They found such a place and hid their boat in the nearby willows. Then all went into the woods to search for berries and edible roots. There would be no fire and therefore no fresh meat that night. They were not yet far enough from the village.

While they ate their berries, they sat on driftwood logs in the dim moonlight that filtered through the trees. Philo insisted that they speak in whispers.

"You have done well, little one," Biocles said to Arn. "You found more berries than the rest of us. No doubt you know these woods." He pointed to the berries and gave a broad smile that revealed childlike dimples.

Arn threw his arms around Biocles and gave him a tremendous hug, then sat on his lap. Biocles hugged back. He could hardly believe the immediate affection of this child. He had no idea he was equated with the most kindly of Celtic spirits.

By now Arn knew that the Greeks didn't understand his language so he spoke to Marlena. "Do you think they will go away when we're out of danger?"

"I don't know, Arn. Maybe we'll be in danger for a long time. You know the high priest won't be satisfied until we're captured."

"Do you think they'll try to kill Philo and Biocles? Do you think Philo and Biocles can be killed? Are they spirits immortal?"

"We'll have to wait, Arn. For now let's be thankful. I'm just glad to be with you and for you to be alive."

With this Arn got up and went to her. She kissed him on the cheek and held him close.

Philo said to Biocles, "I'll take the first watch."

What he watched mostly was Marlena.

Men who served under Otto knew that he would not only stand with them in battle, but that also he would use good common sense in strategy. Now he spread his men to comb the area along the river until they found not one, two, or three but four sets of tracks. Who could the fourth person be? Then they lost the tracks in the reeds near the river. Surely, thought Otto, they had not taken to the river in the dark. The rapids were only a short distance. They would not have survived them.

So Otto's group searched below the rapids. When they found no signs of wreckage, Otto assumed their quarry had gone either across the river some way or had circled back and crept up river staying in the shallows. Of course, they could have lost the tracks as the group came out of the small marsh. If they had gone up river, they would be the responsibility of Karl or Herman. So he sent some of his men across the river. Most of the group went parallel to the river but away from it to try to pick up the most likely trail. Otto was cautious, however. He sent two men down the river along the bank and three others down stream in a boat.

Around midnight, while Biocles snored and Arn slept peacefully in Marlena's arms, Philo heard a bush move just ashore of the gravel bar. Quickly he placed a hand over Biocles' mouth and put his index finger across his lips to shush him when he awoke. Both sat silently and listened.

Another bush moved not fifteen steps away. Philo rose and pointed to Biocles then to one side of the thicket. Then he motioned that he would go to the other side. The willow thicket grew in a small stretch of shallow water that lay behind the gravel bar and in front of the shore bank that rose above the river surface. To one side of the thicket another willow moved. There must be two men coming, thought Philo. He turned to hold two fingers above his head, but Biocles had already disappeared into the thicket. There was a gentle splash to Philo's left. He froze. Then, there was the smell of heavy sweat on the breeze. He looked directly upwind and a huge shadow moved. Philo struck with his knife, and the warrior cried out. Almost immediately a huge weight fell upon Philo's back, and he stumbled into the shallow water twisting and fighting the second Celt. Philo's head was forced under the water. He choked and gasped for air, but he inhaled water instead. Then all was darkness.

Biocles came to the splashing with his ax raised. He split the skull of the giant on top of Philo then dragged Philo to the gravel bar. Arn and Marlena forgot caution and cried out when they heard the scream of the first warrior.

Biocles placed Philo, belly down, across one of the driftwood logs. He let Philo's head dangle near the gravel then emptied him by smacking him on the back. Philo coughed up water and sputtered himself back to consciousness. Then Biocles lowered him to the bar and knelt beside him.

"We nearly lost you, old Phil. I thought you knew better than to let a hulk like that blind side you."

Philo's head was ringing. He couldn't hear Biocles and couldn't have answered him if he had. He continued to cough for life.

Arn ran and hugged Biocles' muscular leg. He gawked at the reviving Philo.

Marlena stared in awe of the two men. These were not nymphs. These were human. They were men who loved each other, and they were men who for some strange reason had given themselves to rescuing her and her brother. For the first time, she considered the fact that at least one of them was a man whom she could love. Well, she could love them both, but not the same way.

CHAPTER IV

It was not a good report that was brought to the oaken lodge in the village of Kresboden that night. For two full days the three search parties had patrolled to little avail. Otto alone could report anything positive.

The council of Druid priests, five in all, sat before the huge stone fireplace in chairs of polished, light birch. The night was warm so the trap door windows were flung open and there was no fire. A gentle breeze blew through the windows, circulated air in the lodge, and caused the flames in the oil lamps to flicker from time to time. It was not a time for assembly of the whole village, so only the search parties were present. The mood was tense.

Otto stood before the council giving his report. He gestured with his huge arms in smooth, confident motions. Covered in red hair as they were, these arms were hard to ignore. Otto had everyone's attention, and he knew it. His voice was not loud, but solid, clear.

"The fugitives have gone down river. Another person has joined them, probably a man judging from the depth and size of his footprint. We have eliminated escape across the river or circling back, also up river or around our village."

"I sent five men down river. The three in the boat have reported no sign, but the two ashore have not returned. I'm afraid harm has come to them. As we have seen by our companion found dead in the bushes, we are not dealing with weaklings."

"Enough, enough," shouted Daga. He bent forward placing one bony, gray hand on the front of the chair handle. He thrust his other arm into the air causing his robe to collapse around his shoulder. This revealed the entire length of his arm, a knotty dead cypress branch. He pointed to the door. "We must decide what to do. Out with all of you."

So Otto, Herman, and Karl took their leave, and the priestly council conversed into the night. Before daybreak the next morning, they called for the three to appear before them.

Daga, as usual, sat in the largest birch chair in the center of the council. As Otto, Herman, and Karl stood before him, he drew himself up to his most erect stature and summoned his most authoritative voice, a strident sound at best.

"We haven't changed our minds about the stolen sacrifice or those infidels who chose to desecrate the altar of Wodan. They must be found and punished. But, since these heretics have over a two-day lead, we anticipate the search for them will be long and difficult. We don't choose to weaken the defensive capability of our village by sending a troop after them but rather choose to send two devout men, strong, and courageous to avenge us. These men will dedicate their entire lives, if necessary, to avenge Wodan. They will seek every ally, use every skill of battle, go to the ends of the earth, and do whatever is necessary to catch these foul pagans. Is this understood?"

The three warriors nodded solemnly.

"We have chosen Otto and Karl for this sacred task. Tonight we will have a dedication service so that the power of Wodan will go with you. Now rest and prepare for your journey."

Otto had assumed he would be chosen. Between Herman and Karl he had no preference for a companion. Both were good fighting men but, unfortunately, a bit simple minded. Otto could foresee many days ahead when any decision made would have to be his alone. The time would be tolerable enough if he could force himself to look away from the skinny Karl as much as possible. The plain-faced and weak- eyed Karl had the unconscious habit of picking at his nose. Otto would try to appoint his hands to other tasks.

24

The four fugitives, still floating down the river, were nearing the small village where Philo and Biocles had purchased the boat. Philo insisted they wait, hidden in a willow flat, until after dark. No one in the village was to see them. When darkness came, they paddled quietly to a well used area along the bank and disembarked. There the Greeks punched large holes in the bottom of the craft, loaded it with stones then pushed it into deep water. They stood watching until the little boat that had served them so well sank out of sight. Then they blended their tracks with those of the villagers, crept through the patch of dwellings, and headed for the mountains.

Philo was edgy for a night or two, and then he relaxed. Biocles seemed never to have a nervous moment. His faith in Philo's discretion appeared complete. If his experiences bordered on death, no one could discern any effect on his disposition.

Beside a small, clear brook secluded in highland forests Philo decided that they could at last rest. They cleared a small area near a deep pool and made a little fire.

Marlena made it clear that she wanted to bathe while the men hunted hares for supper. Arn was eager to know how the Greek bows functioned so he went along with Biocles and Philo. He wondered if they could hit a rabbit at thirty paces. When the hunt had proven successful, he begged to shoot the arrows.

"Please, I will be careful." He pled with his pale green eyes and made motions to the Greeks that they understood.

"I wonder when Celtic boys begin to hunt," said Biocles.

"He must be about right. You can see his heart is in it. Why don't we teach him? It will help us pass the time on our journey."

25

Communication between the Greeks and the Celts improved as the days went by.

"We'll begin to show you some things after supper," Biocles told Arn. "But first we eat, then we must also bathe."

Philo and Biocles were surprised when Marlena took the two rabbits from their hands.

"I'll clean and cook the rabbits," she said. "Give me your knife. You go to the pool. I want you to smell better at supper," she laughed.

Arn held his nose then pointed toward the pool. The Greeks laughed, too. It was the first laugh they all had together.

The roasted rabbit smelled wonderful to fugitives hungry for meat. The Celts watched with wonder as Philo and Biocles took small vials from their pouches and salted it.

Arn and Marlena tore at the rabbit like ravenous wolves. Philo and Biocles ate heartily, but with care.

Arn, with his last mouthful still not swallowed, strings of the meat hanging between his spaced teeth, and a leg bone in his hand, renewed his plea to shoot arrows.

Just before twilight, Biocles began to work with Arn showing him the art of using the bow and arrows. Philo and Marlena sat on logs beside the small campfire and talked. Marlena's long, blonde tresses were beginning to dry from her afternoon dip. Now and again she fluffed her hair and held it momentarily above her head as if to let her smooth and slender neck dry, a swallow preening. Philo planted his elbows on his knees and rested his chin in his hands, making no attempt to conceal his admiration.

Marlena seemed pleased to let him watch for a minute. Then she dropped her gaze from the sky and looked directly into Philo's eyes. The look was one of marvel on her own part, too much for Philo to assimilate. He dropped his gaze to the ground and with a stick drew a map in the dirt.

"Here is Kresboden," he stabbed the stick into the earth. "We have come mostly east since leaving Kresboden. Soon we will turn south." The marks were being made. "We'll have mountains, then a broad river, the Danube, then we will descend into the Hellenistic territories. It's a long journey, but we can make it. Biocles and I live in Athens, home of the greatest gods and world center of culture."

"Ath-, Ath-, Athens."

"Yes, yes, Athens."

Marlena pointed to herself. "Kresboden." Then she pointed at Philo, "Athens."

"Exactly," beamed Philo. He rose from the log, went to her, took her face in both hands and turned it up to him. "You are the most beautiful human I have ever seen," he said. Then he kissed her lightly on the nose and turned away. He wondered if she could tell that he had loved her from the first moment he saw her, heartbroken, at the edge of the forest.

The lower eastern side of the Bavarian Alps burst into colorful splendor as spring began. Wild flowers without number covered the open meadows. Blue Gentians were the conspicuous part of the flora but as though one color couldn't express all their loveliness, they also sprang forth in patches of purple, white and yellow. One didn't have to wander far in any direction to find crocus, narcissus, and alpine roses. It took a closer look to see the diminutive, low growing saxifrage with their basal clumps of leaves and tiny flower clusters on short stems, but they were there, especially in the more rocky soil. White, yellow, pink, and purple, they could make their own display without help if need be. Rare white edelweiss with its long leaves and star-shaped blossoms grew in the higher elevations. Low evergreens took on a lighter hue of new growth. Grass sprang forth from every crevice between stones and blanketed the leas with green, giving the flowers a natural contrast.

Amidst all this beauty, the four fugitives, now with hiking sticks, traipsed along the side of a mountain exchanging songs of their own culture. Biocles burst forth the scolions of Athens.

"By Zeus, the gods have outdone themselves," he declared. "I've never seen a place so beautiful even in the hills of home. Finally, I have a reason to thank you for this trip."

"Aw, come on, Minotaur, you've loved every minute, except maybe the dunking in the rapids."

"Tell me again why we've done this."

"If it never made sense to you in the first place, why do you think it would make sense now?"

"I have an entirely new aspect on it. I suppose the new god you were looking for isn't Wodan."

Philo's blue eyes opened wide, and he gave a quick frown of deep thought. "I can't be sure, but I don't think so. We've challenged him and he hasn't struck us down."

"What do you mean by that, Phil? What difference does it make? How could you accept a god who demands the sacrifice of small children?"

"He may not demand this. This may be only the imagination of the priests who supposedly serve him. Aren't we told that in the early days of our own civilization our forefathers sacrificed humans to all manner of gods? We aren't far away from the same practice."

"That's the way with you, Phil. You confuse my thinking with the facts."

Both had a good laugh. It had been that way for years.

The fathers of Philo and Biocles owned adjacent farms on Mount Hymettus, one of the hills just outside Athens. It was there that the boys had met, played, and worked together. They had learned how to care for olive trees and tend sheep. They had first ridden horses there and followed after the hunting dogs.

When they were teenagers, they became interested in the way the bee keepers extracted honey from their hives. Hymettan honey was the most prized in the world. The reason was that in gathering the honey, the apiarists never smoked the hives.

The smoking settled the bees so that the keeper wouldn't get stung. But it also gave a slight taint to the honey. Both Philo and Biocles had their own ideas of how the Hymettans got by without smoking. Biocles believed there had to be a slow and gentle movement to the keepers hands. Philo thought the bees could simply smell fear the same as all animals. When they did, they attacked the fearful.

One late spring afternoon in a storm, lightning struck a tree near the hives of Alcandor, Philo's father. It toppled onto the hives, breaking them and knocking the bees along with the combs in all directions.

The boys came upon this chaos and tried to restore order as well as they could. The ground and parts of the tree limbs as well as parts of the hives were a mass of angry bees. As Philo and Biocles retrieved one of the hives and began placing honey combs back into it, they became covered with bees, too. Both were so concerned with the bees that they paid little attention to themselves until the remaining hive was once again filled with honey combs and bees.

As they raised their eyes, they were amazed at what they saw and felt. Both were covered with bees. With wide eyes, they looked at one another unbelieving. Then they began to scoop the bees away from one another in large handfuls and place them in the hive. Not a word was spoken.

When both were relatively free of the bees, they walked away. As they stood in the area beyond the hives, they began to remove the stingers left in their skin. Philo had four, Biocles six.

"I don't feel too bad," said Biocles. "I would have thought this many stings would kill me."

"Maybe we are all right because we were thinking more of the bees than ourselves, and they could tell it. We should have been stung hundreds of times," said Philo.

"Yeah, can you imagine how angry you would be if the wind blew your house down," said Biocles with a laugh.

They both began to laugh at the bees, themselves, the world. They just laughed and in laughing, they learned they had a deep friendship.

Biocles had surrendered his bow to Arn for the time being. It seemed that the lad's strength increased daily, and by now he could draw the bow sufficiently to penetrate a larch sapling with the sharp arrows. They were down the hillside hunting for rabbits. Occasionally they found a chamois or ibex, but rabbits remained their usual prey. It would be a while before Arn could hit a flying partridge or grouse with the arrows, but he surprised Biocles by bringing them down with hurled stones.

Philo and Marlena sat in the soft, green grass of an Alpine lea. Marlena's knees were tucked against her breast and enfolded by her arms. Philo lay propped on one elbow trying not to stare at her. Instead, he looked west at the awesome limestone cliffs, tors, and crags of the Alps highest peaks. Snow never left the crests of these formidable giants, but now there was melting at the lower elevations so that there were towering waterfalls in infinite variations. For a long time they sat wanting to drink in each other and wanting to behold the beautiful mountains.

"Can you believe," said Philo, "that once a general of Carthage, one Hannibal Barca, marched an army of over 100,000 through that barrier of cliffs and chasms? Some say he found a secret passage. Today, no one can find his path."

"It was my countrymen, the Celts, who guided him through," said Marlena. "I know you think we are barbarians, but my people are wise in many ways, and they hate the Romans."

"I haven't so much as heard a whisper of such a thing," said Philo, his eyes wide in wonder. "It's true that in the great halls of learning in Athens and Rome the Celts are considered to be barbarians, but I must tell you that you are the farthest thing from a barbarian that I have ever known. As a matter of fact, when I first saw you I,

I ..."

Immediately Philo recalled that Marlena thought little of deity and religion. "Well, let's just say that from the very first I have thought that you were wonderful."

Then, seeing the blush of pink beginning to rise in Marlena's cheeks, he knew he should change the subject. It would scare her to death if she knew how much he cared for her. "I'm sure you know that Hannibal took battle to the very gates of Rome."

"I've heard. But no one seems to know why he didn't assault Rome. Do you know what happened?"

"I've heard the plush life of the Po River Valley weakened his resolve. Perhaps he found a woman with whom he fell very much in love. At any rate he hesitated, then faltered. The Romans regrouped and eventually drove him into the sea. Later they burned Carthage and plowed it under, actually salting the ground as an example to all who would rise against them."

"Do you think a man could love a woman enough to go aside for her at the point of accomplishing his greatest goal?" she asked looking him directly in the eyes.

He withered. "I, I, I've heard of such love," he said. "But the women were exceptional. Someday I'll tell you the story of Helen of Troy. For now, I would like to know what your family was like."

Marlena sensed that Philo was evading her question. Why? Weakness? Embarrassment? She could see it in his eyes. She knew he liked her, but she didn't know how much.

"My father was a great warrior. He was killed by a Roman search party. It was said that he took most of the Romans with him."

"I never had occasion to know how fierce he was in battle. I only knew he was strong and gentle. He always brought Arn and me little gifts whenever he was away from home for very long. He would lift us high into the air and tell us, 'Someday you will be this tall and all the men will love you, or all the people will fear you if it were Arn.' Then he would hug us until we almost popped."

"Mama couldn't stand it when he died. She grieved until she starved herself. Arn and I were too young to understand. One morning we awoke and we were alone in the world. The village people are good, of course. They brought us all we needed to live on. I was old enough to care for Arn so they left us to our cabin. We clung to one another and survived. Two years later, the priests came and said now they must take Arn, too. I wanted to die with him."

Tears flowed down Marlena's cheeks as they had that first night at the ceremony. She knew she couldn't tell Philo her whole story, not now. Since those fateful nights over a year ago she hadn't been able to stand the sight of a man. Philo and Biocles were changing that. She looked up at Philo and smiled through the tears.

Philo wanted to take her into his arms and cover her face with kisses, but there were things he must know first and things he must tell first. Yes, those things that surely must make her run away. How could he start to tell? These things would have to come on another day. This was too bright and happy a day to spoil.

"What about your god Wodan?" he said. "Are you happy with him? Does he bring power and peace into your people's lives?"

Marlena's face straightened.

"Power, yes. Didn't our people defeat and destroy the three Roman legions of Varus, the great Roman general. Have any other people done such a thing? We remain free of Roman rule. Wodan has breathed his fighting fire into our warriors. They are both brave and cunning."

"But you ask also of peace. That's strange. The only peace I've found has been in the home of my father and mother. They were strong, but they were also kind and loving. Wodan is surely not like that. Our people fear him with a great dread."

"Exactly," said Philo. "You have put into words what I've been trying to tell Biocles for weeks."

Then it occurred to him that he and Marlena were communicating almost completely.

"You are perceptive. You've learned this much Greek in these short weeks."

"You mustn't be impressed," Marlena said. "I have a little gift of listening well, that's all."

"Would you close your eyes for a little while?" Philo asked.

"Why?"

"Please don't ask why."

"No, I must, why?"

"Because I want to look at you, and I would be embarrassed if you saw all that will be in my eyes."

"I'll shut them, but all the time I'll be guessing, you know. The guesses may be worse than what is really there."

"You misunderstand. It is not 'how bad' I wish you not to see, but 'how much.'"

Fronds of evergreens made warm beds that night. Philo lay staring at the stars. It was true, he thought, the Germanic tribes had caught those legions of Roman troops in the swamps of Teutoberg Forest and had slaughtered them to the man. A traitor named Armenius had been involved. The story was one of woe told around the Roman world. Publius Quinctilius Varus, Roman imperial legate, governor of Germany, went down with his legions. Even Augustus, emperor of the empire, had loathed to say his name.

The Germans had done this. Was it because of the power of their God? Most people didn't care. Philo did. He thought of the altar in Athens to the "Unknown God." It was set beside the way to Mars Hill. Could Wodan be that God? Somehow, he didn't think so. But there stirred within him a passion to find that god. He had always wished he could explain to Biocles. Now, he wished he could explain to Marlena.

Marlena, at first slept serenely, then into the night, the terrible dream came reminding her of the past. It had been one evening only a couple of months after her mother had died. In their little cabin she and Arn sat on the animal skins before the open fire. She was telling Arn one of their father's stories from the battle in Teutoberg Forest, the greatest defeat of a Roman army ever known.

There came a knock on the door. Marlena had lifted the wooden bar and opened to a sight she didn't dream possible. There stood Daga, the high priest of Wodan, dressed in full regalia, the great black robe with the fiery red bear, the helmet, and around his neck the sacred amulet. His eyes burned with an emotion Marlena had not known.

"I have come to place a special blessing on your home Marlena," he said with honey sweetness.

"Come in then," Marlena said and closed the door behind him. Arn, only nine years old, stood in awe.

"Come sit beside me before the fire," he told Marlena, ignoring Arn altogether. "Your house will have special protection. Special gifts will be brought to your door." His eyes grew wider and wilder. Marlena's respect began to change to fear in spite of Daga's words. "You will be given a special place of honor in the village. But first you must give your body to Wodan. I, his priest, on his behalf, will take your body to do as I see fit." Then he fell upon her with all his lust, tearing away her frock and flinging his own great robe aside.

Marlena's mixed emotions now became fixed. She was terrified. She screamed and escaped Daga's grasp. She couldn't remove the huge bar across her door without stopping so she circled the room, nude, screaming, turning over the few items of furniture in the cabin.

Daga dove at her, brought her to the floor, then slapped her repeatedly. "This is why we don't have more power in our village," he shouted. "The people do not submit to their God."

Little Arn sat in the corner stunned. Knowing nothing of sex, he still realized that Daga was violating his sister in a cruel and horrible way. But the scowl on Daga's face froze him in fear. There he sat trembling, unable to move, unable even to think, tucking himself against the corner wall, wishing he couldn't see what he was seeing.

Marlena knew she was beaten physically, but she would have a last word before her virginity was stolen. "This doesn't have anything to do with Wodan," she had said, "This is the evil act of a lecherous old man."

Then she was struck again, and by gift from some anonymous god, went numb. Still her eyes beheld what her body did not feel — a madman in the act of rape.

Late in the afternoon three days later, Daga attacked Marlena again. He dragged her behind the cabin and threw her to the ground. But this time someone heard Marlena's cries. She had squeezed her eyes shut when she heard a smashing noise, and suddenly Daga was no longer upon her.

When she opened her eyes, she saw Otto, the red giant, standing over Daga.

Fire shot from his eyes. He grabbed Daga by the throat and pulled him up into his face. First he spat into the cheap, cowardly countenance he beheld. Then he shouted into Daga's ear.

"You phony dung of a priest. I ought to kill you here and now. For the sake of our people I will not. But I'll hold you in my power from this moment forward. And this child, if she survives, will be forever a witness against you. You are just fortunate I didn't let you complete this act."

Then Otto threw Daga down, knelt to Marlena, and gently covered her. Terror froze her face.

"Can you hear me child?"

Marlena could not speak. She nodded her head. Then Otto scooped her from the ground and carried her as though she were a baby into the cabin. There he cleaned her wounds and told her she must rest.

If only Marlena could have remembered Otto more than Daga her reverie would have been less fitful. But the depths of evil had been so overwhelming in Daga that all charity she had known was crowded from her subconscious by it. Lasting terror seemed always to hover just below the surface of her consciousness. And when she slept — the dream — oh god, the dream. Sometimes it was so unbearable that she feared sleep because of it. Insomnia had become a disability that she welcomed.

CHAPTER V

Otto, the red giant, had little use for religion. He had never known a high priest who hadn't used his position and power to satisfy his own appetites. Daga had proven to be the worst, however. He knew Daga wanted Marlena alone, to himself, but he never dreamed he would go so far as to eliminate her small brother until Arn was brought to the sacrifice altar.

Now, as he and Karl searched for the two, Otto found he had to make decisions he had rather put aside. He knew if he found Marlena and Arn that he could never return them to Kresboden. However, if he had refused to go on the search, he would have had no control over such a return.

Perhaps, he thought, I could tell Karl what kind of person Daga is. Karl and I could return to the village and simply say we were not able to pick up the trail. The problem he faced in doing this was the problem seekers of truth had faced for centuries. Karl, like most worshippers, preferred to equate the priest with their god. This made any personal contact with actual deity unnecessary, and eliminated the knotty problems of individual spirituality. The worshiper accepted the perfection of the priest and obeyed him. He overlooked many indiscretions on the priest's part for fear of the awesome task of having to face his gods himself.

So, Otto, passing the evenings with such thoughts as these combined with concerns for his family, spent days looking carefully for more signs to direct him to Marlena and Arn. He and Karl had found signs the earlier party had not. Cut willows on the gravel bars, a tag of cloth here, or scuffed footprints there led them eventually to the small village down river from Kresboden. There they questioned the townsfolk to no avail until, on the outskirts of the village, they met the local tanner. He had told them that just about dark a couple of weeks before, he had gone to the edge of the woods to relieve himself and had just caught a glimpse of four people climbing the hill behind his house. One seemed to be a child.

Otto kicked at the remains of a small campfire. It was days, perhaps weeks, old. He looked up at Karl.

"It'll be a while, but we'll find them. They're no longer careful."

With curious, gray eyes, Karl stared at the campfire remains obviously wishing he could build a campfire himself. He pulled at his sandy brown hair, then stabbed at his right nostril with his index finger grabbing his nasal septum with his thumb.

"How long ago were they here?" he asked.

"Ten days or so, but they're taking their time. See these rabbit bones?"

Karl nodded.

"They've taken time to hunt. We'll not have to hunt for a while yet. We still have provisions." He looked directly into Karl's eyes. "Do you really want to turn these children over to the priest?"

"The decision's not mine," said Karl. "The high priest has spoken." He rolled the object of his nose picking between his fingers.

"Karl, would you quit that," Otto said abruptly.

"Quit what?" asked Karl blank faced.

"That absurd nose picking," said Otto.

"Oh, uh, —-sure," said Karl as though what he was doing was a surprise even to himself.

Otto thought a minute then decided to take the chance. "What if I told you that Daga is an adulterer and a rapist? I have caught him red handed."

"No, surely not. I trust you Otto, but how can that be?"

"Have you ever tried to look directly into Daga's eyes?"

Karl was still squatting beside the campfire remains. What made Otto say this? Some months before he had come upon Daga beating a dog behind his house. Daga had not known he was there when he turned suddenly with rage in his face. Karl tried to interpret this rage as power, but, when he was honest with himself, he had to admit that what he had actually seen was evil. And that evil was beyond any evil he recalled. He stammered, "Maybe, but who am I to question the high priest."

"Either you question the high priest or you place no value on your religion at all. Do you worship Wodan, or do you worship a person who says he knows Wodan?"

"I've never spent time thinking of such things."

Arn couldn't draw Biocles' bow all the way, he had neither the arm span nor the strength to do it, but he could make it work for small game and target practice. Biocles let him use it sparingly. There was not time to stop and make more arrows. But, Biocles did teach Arn the names of the bow and arrow parts and the reasons for correct positioning.

One bright, spring morning, they stood in an alpine meadow at the edge of a grove of pines and hornbeams. A squirrel jumped from limb to limb in the trees. Two skylarks sang to one another, flew into the air, then swooped again into the cover of the hornbeams.

"You must stand square to the target," Biocles said. "Spread your feet comfortably until you feel your best balance. Your body and shoulders should line up with the intended flight of the arrow. The pressure of the bow when the bowstring is pulled should come in the V of your hand between the thumb and forefinger."

Arn fastened onto every word. "What about the arrow?" he said impulsively.

"Line up your body for now at, say, that tree over there."

Arn complied. Then Biocles checked him from all around, moving Arn's small figure only slightly. The lad was getting a tan and growing stronger by the day it seemed.

"I suppose we can spare one arrow," Biocles said. "This has to be right. Hold the bow across your body." He motioned horizontally. "Now, nock the arrow and be sure the cock feather is up this time," he said with a grin.

"Aw. You remember every mistake I make. I know about the cock feather."

"Just kidding, little guy, just kidding. Now swing vertically and draw. Remember, your drawing power should come from your shoulder and back."

Arn drew as far as he could.

"Keep your elbow up at shoulder level. I know it's hard, but it's better to start right than break bad habits."

Arn moved his arm up keeping the fingers of his drawing hand resting along his jaw.

"Arn, you have a natural shot. The gods have given it to you. Don't aim. Just watch the target intently and point. Good, now relax those draw fingers."

The arrow went sailing and struck the tree dead center.

"You're getting stronger. I don't know if I'll be able to get that arrow out or not."

Just then Philo came ambling down the mountain. "You two come on. Marlena has roasted grouse for dinner."

"I'm starved and that sounds wonderful," said Arn.

"Yes, we will come," said Biocles. "But, first I must do something. This lad is getting too big for his tunic."

Then Biocles took an arrow from his quiver and nocked it as he had just shown Arn. His huge muscles bulged. Then he raised his aim half skyward and relaxed his fingers. The arrow disappeared into the blue.

"Did you mark the direction?" he asked Arn.

"I did, as I always do."

"Very well, I want you to count the steps until you come to the arrow. Bring the arrow, and we'll eat."

"Why must you do these things to me," complained Arn.

"A true warrior learns discipline," said Biocles with a laugh.

As Arn paced and counted, he threw back, "Well you don't have to enjoy it." The truth was that he would walk over the Alps for Biocles. What was retrieving one arrow!

Marlena, Philo, and Biocles sat relishing their grouse when Arn came dragging up the hill with the arrow. He plopped down exhausted.

"Would you believe five hundred and sixteen steps."

"Ah, yes, my boy," came Philo's agreeable voice. "I've seen it many times. I would believe it. Of course, your steps are shorter than a man's, but even a man would have stepped well over three hundred times."

As Arn began to hungrily eat the grouse, Biocles mused softly, "When you can shoot an arrow that far, then you will be a warrior."

"Celtic or Greek?" asked Arn through a mouth full of grouse. Then, before Biocles could answer, "This bird is wonderful, my sister."

"Thank you, little brother," said the cook. "I hope it's enough for you to stay strong. Now, I, too, am interested in the answer to your Celtic or Greek question."

Philo answered for Biocles, leaving him to his modesty.

"My boy, when you can shoot an arrow that far, you can choose your side … just hope the Romans don't find out about you." They all had a hearty laugh.

Every day was a day for Philo to fall more deeply in love with Marlena. He thought, as a matter of fact, that he had been in love before. As he lay drifting into slumber that evening beside the little campfire he admitted that he had never felt like this. But how would he ever tell Marlena

41

what he must, that no son of true Greek aristocracy ever chose his own bride. "Real Greeks do not entrust the sanctity of marriage to such a fickle thing as romantic adoration," his father had told him.

Philo could see the old man pacing before him, scratching his chin and speaking in chopped phrases. His short, white hair and beard set him apart from any pretender. In his sixties, he still had the erect stature and precise manners of a patrician. The Romans may rule the government, but society was still Greek. His father knew it.

"Philo, my son, the glory of Greece is gone, but the honor isn't. Nor shall it be as long as a son of Alcandor of Trapezus remains. You will marry Theana, as your mother and I wish. She is intelligent, well-mannered, and most important of all, she will bring a handsome dowry. When you are older and more comfortable with yourself, you will see the wisdom of these things. In the meantime, enjoy yourself with lovers, but don't make the mistake of thinking you may take one permanently, except as a slave."

Philo sat eyeing his father's movements as he walked the stone floor before the stucco wall in the courtyard of their home in Athens. "Why do you suppose the Gods would have us attracted to one woman but supposed to have children by a different one?"

"The gods are not to be trusted, and certainly desire is not to be trusted. Only the wisdom of the ages is to be trusted. Spend your desires on lovers and courtesans, but entrust your family to a good wife."

And, thought Philo, that means one chosen by you. He knew perfectly well that "the wisdom of the ages" had failed at marriages as often as anything else. His resentment about this would have been complete except that, as was occasionally the case, he was allowed to meet Theana.

So it was, that while Biocles slept like a baby, Philo wrestled with his bounds to Greek tradition. Both slept better than Arn and Marlena.

The next morning Biocles rose early only to find Arn missing from his bed of evergreen boughs. His bow was missing, too. He leaned over to Philo. "Get us some breakfast together, Philo," he said. "I'll try to find the little one."

He came upon Arn in the meadow below, hardly believing what he saw. Arn lay on his back. The bow was tied to his feet, and he was drawing the string with both hands. "That is amazing," he said, as Arn more than doubled his draw length.

"Give me an arrow, please, please," said Arn. "Maybe I can shoot as far as you."

"I have to hand it to you, little one. You'll be able to shoot much farther. Let's go get something to eat, then we'll see how much farther. How did you come up with this?"

"When Philo said what he did about how far you shot the arrow, I began to try to figure a way to do it. Once I thought, if only my arms were as strong as my legs. Then I thought, hey, wait a minute, maybe, just maybe, I could draw with my arms and legs. I began to try. Then I got the idea of tying the bow to my feet. I think it will work."

"I do too. We'll see."

After they ate, they returned to the meadow with Philo and Marlena as an audience.

Arn lay on the soft grass and laced the bow to his feet. He gave a few tugs of the string, then Biocles provided the arrow. The bow, now horizontal, not vertical as usual, took on a different contour when braced against both feet, but still it showed flexibility. Arn rested the arrow across the bow. Now, in essence, his whole body was drawing the bow. He pushed with both legs, using not only leg but also back strength. Mostly, he held on with his arms. Then he raised the bow toward the sky and released the arrow. It flew out of sight.

Philo and Marlena sat watching in a shady grove of spruce trees. "That is the most incredible thing I've ever seen," said Marlena.

"Incredible it is, no doubt about it," said Philo, "but no more incredible than the way those two are bound together. Biocles has done more than rescue a lad. He has found a son before his own."

"It is evident," said Marlena. "In a way, it's sad too. It's sad that we four are so bound together."

"What do you mean?"

"You know only part of the evil of Daga. He'll not leave us alone."

"We've been free for weeks now. How can you say that?"

"I only know what I feel in my heart. Evil runs deep in that monster."

"And I know what I feel in my heart," said Philo, looking tenderly into those eyes the impossible color of violet he adored and wanted to protect forever. "I love you. Sometimes when I look at you I think my heart will pound out of my chest."

He took her hand. "Here, feel," he said. Then he placed her palm to the middle of his chest.

She giggled, "You make me blush," she said. "But I want you to know that your heart is not the only one pounding so." Then she took his hand and placed it between her breasts. He drew her to him, and slowly, gently they reclined into the deep, green grass. Flowers bloomed all around them, crocus, narcissus, alpine roses, and gentians painted the meadow a sea of red, yellow, pink, blue, violet and white. Even in the rocky places, the saxifrages seemed to crack the stones with their thick, fleshy leaves and push their little bare stalks upward to support clusters of tiny blossoms. The fragrance of clove pinks filled the air as irrepressibly as the emotions of love that filled the hearts of Philo and Marlena.

A yellow-throated bee-eater with its beautiful blue-green and brown plumage sailed from a tall spruce and sat amid the green grass and flowers not two meters from the kissing lovers. He felt no danger whatever, sensing the total distraction of the people so near. He stretched his yellow neck and turned his head this way and that staring curiously through the beady black pupils of his blood red eyes. He hopped close enough to hear whispers of love and saw the beginning of the inevitable mating. Then, as though the bee-eater were a messenger from the gods pleased with the completion of a project, he gave a couple of satisfied chirps and ascended back to the heavens.

Both Philo and Marlena had hoped this would happen, and both had hoped it wouldn't happen. Neither had planned it, but there had been so much fear, so much peril, so much togetherness, so much emotion. And they were so young.

When the height of passion was passed, neither wanted to release the other.

"If only we could be together like this forever I would gladly stay on this mountain," Philo said. "You my dear, are lovely in ways I never knew a person could be lovely."

"And you, my Philo, are the only man I will ever give myself to. I love you as I thought I would never love a man."

She hadn't told him about Daga. He hadn't told her about Theana. But for this brief time, nothing else mattered. There was only the love Philo and Marlena felt so powerfully.

When they slept that night, the bad dreams were banished from that part of Marlena's mind that had refused to surrender them before.

CHAPTER VI

The gray light of dawn crept down the mountain side and found four content travelers fast asleep still at the edge of the little meadow that none of them would soon forget. Their beds and covers were fragrant pine boughs. Arn lay close to his sister on one side of the dead campfire, and Philo and Biocles completed a circle around it. Slowly, the bed of Arn and Marlena darkened. Shadows, barely perceptible, hovered over them.

A speck of dust rose and caught in the corner of Philo's eye. He blinked and saw two huge hulks making off with Arn and Marlena. "Minotaur, quick," he shouted.

Biocles rolled left and grabbed his bow. A beam of moonlight shone into one spot on the meadow and he got a clear view of Karl with his hand over Arn's mouth. The arrow went straight through Karl's skull. He plunged forward onto the ground like a swimmer starting a race. When he released Arn, Arn dove at Otto who held Marlena. He tripped him enough to slow his run. Then Biocles and Philo were upon him.

Otto released Marlena and threw Philo through the trees as though he were a rag doll. Biocles hit Otto next. He blasted Otto's belly with his shoulder and knocked him to the ground. In the early dawn, they struggled in the grass. Marlena had regained control of herself and stood over the two crying, "no, no," pulling first at one then at the other. "Please, you don't understand," she screamed into Biocles ear. Then Otto slammed Biocles into a huge oak and raised his war ax over him.

Philo came running, leaped into the air, and struck Otto in the back with both feet, knocking the air from his lungs and folding his massive body. Philo took the ax and prepared to strike.

Marlena threw herself across Otto's body. "This man saved my life. He would never harm me."

"He was taking you away, why?"

"I don't know why, but …"

Otto began to cough, "Please let me speak," he told Marlena.

Biocles was getting off the ground still with a stunned look on his face. Marlena fixed them all with a gaze of determination and control. "We're going to let Otto tell us what this is about," she said. Then she turned to Arn, "Come, make a fire," she told him. "We'll talk."

So the five sat there in the early morning light as Otto told what had happened in the village of Kresboden. Occasionally, Marlena stopped Otto and interpreted for Philo and Biocles.

"I would never have taken you two back to Kresboden, Marlena. You know that. But if someone else comes, they will. I had Karl about convinced to go along with me, but I needed a little more time. We caught you too soon. Karl was a simple man but good man. We must bury him."

"We will do that tomorrow Otto. What did you plan to do? Where could you go? Where could we go? What about your children?"

"I don't know the answers to these questions. I only know that Daga will never give up the search for you. He was willing to kill Arn to get you. Now, too, his pride has been insulted. He'll send men after you as long as he lives."

Marlena did not interpret this last part for Philo and Biocles. Arn had started to say something to them when Marlena spoke to him. "Arn, you must go for the firewood. It's off to the trees for you." Then she turned to Philo and Biocles. "You have nothing to fear from Otto. Believe me, he's the one good man in all of Kresboden. He saved me once from complete destruction. I'll tell you about it later. We've all had a hard night. Let's have something to eat."

"All right," said a displeased but trusting Philo.

"I love you with everything that is in my being," Marlena said openly to Philo. "Trust me just this day."

And so, when they had eaten and Philo was with Biocles in the woods, Marlena went casually to Arn's side. "You know what we must do, my little brother. As long as we are with Philo and Biocles, they will be in danger of Daga's treachery. If we love them, we must leave them."

"No," blurted Arn, and Marlena's hand was quickly over his mouth.

"Think, little brother, think." Tears rolled down her face. She couldn't stand to leave Philo, or Biocles for that matter. Nor could she stand to ask Arn to leave them, but she had no other choice. Then the tears came to Arn's eyes and he began to shake. Marlena took him in her arms then led him into the trees. Otto was waiting.

A month later Daga, the high priest of Wodan for the village of Kresboden had found no peace. His garrulous shrew of a wife, Brunhilda, had given him no comfort for years. Then, adding to his consternation, she had raised two daughters, replicas of herself. He had found an outlet for his lust in the beautiful maiden, Marlena, but he had overplayed his hand by trying to take her in broad daylight. Things would have worked if it hadn't been for Otto. The little brother was certainly no problem. Daga could keep him terrified one way or another. Then the blasted Greeks, and they most certainly were Greeks, not Romans, had to come along. Well, at least I have Otto out of my hair, he thought. But where are he and Karl?

At last, Daga's longing for Marlena was overcoming him. He gathered the town council and sent out two more emissaries of his wrath. He sent two younger men this time. Younger men had more religious zeal. Why hadn't he thought of that in the first place? Was he too eager to get rid of Otto? Too, the new pursuers were to send reports back. He must know what was happening. He thought he would have Marlena back by now. Maybe he could find a substitute until his men returned her to him. It could be that he already had someone in mind. Were not his teen-aged daughters bringing their friend right into his house? He, of course, would have to be more careful.

CHAPTER VII

Philo and Biocles had searched the mountains for weeks looking for Marlena and Arn. They would have searched longer, but as they climbed rocky gorges and swam streams, questions kept sweeping through Philo's mind.

How could Otto abduct both Arn and Marlena against their will without either of them making a sound? How could Marlena be so wrong about her trust in Otto? Hadn't she said, "Trust me for just this one day?" That was the thing that kept ringing in his ears and stabbing his heart, "just today, just today," and that day she was gone.

Otto was the one good man in Kresboden she had said. Had she been waiting for him all along, knowing he would come? Was she in love with Otto? It seemed unlikely seeing the age difference and the fact Otto was married and had a family. But he had rescued her. He was the one good man. What was age? What was being married or having a family if he was the only source of kindness she knew?

After three weeks of such questioning, Philo decided that Marlena had only feigned love for him in exchange for his protection. He probed through his shining black hair and scratched his scalp. He rubbed his square chin until it was raw. He cried out in agony with a great baritone shout of anguish that reverberated through the Alps echo upon echo.

There was all the love he thought he had seen in her eyes. There was the sincerity of words she didn't have to say. There was the afternoon when love became passion and the peace he felt in it all. And yet she had gone, apparently of her own will. There was no sign of struggle. And Arn had gone, too. It was impossible to believe, yet all the evidence was there.

Biocles couldn't believe it either. Arn and Marlena had become as close as family in only a few weeks. He knew they had. There was no doubt in his mind whatever.

Nothing was fake to him. There was something he and Philo didn't understand, would probably never understand. But one thing he knew. He would never, ever forget them. They had become too much of what made him exist.

Athens was beautiful in the fall. Rome may have been larger and more powerful, but no city in the world would ever have the graceful charm of Athens. Esthetics would always be high priority for Athenians. These creative people had seen need to preserve trees in the midst of great stone buildings and streets. Now the reds, yellows, and browns of deciduous trees made a beautiful blend with the evergreens. The constantly experimenting Greeks had brought conifers from the hills in hopes of having some green through the winter. These transplants didn't survive near the sea, but they took root on the hills of Athens and served their purpose well. Now spruce and pine lined some streets and dotted garden spots amid the changing cork oaks and beech trees.

The people of Athens laughed at themselves about the larch trees. They had been transplanted in the summer as had most of the needled conifers. Athenians loved them for their slender, graceful perfection of shape and their deep green boughs. But, alas, when winter had come they shed their foliage just as the oaks did. The larches were the only needled trees to have this change, a fact any woodsman could have told them. But the gardeners of Athens, in their haste to beautify the city, had neglected consultation on the larch trees. They felt, indeed, that nature had tricked them. The larch were not evergreens as they appeared to be.

Philo stood on the portico of his hilltop home. He leaned forward with both hands resting on the balustrade and looked out over the city's famed Agora with its hundreds of tent kiosks.

Over roofs bordered in acanthus tile, he could see the High City. These buildings changed from stucco to stone and between the winged roofs of the temple, he could see a point of gold, Athena of the Vanguard lifted her spear toward the sea. As his eyes fell again, they found a row of larch trees situated down his own street. "I live among the larch," he said to himself. "I can't tell the real thing from an impostor."

His thoughts never left Marlena for very long no matter what business was at hand. Now, with time to meditate, he tried to find a way to exorcise the memory of her. Maybe his father had been right. Romantic attraction was not solid enough stuff on which to base a marriage. The marriage to Theana was set. It was time. A lover would probably never make a good wife. So he loved Marlena as he would probably never love anyone again, but now that was finished, over. Why couldn't he forget it? Briefly he had known what it was like to love a woman with all his soul. And, even if she hadn't loved him, at least he had thought she did. Yet, as precious as those days were, they didn't seem to be filled with the same passion he had toward his own God, as unknown as he may be. Philo had dragged Biocles to Egypt, Persia, and even once all the way to Spain searching for the "Unknown God." Why such a thing was a passion for him he couldn't understand. He only knew about the deep longing in his heart, as though a vacuum were there that had never been filled. Strangely, he had felt nearer this deity when he was with Marlena. Why was it? Why did it seem that everything kept coming back to Marlena? Was it her physical beauty? Was it her sharp mind? He still couldn't believe she comprehended Greek so rapidly. No, it was these things and more. It was all of her. It was what he saw when he looked directly into those bright, crystalline violet eyes, clearer than the sky, softer than small flowers, more loving than any he had ever hoped to see …

"Don't do this to yourself, Philo," he uttered.

"Do what?" came a gentle, matronly voice from behind him. Philo's mother had slipped quietly onto the portico. Penelope was as gentle as Alcandor was irascible. She thought of her own happiness in terms of what made her husband and children happy. Streaks of gray hair enhanced the beauty of her light olive skin and oval face. She stood taller than most Greek women and always wore modest clothing over her comfortable, matronly figure. To Philo she was the embodiment of what he understood grace to be, the intended outpouring of benevolence blended with an uncanny understanding of human nature.

Philo stared at the Athenian skyline. "What are you doing to yourself?" Penelope asked again.

"Mother, you would understand. I'm sure of it. But now isn't the time to speak of it. Rather, now is the time to forget it."

"You may not understand this, but it may be easier to forget if you do speak of it."

This was not the first time Penelope had found Philo brooding. She put a hand on his cheek and let it fall away, but held him with her eyes. "Sometimes the things we try to bury within ourselves only become more powerful, as if they were—plants sending out deep roots. Roots exposed to the sun, however, usually wither and die."

"Why is it that I can never resist your wisdom?" said Philo. "I suppose it's because it's given in love." He answered his own question and gave his mother a warm embrace. Standing there at arm's length he told her, "As unlikely as it may seem, I love a Celtic woman."

Penelope didn't fall away in shock, but gave him a look of perplexity. Her brown eyes narrowed and furrows showed across her forehead. "A—, a barbarian?"

"We call them barbarians. They call us barbarians. No matter. I'm convinced all human beings have similar capacities given similar circumstances. Marlena was certainly as intelligent a person as I've ever known. And brave, and so beautiful I thought at first she was Athena come to visit me."

So Philo told Penelope some of the story including how Marlena and Arn had disappeared. As he finished he again leaned over the balustrade, staring at the building that stood atop the Acropolis, the Parthenon, temple of Athena Parathions, epitome of Greek architecture, standard of excellence for all time. An arrow whisked through the air before him and pierced his right shoulder. He cried out in great pain and fell to the stone floor of the portico.

Penelope screamed, "Philo! Philo! Help someone! Come quickly, Caleb, quickly."

In a matter of seconds Caleb, the chief household servant, was at their sides. Caleb was somewhere in his early fifties, exactly where no one could tell, not even Caleb. He was a Jew with a lean body and brown eyes that seemed to strain for a deeper look at things. As a child, he had been captured by the Romans and sold into slavery. For over forty years he had served the household of Alcandor. Not only was he a loyal servant, but he had been a careful student of many useful things. Now he bent over Philo and examined the arrow. "Please, my lady, go inside," he said to Penelope.

"I'll stay here, Caleb. I'll be all right. Do what you must. You know I trust you."

Without a further word to Penelope, Caleb turned to Philo, "I must see your back." Then carefully he rolled Philo onto his left shoulder. The arrow had somehow missed the shoulder blade and collar bone. Its point broke the skin of Philo's back. Better to push it through than pull it out, Caleb thought.

"I'll need some clean cloth," Caleb said to Penelope. Then Penelope plunged into the house as Caleb spoke to Philo.

"I think you're going to be all right. There's not a lot of blood as yet."

Philo groaned in pain. "I'll stay with you as long as I can, Caleb. Do what you need to do." From childhood,

Philo had received from and given more love to Caleb than to Alcandor.

Penelope came with the cloth and Caleb tore a corner from it. While he spoke to Penelope, he rolled the small piece into a cylinder the shape of a thumb-sized stick. "We'll need a long band and two large bandages." Then he placed the small wad of cloth into Philo's mouth and across his back teeth.

"Bite when I tell you," he said to Philo. He grasped the shaft of the arrow and instructed, "Bite." As Philo bit, he shoved the arrow deeper so that it penetrated Philo's back, exposing the entire head. Caleb grasped the arrow shaft as near Philo's chest as he could. It took him a few seconds to get the base of his thumb squarely against the wood.

"Feels like you have a fire poker twisting around in there," Philo sighed.

"I'll stop when I see the flames," teased his old friend. This evoked a weak smile from Philo. Caleb broke the arrow shaft where it entered Philo's chest.

Philo was becoming pale. "Much longer?" he whispered as Caleb got completely behind him.

"Hang in there," Caleb said in his ear as he grasped the arrow head. "Now bite," he said loudly and pulled the arrow out Philo's back.

"Awhhhhhh," moaned Philo as he clinched the small cloth, then passed out.

Blood now flowed at both Philo's chest and back. Quickly Caleb applied the bandages and strapped them on with the cloth. He then turned to Penelope, "He was lucky. The arrow came through clean. He'll come around in a few minutes." Caleb looked at the arrow a bit then asked Penelope to excuse him.

Penelope gave Caleb a look of uncertainty as he left. She sat on the floor beside Philo, held his hand and prayed.

Ten minutes later her vigil was rewarded. Philo blinked his eyes then opened them, "Mother I, I ..." "Shush," she said. "Don't speak. You need your strength."

Caleb returned with other household servants who bore a small bed. They lifted Philo and placed him on it. There Philo lay in pain wandering what could have happened.

Dorea came running to the bedside panting breathlessly, "My Philo, my Philo, what has happened to you?" She was fully ten years old and was a true gift from the Gods. Every feature of her frame was delicate, petite. Despite the daintiness, however, she had an angular jaw which she often raised in disdain upon consideration of distasteful things in the world about her. Her little nose was pointed and her brown eyes were disproportionately huge, the windows of a hundred expressions. Her light brown hair was fine of texture. She preferred to keep it swept back into a barrette that let the ends hang free behind her.

Dorea, the daughter born out of season, was an actress from the moment she was able to take her first steps. It were as though she had studied at the feet of Euripides when she was in Penelope's womb. Her dramatic birth quickly evolved into the life of a melodramatic child, her feelings of compassion so completely overstated that few could help but chuckle at her on the one hand and love her on the other.

"I've just had a little accident here, Sunshine. I'll be all right," said Philo with great effort.

The effort was sensed immediately by Dorea. "Oh no, no," she said placing both hands over her mouth.

Penelope appeared looking apologetic. "Dorea, Philo needs rest. You must come away and let him be quiet."

"But, Ma, I love him so, and he has been away so long. Why did this have to happen?"

"We don't know that, Dorea. All we know is that we must let him rest so that he can heal."

Dorea looked from her mother back to her brother. Tears streamed down her cheeks. She took the edge of the bed covers and drew them gently over Philo. "Love of my life, you must keep warm," she said. "Evil spirits enter the body through cold shoulders."

In spite of his pain, Philo gave her a smile. "Where in the name of Zeus did she get that," he was thinking.

Then Penelope led Dorea from the room.

Only a few moments later Caleb looked in. "I've cleaned the arrow," he said. "I've never seen one like it." Then he handed the two pieces to Philo.

Philo took them with his left hand, held them up for inspection and incredulity swarmed his body. He lay stunned and stared at the arrow. All he said was, "Celtic."

CHAPTER VIII

In the small alpine village of Melz lived a cloth merchant named Hans Helvet who had gained a relatively comfortable position for himself within the community by perfecting dyes for wool thread. It had been the custom of the area to dye woven cloth. Now, Hans' workers could weave beautiful materials of various patterns. His varicolored woolens were sought through all the mountain regions.

Hans was a plump little man with arms and legs like fence posts and imperceptible wrists and ankles. His face stayed a rosy red. It was said that this rosiness was due to Hans' consumption of the product of his second business, beer. It seemed that Hans could take the natural products of his region and lift them to more profitable heights. He had taken wool from the hillside flocks of sheep, and now he was taking the mountain barley and combining it with hops he had started himself, to brew some very good lager. "I make the wool for a profit," he had said. "I brew the beer for pleasure." Nevertheless, pleasure or not, Hans earned a tidy sum from his brewery.

The townsfolk, for the most part, admired Hans and appreciated him. After all, he brought prosperity to the area, and he seemed to pay a living wage in a country with few slaves. But little was known of his family life. He lived in a small, walled villa at the edge of town where his wife and teenage daughter remained recluses. Servants whispered that they both were quite insane.

In recent days Hans had employed two new workers who seemed to be learning their work at the looms very rapidly. Hans had reservations about them when they had first applied for work. The boy was only twelve and the young woman, though strong and obviously more attractive than any one in all of Melz, was, alas, very pregnant. He had refused to hire them.

Then the red haired giant had appeared to vouch for them both. He was a figure one could hardly ignore. Being refused entrance to Hans' offices by his six personal guards, the giant had overcome them all and stacked them, unconscious, like cord wood, at Hans' door.

Standing before the startled Hans as he sat at his working tables, the giant had begun, "I didn't want to intrude, but I had to talk to you. My friends, Arn and Marlena, need work. I'll personally take responsibility for their performance. If they don't make a profit for you, then fire them, and I'll come and repay your losses."

Though taken back, the round little Hans refused to be intimidated. His slit-like, hazel eyes narrowed even more, "I suppose that would be a very good deal for me if I had any assurance of your assets," he said.

"I live far from here, and I go, but I will return," said Otto. He unsheathed his sword and placed it before Hans. "This is the only asset I have with me. Take it as a bond. If Arn and Marlena have worked well, I will retrieve it when I return."

"You're willing to give up your only means of protection and make a journey?"

"I am."

"My name is Hans. I don't think I've ever met a man like you." He extended a hand to Otto. "It's a deal," he said.

"My name is Otto," said the big man. He shook Hans' hand and turned to leave. "There is one other thing—."

"Yes?"

"I'll take it as a personal affront should any evil come upon my wards. Do you understand?"

"I can't control the whole world," blurted Hans as he leaped from his chair, but Otto was out the door and gone.

Hans Helvet was a reasonable man. He had cut working time to twelve hours a day. And, of course, there were holidays: Yule, New Year, Mayspring, and best of all, Harvest's End which involved a whole week of merrymaking.

Marlena worked her loom over her protruded abdomen as though things were supposed to be that way. Arn performed better than most adults, then had energy to spare. They lived in a room above the Hog Jaw, one of the local taverns, and went in by the outside stairs.

Marlena spent her spare time preparing for the baby. She sewed little gowns and booties. She made blankets and a warm hat. She had learned to hum as she sewed. The sound of the gentle music seemed to calm and cheer her. Arn liked it too. She hummed songs taught her by her mother when she was a child. They were quiet lullabies and play time songs. Once in a while, she hummed the merry Greek songs Philo and Biocles had taught her.

As she hummed and held the things she had made, her mind always returned to Philo. His face appeared before her, happy, laughing, full of love and speaking words she would never forget. "Marlena, you're more of a woman than I have ever imagined there could be. I look into your eyes, and I see all the happiness I've ever wanted. I see beauty inside and out, beauty of countenance, beauty of soul." Then Marlena would stop humming.

One evening as she sewed, tears came to Marlena's eyes and silently she prayed, "If there are any gods, would you please make this baby like Philo. I'll never see him again, but I have his baby. If it's a boy, I will name him Philo, yes Philo." The tears came freely, and Arn came to his sister.

"It's hard I know, Marlena. But I'll help. I'll learn. We'll not always be here under bond. Someday we will have enough to go free, and I'll make a living for us all."

Marlena took Arn in her arms and held him for a long time. "We have things to be thankful for. We have each other. Both of us could have been killed. We were close more than once. And we have Otto. He won't forget us. And we'll have the baby, a part of Philo and a memory of Biocles, those brave men who saved us."

"Someday, Marlena, we'll see them again. I know it."

"There's no way, my little brother. The world is too big, and our means are so small."

The subject of archery was never far from Arn's mind. In his reverie, he saw himself with the amiable and muscular Biocles learning to shoot arrows more accurately and farther. He remembered learning to hunt. He remembered the strong bow bending and sleek arrows sailing through the air. He remembered Biocles saying, "You have a natural shot, little one. It's a gift from the gods."

That night on the mountain when he and Marlena had left with Otto, he had been tempted to take Biocles' bow with him. He felt Biocles would understand. But he couldn't do it; Biocles had been too good to him. He had taught him all he knew about bows and arrows. Somehow he had to get his own bow. Now, with some time on his hands, Arn decided to make his own bow. He began the tedious process of choosing just the right wood and shaping it a bit at a time, never cutting errantly. In Arn's mind there was never the idea of making another bow if this didn't turn out well. There was an urgency in him that kept saying: This will be your bow. Think as you go. Choose well. Work carefully. Don't make provision for mistakes because if you do, you surely will make them. And so, day by day, the bow took shape.

Arn didn't forget the baby. He made a special toy with the knife he had purchased for making the bow. The toy was a small, wooden horse carved of hardwood and colored with dyes from the cloth factory of russet red, deep blue and bright green. When he finished it, he polished it with bees wax and showed it to Marlena.

She stopped her humming, put aside her sewing, and examined it carefully. "You're artful, my brother. The baby will like it. What made you think of these colors? They blend so well, and yet they're so bright and cheery."

"They're the colors from Biocles' arrows. I hope you don't mind. I know you don't like weapons."

"I don't mind, Arn. It's true I don't like weapons, but I know that sometimes they're necessary. And, after all, the baby will never know the difference."

As time approached for Marlena's delivery, she began to be ill. Pains pounded through her belly and up her back. Nausea swept what seemed to be her whole body. Curled around her unborn child, she lay in bed with a fever, and sweat oozed from every pore. That is when Hans Helvet summoned the midwives.

There were two of them, Helga and Frieda. Two eggs in a basket they were, plump, blonde, huge bosomed and wide bottomed. Most of the villagers assumed they were twins, but they were not. Helga, at forty-two, was a scant year older than Frieda. Both believed life should be as happy as possible. They had huge mouths and big square teeth that showed often as they teased one another through life's vicissitudes.

Outside it was a frigid mid-January night. Deep snow covered everything like a great crystal white banquet cloth that reflected the moon and stars a million times from every tree or bush. The smooth curves of the snow rose gently in drifts against any obstacle it met in its blowing. It was a spectacle of beauty; it meant life; it meant death. Out of winter spring would come, too soon for some, too late for others.

In the room over the Hog Jaw Tavern, Arn hovered over Marlena consoling her and washing her face. There came a banging at the door.

"Hello, in there. Is anyone about to have a baby?"

Arn swung the wood plank door open and got his first look at Helga and Frieda. They stood there in the snow, wrapped like giant fuzzy caterpillars, their cheeks rosy, their big teeth glowing in bright smiles and their eyes beaming as though they knew some wonderful secret.

"We've come to help," blurted Frieda.

"Where's the momma?" asked Helga.

Arn was so relieved and delighted he gasped. "Please come in. My sister is very sick. I'm afraid something bad is happening."

"My name is Helga. This is my sister, Frieda. Herr Helvet sent us. We have helped with many babies."

"I'm Arn," he said as the ladies entered the room. He shut the door and walked to Marlena's side. "This is my sister, Marlena. The father of her baby is very far away."

Both sisters were shedding their huge coats. "Yes, we know all about this sort of thing," said Helga. "The sorry cowards don't deserve to be called men."

Frieda was hanging the coats along with their thick head scarves on pegs in the wall. "Pigs maybe," said Frieda.

"Oh, no," said Marlena softly between her groans. "You don't understand. It isn't his fault. We were forced apart by circumstances. Neither of us knew about the baby."

Helga could see a fierce loyalty in Marlena's face, and she knew she shouldn't argue. But she also knew men had all kinds of excuses, and women wanted to believe them despite the obvious facts. Hadn't it been that way since the first shepherd yodeled out across the wide Aare valley?

Frieda had hung the wraps by then and went to Marlena, "There, there little one. What we must think about now is the baby. Let me look at you." She placed a hand on Marlena's forehead and held it there for a few moments. Then, she reached beneath Marlena's gown and felt her abdomen. Up and down she felt with both hands, then across. She turned to Helga. "We have to talk."

Leaving Arn to hold his sister's hand, the two went to the corner of the room and whispered to one another. Frieda spoke first, "It looks like it will be a hard one. The baby is still head up, and the poor child is sick."

"How long do you think?" asked Helga.

"I have to see her opening."

Helga turned to Arn. "Go down stairs and tell the innkeeper that you must stay with him tonight. If the blockhead doesn't understand, tell him Herr Helvet will explain later."

"I have to stay with Marlena," Arn said. "I know about babies. I helped my mother with our cow once. She had a beautiful calf. And it isn't just that, Marlena is all I have, and I know she's in trouble. I love her more than anything, and I'll not leave her when she may need me."

The midwives stared at him. "How old are you, boy?" Helga asked.

"Twelve."

"You have courage. Take the buckets and bring as much water as you can. Start a pot to boiling."

Marlena lay hurting, wondering, but she was not indecisive about letting Helga and Frieda help. She sensed compassion in their voices and had felt gentleness in Frieda's touch. She was reluctant to be so physically exposed to her brother, yet she knew he was desperate to be with her.

"Raise your knees and spread your legs," Frieda instructed her.

It was a long night of labor. The next morning found Marlena screaming in agony while Helga and Frieda tried to help. Arn kept the cloths and warm water coming. Several times he stayed out by the well much longer than he needed to, even though he nearly froze. Seeing Marlena suffer was almost too much for him.

By evening, the sisters realized that though the baby was not in position, they would have to try to take it to save

Marlena's life. The baby could not be saved. Then pulling first a foot, then an arm, then whatever part she could reach, Frieda wrest the baby almost asunder but delivered her from Marlena's womb. It was a girl, limp, seemingly lifeless. Both sisters shook their heads. Frieda left the care of Marlena to Helga and wrapped the baby in a blanket. Staring at its lifeless form, she began to weep. Slowly she placed the little girl into a nearby chair and covered her entire form with another blanket. Nothing more could be done. The baby would never know what life could have been, but now there was an urgency to save one who knew life. Blood was everywhere. It had covered the baby. It was smeared up Frieda's arms and onto her apron. It coated Marlena and pooled in the bed beneath her.

Marlena had fainted. The sisters cleaned her, bathed her, and wrapped her in warm blankets. Frieda turned to Arn, "I'm sorry we couldn't save the little girl," she said. "We had to give Marlena a chance to live."

"I understand," said Arn. The blood scared him. He had never seen a creature lose so much and still live. "Will my sister be all right?" he asked.

"It's hard to say. We've done what we can for her. We've seen this bad before. It can go either way. At least she has a chance. The bleeding is stopped. Again, we are sorry about the baby."

Then, from beneath the blanket cover, the baby girl coughed and moved. In a flash, Frieda threw aside the cover, grabbed the baby and ran her finger down its throat to clear its mouth of mucous. "Helga, Helga, this baby is alive! This baby is alive!" When the baby was breathing well, she tied its cord and began to bathe it. Helga and Arn stood by overcome with emotion. Both wept.

By that evening, Marlena lay in a coma. Helga and Frieda tried in vain to force feed her broth. They checked frequently to make sure Marlena's bleeding was still stopped, and they continued to bathe her fevered body.

The baby had screamed constantly for hours. "She will die unless we feed her," said Frieda as she held her and walked the floor.

"It's better that way," Helga reasoned. "What kind of person would that poor, twisted, disjointed little babe make? And who knows what damage is done to her insides? We've never seen a child live through a delivery like this. It's better that she die now, before Marlena awakes." She stroked Marlena's brow.

"But she has such spirit," answered Frieda. "Listen to her. She is pleading with us."

"Her mother can't feed her. It's that simple."

"It is not and you know it. I'll not refuse her when I make more milk than a farmer's cow." She unbuttoned the front of her frock and raised the infant to her bare breast helping her find the nipple. The crying stopped so fast that one would have thought the baby's head had been thrust under water. She fed ravenously, and Frieda hummed with pleasure. A quirk of nature had left her in continued lactation when she had lost her baby and husband three years before in a village fire.

This is what Frieda had come for. She was sustaining a life. She knew few physical satisfactions like holding a warm little body next to her own and feeling life flow between them. The emotional connection was also complete. The baby needed her, and almost as much, she needed the baby, her beautiful smooth skin, her full shocks of raven black hair, her searching eyes, her wild gyrations of happiness. She looked like a rag doll, all disjointed and distorted, but Frieda would help her heal. She began to set the joints back in their sockets and to massage the limbs where they were bent. For three days she studied and memorized every deformity. She pulled and pushed and massaged and loved, drawing the babe to her and softly singing lullabies of the Alps.

Arn and Helga did all they could for Marlena. More than once Arn wept and cried out to whatever gods might care. Then, Helga held him in her arms and told him, "There are gods who care, and somehow I feel they can hear you."

"We've come so far," said Arn. "I just can't bear to lose her now." Then, he lay back onto his bed and fell asleep from exhaustion.

On the fourth day the fever broke, and Marlena fought for consciousness.

"My baby, my baby," she whispered. "Let me hold my baby."

Frieda had wrapped the infant in a small blanket so that only her head appeared. "You have a beautiful girl," she said. "Her father must have had dark hair." Then she placed the babe on Marlena's pillow while Helga scowled.

Marlena, too weak to move, looked directly into the curious eyes. "I'll call her Nixe," she said weakly, "After all, I thought her father was a forest nymph." Then she fell into a deep sleep.

CHAPTER IX

A self-satisfied Daga lay half prostate on the huge bear skin before the warm hearth, drinking mead and reviewing the successes of his own wise planning. Brunhilda had taken the girls to Obenstat to visit her relatives. He had the peace of solitude and the pleasure of high anticipation.

Otto had returned with news about Marlena and Arn and their abductors. It seemed that he and Karl had actually seen the four of them across a deep mountain ravine, but Karl had fallen to his death in his eagerness to climb the escarpment that separated them. Grieved and disappointed, Otto had buried Karl and returned to Kresboden. On his return journey, he had encountered Adolph and Franz, the young zealots Daga had sent.

Adolph and Franz had followed the easy trail Otto and Karl had left. Otto and Karl obviously had no idea anyone would come after them.

Daga had never trusted Otto since that afternoon behind Marlena's cabin, so he was more than pleased that others were in pursuit of the blasphemers. Adolph and Franz were sworn to avenge Wodan. They were capable of great hatred, and Daga knew exactly how to use them.

But that certainly was not the half of Daga's good fortune. One fall afternoon while his cantankerous wife and daughters were out gathering nuts, Gretchen, the teenage friend of his daughters, came knocking at his door. It was exactly the chance he was waiting for. He deftly seduced Gretchen. There was no chasing, and wrestling, and screaming as there had been with Marlena. He was so smooth, in fact, that he found Gretchen eager. When they were finished and had rested a bit, Gretchen once more became amorous. He smiled as he thought of it. He had given so much of his energy to the experience that he was unable to respond, but he promised Gretchen he would see her again later.

Daga had been so pleased with himself that he overlooked the fact that he had not seduced a virgin. If he had been privy to the common gossip of the village, he would have known what the hunters in the forest and the warriors in training camp already knew: Gretchen was easy and was seldom satisfied.

The door to Daga's house was not bolted. As he lay staring into the flames of his fireplace, the bar lifted and the door swung open. Gretchen paused there, taking in the warm room before her. She was not a small girl, but she had long, flaming red hair and smooth freckled skin that made her attractive. Her hazel eyes panned the room finding no one but Daga. She closed the door behind her and bolted it. Throwing her coat onto the floor she went straight to Daga without so much as a word. She knew what he wanted, what she wanted. She began to tear at his clothes.

"Careful child," he said with a laugh. "You upset my dignity as the high priest of Wodan."

Then she drew aside her frock revealing the nubile breasts of youth, and she gave him a long, seductive stare.

His heart pounded; a warmth swept his body; his lecherous eyes bulged.

"The devil can take dignity," he whispered.

As the sun began to touch the hilltops of Athens' outskirts, Adolph and Franz stood before an open fire. This was not the dense forest of home, but at least, it was a secluded spot amid the evergreens and rocks. Adolph and Franz lifted their arms to the heavens and began to chant a tribute to the mighty god, Wodan.

Adolph was of medium build. He had light brown hair and gray, penetrating eyes that seemed to stare completely through objects of his concentration. Franz was a red man, red curly hair, pink skin, mild amber freckles, yellow teeth, and an irritable disposition. They had shed their skins of the north and replaced them with typical Greek clothing. Each wore a cloak, a Chlamys. They had paid a tax and become legal aliens, metics the Greeks called them.

When their prayers were finished, they sat on large rocks and faced the small campfire. They dragged morsels of dried meat from their traveling pouches and began to eat.

Adolph spoke first. "I know he's dead. Wodan guided my arrow. Have you ever seen such a good shot from that distance? He'll roast with the cursed."

Franz was not so sure of all of that. "You're too cocky. So it was a good shot. I could have done as well. I think you hit him too high. His roasting may be delayed."

"We haven't seen him on the porch in days, have we?"

"No, but he could be only wounded. You know that as well as I. Besides, they may have decided that the porch is a dangerous place, at least for a while."

Adolph was disturbed. "Why can't you have faith. The man known as Philo is gone. We need to find the other one."

Franz was the enigmatic kind of person with both intelligence and temper. "Why can't you have some sense? Do you think Wodan wants us to behave like a couple of idiots just because you made a good shot?"

Adolph fixed Franz with a stony stare. "We may both be idiots, but I have a vision of Wodan's power. I thought you did too. Now I wonder." Then he took command. "Tomorrow we start the search for the man called Biocles."

Philo had been very ill. Now his fever was receding, and since it was a beautiful spring day, the servants brought his bed to the edge of the peristyle. There was a small colonnade and a fountain with stone dryads holding torches. A fig tree sprouted in a garden with flowers beginning to bloom. The columns were painted bright colors of green, yellow, and blue. Caleb had set the fountain to flowing for the first time in the year.

Penelope sat beside Philo occasionally bathing his face with cool water. There was tenderness in her brown eyes, healing in her hands, and gratitude in her heart.

"You never got to tell me what you think of my being in love with a Celtic woman," Philo said weakly.

"I've thought about it. As you know, what women think makes little difference in our society," said Penelope.

Some of the luster was gone from the blue eyes Philo had inherited from his father, but the probity he had inherited from his mother came through as well as ever. He wanted Penelope to understand perfectly what he was about to say, so he fixed those eyes she knew so well directly upon hers. "Mother, you are not just any woman. You've guided my thinking and my opinions since I was born. Yes, I've learned much in school, and I value the teachings of our great men, but I've never known your wisdom to fail. Theirs does."

"My dear son, I'm afraid you value my counsel too highly. I only speak what love says. You know there's only a rare woman who has education."

"But, Mother, life is not bound up in education. Your spirit is the finest I've ever known. It's partly because of you that I search for a more noble God. Don't you realize that?"

"I suppose I haven't realized it. And this woman———."

"Of course, Mother! In spirit she was like you. How could I love her otherwise?" I know it seems strange, but I think somehow the gods are telling me that I am doing the right thing by searching for other gods, even if the searching must stop for a while. And even if I have lost Marlena forever."

"I would like to have known this Marlena," said Penelope as she put the cloth down and stood to go for fresh water. "But I think your last words tell me the true situation. She is evidently gone. And I must tell you that Theana is a remarkable person. If you will but give her an opportunity to have room in your heart she will bless your life."

Dorea came skipping into the peristyle. "Love of my life, you are better. My heart springs with ecstasy. Soon you may tell me of your adventures among the barbarians, and I shall hug your neck at every opportunity."

"You're right Sunshine," said Philo. "The telling will come before the hugging though. My shoulder is still sore. Maybe we could settle for a kiss on the cheek and I could use one of those right now."

Dorea, having been banished from Philo's presence while he recuperated, now raced to his side and placed a slobbery kiss on his cheek. "There, my love," she said. "The touch of your face is like sweet wine."

"And how might you know that, little one?"

"Isn't a child permitted some mystery?"

"I won't tell if you won't," said Philo as he looked up at Penelope.

Penelope, standing behind Dorea, rolled her eyes and tilted her head while turning up her palms in a quasi-permissive gesture. Everyone indulged Dorea. Not to do so would mean the sacrifice of much entertainment.

Only a few days had passed when Franz and Adolph discovered both good news and bad. By watching the house of Alcandor, they found a frequent visitor, young and strong, to be addressed as "Biocles" when he entered or left. But they also found that the reason for his visits was his wounded friend, Philo.

They were, as yet, not sure what to do about Philo, but their plan for Biocles was simple. They would wait in the dark street for him to complete an evening visit with his friend. One of them would stop him to ask a question while, from behind, the other would slip a dagger between his ribs. The one doing the talking would cover Biocles' mouth so that no sound would be made. They would hide the body so that it would attract no immediate attention, then be on their way. The streets were not lit, and there were few people who traveled by night. Those who did, carried torches or lamps so their approach was easily seen from a distance.

Franz and Adolph were not sophisticated people, but they had thought of these things as well as others. For instance, who should do the talking and who the knifing. Both were killers at heart. They had finished their evening meal and sat at their small campfire talking about it.

"It isn't a simple thing," said Adolph. "If you hit a rib first, you'll dull your dagger and give the victim time to react. Not only that, once you have penetrated you must turn the knife to cut the big blood vessels."

"As always, you act as if you're the only Celt who ever wielded a knife. Hey, I'll just carry a battle ax and split his skull. How'll that be?" said an irritated and frustrated Franz.

"You'd probably try it," said Adolph. "What would you look like traveling the streets of Athens trying to keep a battle ax hidden. If I could trust you to ask the questions, I'd do the stabbing. "I'll have my dagger along because I'll probably have to finish the job anyway."

"Yeah, like you finished the job on Philo," said Franz, one who never missed a chance at sarcasm.

Adolph rose from his seat, walked to Franz, and put a finger in his face. "When this is over, I may just finish you, but right now, we have to think of our mission and Wodan," he said.

Franz was afraid of Adolph. He always ended up doing what Adolph said, but hardly ever without objections.

73

Sometimes, when he was angry enough, he thought he just might take Adolph, but in his saner moments, he knew better.

Biocles sat looking into Philo's weak face wondering how soon he would recover. Philo seemed better this night.

"We haven't talked about what there is to do about the Celts who shot you," said Biocles.

They were in the peristyle again, and Philo lay propped up on his portable cot. "What is there to do? We could have our friends watch for them, but there are so many aliens in Athens that they will blend with the rest. Besides, I'm sure they'll keep to themselves for the most part."

"I have some friends who do little but wander the streets keeping their eyes and ears open for rumor," said Biocles. "I'll describe Celtic accents and customs to them the best that I can. Maybe they'll pick up something."

"In the meantime, you must be careful, Minotaur. The evil of those people seems to reach into the whole world," said Philo as he lay back on his pillow.

"I'm not sure it's the evil of those people as much as it is the evil of one man, that priest. Did you notice the smile on his face as he prepared to kill Arn? It was a pleasure for him."

"Yes, I saw it. We've never spoken of it. How do you suppose a person could get so twisted?" Philo mused looking at the open sky, the moon barely making a faint glow on this foggy night.

"In a way I hope I never find out," said Biocles. "I still think it was that evil that has separated us from Arn and Marlena."

At the mention of Marlena and Arn, Philo groaned.

"It's getting late," said Biocles. "I have to go. You rest and leave the Celts to me for now."

Caleb saw Biocles to the door. As he opened it, both men experienced an unusual moment of silence. As Caleb lit a small torch and handed it to him, Biocles bent his head toward the dark street. He thought he heard a low, mumbled conversation. Probably not.

"The fog is getting worse," said Caleb. "Keep a sharp eye. It's the kind of night brigands love."

When Caleb had shut the door and Biocles was left standing alone with his torch in the deserted street, he again listened for the whispers he thought he had heard before. Nothing. Head erect, he walked out into the street.

Franz and Adolph huddled together between two buildings across the street and watched the entrance of the house of Alcandor.

"We had better do this right," said Franz. "Did you see the bodies of our countrymen who had met these Greeks? One had his neck broken with hardly a mark on his body."

"Will you keep quiet," whispered Adolph. "One of the things we need to do right is keep silent." He felt like kicking Franz, but the oaf wouldn't have any better sense than to cry out.

Franz lowered his voice. "I just wanted to remind you. I …"

Adolph slapped a hand over his mouth and held his face against Franz's ear. "If I hear another sound from you, you will feel my dagger across your throat," he said.

Franz froze and slowly Adolph lowered his hand. The door of Alcandor's house opened and light shone forth.

"Look, he's coming," said Franz before he realized it.

Adolph couldn't help it, he kicked Franz with his thick boot and at the same time shoved his fist in his mouth.

There was a low grumbling from Franz as Adolph hissed into his ear. "We do it now—silently." He twisted his fist over Franz's lips as he withdrew it.

Biocles had walked only a scant twenty steps from Alcandor's door. The admonitions of Caleb and Philo and the soft sounds of mumbling were still fresh on his mind when a robed figure bearing a small lamp appeared in the street before him.

"Excuse me, sir. I'm a stranger here, and I seem to have lost my way."

The accent was Celtic. Biocles never broke stride. He didn't rush forward either, however, this causing a few seconds of indecision on Adolph's part; and before he reacted, Biocles threw his torch and slammed into him, kicking him in the groin with his knee and slugging his jaw at the same time.

Adolph went flying onto the stone street and Biocles, realizing from the whispering he had heard that there were at least two assailants, wheeled quickly to face whatever was in store for him from behind. He caught the forearm of Franz that held the dagger only inches from his body. Grabbing it with both hands, he smashed it across his knee breaking it in two places. The knife went sailing. Still holding the arm of the now screaming Franz, he twisted his body to the ground and placed a foot on his chest. Slowly pressing, he heard ribs begin to break.

Few men his size were equal to Biocles in strength. Now anger infused his muscles with added vigor. He pulled Franz's broken arm and pressed his heavy foot against Franz's chest. Another rib broke and Franz screamed a sharp cry that pierced the foggy air like a lightening bolt.

Biocles eased the pressure but held his position. Looking down into Franz's face, he began to speak. "I hope you can understand what I am telling you. I will only say this once. If I ever see you in Athens again, I will kill you with no hesitation whatever. You go back to that sorry priest in Kresboden and tell him if I ever see another Celt again in my lifetime, I will come to Kresboden and break every bone in his body just as I now break yours. He will never know I'm coming. He will never know I'm there. He will walk into a shadowy place some day and feel an arm around his neck. Breathing will become difficult; bones will begin to break, and the last one will be his neck. Say you understand."

"Ya, ya," screamed Franz.

Biocles glanced at Adolph. Blood ran from the side of his head where it had struck a sharp stone on his falling. He lay limp and lifeless. It hadn't been Biocles intent to kill the man, but he felt no remorse in destroying one intent on killing him. He picked up his torch and turned toward home.

CHAPTER X

Four years later Little Nixe's arm was withered, her shoulder drooped, and one of her legs was shorter than the other. The surprising thing was that few people noticed because she had the face and the smile of an Egyptian princess. She had learned to talk much earlier than other children; and the simple, yet deep, insight of her observations had the entire village of Melz bewitched. It grieved them all that Nixe was four and had never walked.

Marlena sat on the floor with her arms extended to Nixe who stood bracing herself against a small chair Otto had brought. Her violet eyes pled. Her fingers said, "Come."

"All right just two steps, Nixe. Come on, darling, you can do it."

"I can't do it, Mommy. I can't do it."

"Never say you can't do it. Say you'll try. You have learned to stand, now you must learn to walk."

"I'll fall and bust my front or my back."

"If you fall I'll catch you. Do you know your Mommy loves you more than anything in the whole world?"

"I'll try, Mommy, "said the reluctant child. She looked into her mother's eyes and took a step and a plunge.

"Yea," they both exulted. Marlena took Nixe in her arms and gave her a huge bear hug.

"I did it, Mommy. I did it," cried Nixe just before she planted a kiss on the cheek of her radiant mother.

"Yes, darling, you did it. You can do anything you make up your mind you are going to do. Some things will be harder than others, but you must never give up."

Marlena never looked at Nixe that she didn't see Philo. She never heard the music of her voice that she didn't hear Philo. Where could you be, my Philo? What could you be doing, she thought.

Arn burst through the door. Now sixteen, he exhibited most of the characteristics of manhood, or so Marlena thought.

"I have good news," he beamed.

"Well so do Nixe and I, but you go first."

Arn couldn't have throttled his exuberance anyway. "The city council has announced an archery contest. Herr Helvet will donate ten gold pieces for the winner's prize."

"Ten gold pieces? Are you serious, Arn? Do you think you can win?"

"Marlena, it's like I have been practicing for this for five years. I know I can win if they will just let me try."

"Against mature warriors?"

"It doesn't make any difference. I know they will have the experience, but Biocles said I have a natural talent."

"You still remember Biocles?"

'I'll never forget him. You know that."

"What would we do with all that money? We really have all we need right here."

"You don't want freedom? We could start our own business. We could travel."

Arn never said it but he suspected that Marlena must feel it would be safe now to look for Philo and Biocles.

In truth, it was Hans Helvet who thought of the archery contest to be held at the Harvest's End festival. He was trying any project to keep himself distracted from two salient truths that plagued him almost constantly: His wife, long since no longer a wife in practice, was having horrible hallucinations and with terrifying screams was disrupting any semblance of peace in his house. To make things worse, he had fallen desperately in love with Marlena with no encouragement whatever coming from her.

In the weeks preceding the Harvest's End festival, little Nixe had learned to walk, and Arn had convinced the city fathers that he belonged in the archery contest. Nixe held Arn's hand as they walked along side Marlena, the proud and comely sister and mother, through the passages formed by carnival booths. The booths were brightly decorated with banners and pennants waving in the late fall breeze. Clowns performed on temporary stages, and a little band of musicians played happily at the center of the festivities. There were all kinds of good things to eat and plenty of cheap beer.

The farmers brought the best of their crops and animals for display. There were cooking contests. There were wrestling and weight lifting. There were dancers, and jugglers, and magicians. But the main event would be the archery contest. Until then, and probably even then, what most of the men wanted to look at was simply Marlena. She had made herself a new sky blue frock with small flowers embroidered on the hemlines and again at the waist line. Her hair was brilliant in the bright mountain sunlight. Yet, she seemed, somehow, not to be as happy as she should have been, as though some permanent heartbreak lay just beneath the surface of her smile. This mystery only served to make her more attractive. She could have had any man in the village except those that thought she already had a husband, the red giant who showed up periodically. Others thought that Herr Helvet himself had his eyes on her even though he was married. It was no secret that the marriage was an unhappy one.

At just past noon, the horn blew for the main event, the archery contest. The people were directed to a field where the mountainside presented a shelf before it plunged once more to the valley below. On the field they formed what was roughly a huge "U." On one leg of the U was a special viewing tent for the city council and their ladies. On the other was a tent for the contest judges. These colorful tents were set on wooden platforms, affording the officials an excellent view of the proceedings. They were composed of stout goats' wool cloth with broad black and white stripes. Varicolored streamers flew from the crest of each tent pole.

There were phases to the contest. The first phase was an elimination process whereby forty-two entrants would be trimmed to only six. Pumpkins were set on small stands fifty paces from the shooting line. Each entrant had five arrows and six archers shot at the same time. The number of arrows shot into the pumpkin was the archer's score. After each group of six men shot, the crier announced the scores. He stood before the judges' tent with his scroll.

William of Binnengen — three

Urs of Amriswil — two

Max of Chur — zero

Henri of Glarus — three

Emil of Dornbirn — four

And so it went. Arn was scheduled for the last group to shoot since he was considered an unlikely candidate to win.

As the eliminations were underway, a messenger came running to the tent of the city council and whispered in Hans Helvet's ear.

"Sir, there has been a terrible accident at your villa. You should come at once."

"I don't understand. What are you talking about, man? Most of my servants are here."

"I'm afraid it's your wife and daughter, sir."

"Oh no. I'll come quickly."

Chubby little Hans scurried from the tent and headed home in his own special horse drawn cart.

When he arrived at the villa, a single trusted servant, long faced and teary eyed, waited for him at the gate. Ernst wore his white hair short. In his fifties, he showed the lines and calluses that went with hard work. He was still a strong man, and Hans had found him to have a wise and faithful heart.

Hans asked, "Where, Ernst, where?"

"In the back room, sir."

Hans stalked to the back of the house, his servant dogging his steps. When he burst into the room what he saw made him turn away and vomit. Blood was splattered over the floor, the walls, the furniture. The mutilated body of his daughter lay by the south wall, and his wife was hanging by her neck from a ceiling beam.

When Hans could control himself, he turned to his servant, "By all the gods, have they somehow killed one another? You were in charge here, how could you let this happen?"

"I was called to the stables, sir. A mare was foaling and having a difficult time. When I returned, this is what I found. I don't think they meant each other any harm. Apparently Frau Helvet had one of her hallucinations and thought the frauline was some crude monster about to attack her. She evidently took a piece of firewood, there sir," the servant said pointing to the crude weapon, "and beat your daughter. When the vision was passed and she realized what she had done, she must have hanged herself. I'm so sorry, sir. I never dreamed anything like this could ever happen."

Hans placed a hand on his shoulder, "Nor could anyone, Ernst. This is not your fault. It doesn't seem to be anyone's fault. Maybe it's mine. Maybe I drove them both mad."

"Oh, no, sir. None of us has ever known a kinder man than you."

It was Arn's turn to shoot. Little Nixe yelled and clapped and tried to jump only to fall over into the lush grass. Marlena helped her to her feet and brushed her off. Exchanging grins, they returned their attention to Arn.

He was nervous. His first arrow went over the pumpkin.

"Oh no," said Marlena and Nixe in concert. "Come on Arn you can hit it. We know you can."

The rest of the crowd seemed only mildly interested that a boy would enter a man's contest. Only Helga and Frieda stood by with words of encouragement.

"We love you, Arn, yea," they shouted.

Arn told himself that he needed to shut out the crowd and concentrate. He looked to heaven and prayed, "God of Biocles, help me." Then as he nocked his arrow, he could hear Biocles saying, "You have a natural shot, Arn. Don't aim, just concentrate on the target and let the arrow fly."

He brought all his mental and emotional faculties into control and concentrated on the pumpkin. The arrow made a slender arc as it flew the fifty yards and pinned the pumpkin to the stand.

"Yea! Yea! Yea!" shouted his female fans. With this, some of the people began to watch.

"By thunder," said an old mountain man nearby, "the lad has scored an arrow."

By that time Arn was shooting again. There was no waste of motion or strength in his movements. He stuck the pumpkin with the rest of his arrows and the crowd cheered wildly. The home boy, Arn of Melz, had come through. He had qualified for the rest of the match.

Then there was intermission. In the moments when Arn talked with Marlena a whisper went through the crowd. There had been an accident at the Helvet villa. No one knew anything more.

To the great delight of his fellow townsmen, when the six finalists toed the shooting line, Arn again scored with four arrows. But there were two more phases to the contest. To hit the moving targets would probably be the most difficult task of the tournament. It was also the most exciting for the spectators since the men would shoot one at a time. This was done in order to prevent arrows from flying in every direction and endangering people in the crowd.

A special slinger was appointed to prepare five stuffed animal skins. Each was a little more than half the size of the pumpkin. The slinger moved to a distance of only twenty-five steps from the shooters. From there he would sling the targets in any direction he chose as long as the target stayed over the shooting range and did not go into the crowd.

Arn would shoot last. Last, however, was no longer a position of disrespect, but a happenstance determined by the luck of the draw. Arn actually cherished this position since he could tell exactly where he stood in the competition before he came to shoot. He had finished the still targets tied at four with two other archers.

He watched as arrows sailed high, low, and wide of the flying targets. Apparently, none of these men had ever lived off their ability to shoot a flying grouse. The best any could do was score three arrows.

Arn took the line. He knew all he had to do to take the lead was to keep his head. By this time, he had captivated his audience, not only with his shooting ability, but with his good looks, his broad smile, and his open personality. They cheered, and he waved graciously.

The first target was thrown and Arn swung with its flight. He liked the flow of movement and felt one with his arrow. He was reaching out to meet the flight of another object. Two things in space were destined to come together. Ka-pop! The arrow hit dead center and knocked the target from its course directly to the ground.

Little Nixe was beside herself. She couldn't believe anyone could do a thing like that, but her own young uncle, never. She screamed with sheer delight, and she was not alone. Most of the crowd had joined the cause of young Arn.

Arn followed with two more hits and was beginning to win the respect of the skeptics. The slinger then decided he would see just how good this young fellow really was. He threw the next target straight up into the air.

Arn sensed immediately what was happening. None of the other archers had been tested like this. There is a split second when an object thrown straight up seems to hang suspended before it descends. Arn timed it perfectly. Ka-pop! He had beaten his opposition with only four arrows and was ready to retire, but as he removed his hat, the crowd began to chant, "Five, Five, Five …"

He waved. "All right. Five it will be," he shouted. Then he turned toward the target master, "If you will Mr. Slinger."

By now the slinger was irritated. "He'll not hit five in a row," he muttered under his breath. He reared back and hurled the now battered target straight at Arn's face. It was a throw forbidden by general agreement and none of the other archers had to contend with anything like it.

The crowd gasped. Then, only two steps in front of Arn, the target exploded as the arrow went completely through it.

Pandemonium erupted. In all their lives, no one in Melz had ever seen such an incredible feat. They mobbed Arn. Two men lifted him to their shoulders and paraded him about as the crowd cheered, "Arn, Arn, Arn." Everyone wanted to see him and touch him, so see him and touch him they did.

For himself, Arn could hardly believe this. He had a look of self deprecation upon his face. He could hear Biocles saying, "The gods have given you a natural shot."

So he kept telling himself and the throng, "I don't deserve all this. I am only the recipient of a gift." But he waved in grateful appreciation to the crowd. They fell in love with his modesty.

At last the tumult subsided and the crier announced the last contest. "Your attention, everyone. As we all know Arn of Melz has won at moving targets." A cheer arose and the crier lifted his hand for silence. Then he continued. "But there was a tie in still targets between Arn and Emil of Dornbirn. So if Emil of Dornbirn wins the final contest, he will split the prize money with Arn. In the final contest, only two arrows will be shot by each contestant. The contest is for distance. The single longest shot will win."

The crowd began to murmur. "The lad doesn't have a chance. Look at the size of that Emil." And again, "I've never seen such arms on a man. The boy can't win it all, but he has certainly given a good account of himself."

In all the huge gathering only Marlena knew what was going to happen. She knew Arn would surprise them all. But she didn't know if Arn's invention would be enough to carry the day.

Six flags with the contestants' names on them were produced. Then boys ran far out into the open meadow and awaited the shooting. Only the arrow of each archer that went farthest was marked. When Emil, who shot fourth, stepped to the line, he had removed his shirt showing wide leather bands around his biceps and forearms. He nocked his arrow, then flexed his big muscles. Young ladies squealed, and the astonished crowd groaned.

Emil's arrow sailed over the flags of the first three contestants and his second went even farther. The crowd gave a collective sigh of awe when they saw how far out into the meadow Emil's flag was placed. They clapped politely and Emil gave a broad smirk of satisfaction.

The fifth shooter had been unremarkable as expected, and now Arn came to the line. "What's this?" some of the people began to say because Arn carried a longer and heavier than he had used before. Leather laces dangled near the grip of his bow. Then Arn surprised everybody by sitting on the ground. He began to lace the bow to his feet, and the murmuring of the crowd grew to a dull roar. Even the other archers began to gawk.

When the bow was solidly secured to his feet, Arn held his legs just off the ground and tested the bow string. Now it was evident what he intended to do, and the other archers began to complain. The judges looked at each other and scratched their beards.

Arn held his feet up, leaned back and with both hands drew the bow string. He pushed the bow with his legs and pulled the string with his shoulders and arms. Away the arrow sailed. Across the meadow it flew, over all the flags it went, and still it was not spent. Completely across the meadow, the arrow struck a small sapling and penetrated the trunk. It had left sight of the crowd. They hesitated, unable to tell whether to cheer or not.

The arrow boys went running with Arn's flag. They passed the other flags and crossed the meadow. One of the boys spotted the arrow. Quickly he climbed the saplings so all could see. Then he began to wave Arn's flag and shout, "Arn, Arn, Arn."

Greater pandemonium than before erupted. The crowd was ecstatic. Marlena put little Nixe on her shoulders and they began to wave at Arn. But Arn was swarmed by the adoring mob who celebrated for half an hour with cheers, and songs, and dances.

Finally, the crier was able to achieve some order, and he made this announcement: "A protest was lodged as to the manner of Arn of Melz in making his remarkable shot."

Whistles and hisses erupted from the crowd.

"Please, please let me finish. The judges, however, have ruled that the same shot would have been open to any archer had he been clever enough to think of it. The prize goes to Arn of Melz."

A new celebration began that lasted into the night.

The prize, of course, was not given that night. The possessor of the gold sat heart broken, stunned, angry, and still nauseated at his villa. Servants called from the fair had removed the bodies of his wife and daughter and were cleaning the back room.

CHAPTER XI

The wake was held two days later. Though they were not sure of the exact nature of such an event, Marlena and Arn felt compelled to attend. Hans Helvet had been their benefactor and had actually tried to be more, at least as far as Marlena was concerned. But Marlena was afraid of most men. She completely trusted only three on earth, Philo, Biocles, and Otto. Nevertheless, she fixed some tasty sausages, wrapped them in a little cloth with some rye bread and placed them in a small, oblong basket to take to Hans Helvet's villa.

The whole village seemed to have descended upon the place. People stood everywhere in tight little groups whispering mostly about the grim details of the double death. As Marlena and Arn led Nixe slowly through the gathering, they picked up bits and pieces of conversations.

Marlena spotted a servant and gave him the basket. "Where might we find Herr Helvet," she asked him.

"He is seated in the far corner. He tired of standing, poor man. This has been so hard on him."

"I'm sure it has," Marlena said softly. "We'll find him, thank you."

"And thank you for the nice basket. I know Herr Helvet will enjoy it."

This was a strange meeting as far as Marlena and Arn were concerned. In the north woods there was simply a burial of the dead. People mourned, then they went home. Well, not exactly all went home. It was the custom of the Celts for the young couples to go into the woods and make love, hopefully conceiving new Celts and thus defying the effect of death. Now this seemed too public a place for grief, and sadly, Marlena and Arn found more morbid curiosity than grief. How terrible, indeed, it must be for Herr Helvet.

They waited for others to express condolences. By the time they were able to speak to him, the crowd was thinning. Most had gone home.

Arn was beginning to take his place as the man of the family. He spoke first, "We are so sorry for you Herr Helvet."

Hans took the boy's hand. "I understand you won the archery contest. Congratulations. I will get your prize to you shortly."

"Please Herr Helvet, don't worry about anything like that just now. You have been more than kind giving us work and especially sending Helga and Frieda to help with the baby."

"You are growing up fast Arn. I will remember that. Thank you for coming today."

Marlena took Hans' hand as Arn stepped away. "I grieve with you Herr Helvet," she said.

"How many times have I asked you to call me Hans, beautiful Marlena? Do you truly grieve with me?" he asked as he held her hand snugly. A look that bordered on desire came into his eyes, but Marlena didn't notice.

"I truly do," said Marlena. "I know what it's like to lose family."

"Then let Arn help Nixe with some of the good things to eat here and let me show you a marvel we have in our stables. Most of the people are gone now, and I need to get away from here for a few minutes."

"Of course," she said. Then she spoke to Arn, and he and Nixe disappeared toward the food tables.

Hans whispered to one of his servants at the door, "See to it that my guest and I are not disturbed while we are at the stables." Then, he gestured to Marlena, and she followed him out of the house.

The stable was a hundred steps or more down the hill from the house. It was an open affair with only a roof and two rows of railed stalls separated by a central walkway.

When Marlena entered she noticed immediately the good quality of the Helvet horses.

"You have some beautiful animals, Hans. Although my family has never been able to own a horse, I have always liked them." A black mare raised her head and allowed Marlena to stroke the side of her long face.

"The animals sense that you like them. I want to show you a special one." He brought Marlena to the stall of a beautiful chestnut mare. "Isn't she something," he said with pride.

"Indeed she is," said Marlena, holding out a hand and being rewarded with a shy lick.

"Now, look in the dark corner, almost covered in hay."

"Ohhhh, ohhhh," said Marlena with a sigh of awe. She had spotted the foal.

"He is so small. How old is he?"

"Just over two days."

"Hi, little boy," said Marlena as she held out a beckoning hand to the foal. Then he stood, shaky, wobbling. He looked at Marlena with huge brown eyes and shook his head.

Marlena was so enchanted that she didn't notice how close Hans was standing. He was breathing into her ear, "Let me kiss you, Marlena."

She stood straight, and her body stiffened. "No," she cried as she began to fling both of her fists at him in alternate swings.

But Hans pinned her to a stall post and began to cover her face with kisses. Marlena twisted and kicked and screamed. She tried to push him away, "No, no no!"

"You don't understand, Marlena, I love you. Please let me take you."

Marlena began to scream at the top of her lungs. Hans grabbed a handful of her silken hair and forced her mouth to his. With his other hand, he ripped the front of her frock, and in doing so, backed away from her a step.

Without the weight of his thick body upon her, Marlena was able to kick. She buried her knee into Hans' groin, and he bent forward with pain. Marlena leaped free of him and ran screaming to the house. Hans tried to catch her, but alas, his short legs were no match for the nimble Marlena. She ran through the door of the house screaming, "Help, help, help!"

Arn was at her side quickly. The remaining guests gasped. The women placed their hands across their mouths, sensing immediately what was happening, but not knowing who was involved.

"What, what?" asked Arn.

"We have to get out of here fast," sputtered Marlena. She grabbed Nixe into her arms, bolted through the room, and dashed out the front of the villa. Arn was by her side all the way.

Hans was too embarrassed to go into the house. He stopped short of it at a large aspen tree, crossed his arms against it, and buried his head in his arms. "No, no, no, Marlena. You don't understand. I, I've done it all wrong, wrong, wrong." He kicked the huge trunk of the aspen with such a force that he broke his big toe. "Aw," he cried, writhing on the ground in pain. For long minutes he lay there holding his right foot with both hands and moaning, "Marlena, Marlena, Marlena."

Very early the next morning, Ernst, a messenger from Hans Helvet, knocked at Marlena's door. She opened the door only a small crack and peeped out. Her eyes met the sincere gray eyes of a man she felt she might trust if she knew him better.

"I've brought the prize money for Herr Arn," said Ernst.

"We don't want anything from Herr Helvet," said a cheerless Marlena.

"Herr Helvet says he is very sorry. He sends an offering of his repentance." Ernst then turned and gestured toward the hitching post in front of the Hog Jaw tavern. There stood the chestnut mare and beside her the wobbly little colt.

Tears streamed down Marlena's cheek. Such innocence for such guilt she thought. "No," she whispered, and shut the door.

For a few minutes she sat and wept. Then Arn began to stir in his bed.

"Was someone at the door?" he said slowly.

"A man from Hans Helvet."

Arn leaped from the bed, suddenly very much awake. "Did he bring the gold prize money?"

Marlena hadn't thought of the impact her decision about the prize money would make on Arn. So, she hung her head, "I wouldn't take it."

"You wouldn't take it?" he screamed. "What do you mean you wouldn't take it? That's my money."

"You're my ward. I forbid you to take anything from that vile man."

"I earned the money. I worked hard for it. I practiced hours and hours. Now, you won't take it! Besides, Herr Helvet is not a vile man. He does all kinds of good things."

"You weren't buried under his fat little body yesterday. He wasn't ripping your clothes and grabbing your flesh." Marlena began to sob again.

For long moments Arn stood staring at his sister as she bowed her head and wiped her eyes. Time passed, and neither spoke, but Arn began to understand something of Marlena's hurt. Images of Daga assaulting Marlena rushed into Arn's consciousness. Arn was ten again. He was once more standing in a corner of the house of his parents in Kresboden, the evil of Daga terrifying him.

Daga was assaulting the only point of security he knew in his life. He was humiliating the only person he loved. He was devastating Arn's belief in Wodan. Arn wanted to fight

Daga. He wanted to tear him limb from limb, but his courage failed. He at least wanted to scream, but his throat was paralyzed. He hated himself for being ten. He hated being terrified. He hated being a coward.

Surely Hans Helvet was not as bad a person as Daga. Even so, half as bad would be bad enough. He put his arm around Marlena's shoulder and leaned his head into her soft hair. "All right, all right," he said. "What are we going to do?"

"I think we will have to leave this place."

A few days later when Otto appeared, he felt that he was being followed. Then when he heard Marlena's story, he became certain that he should move the little family away from Melz and further from Kresboden.

Further from Kresboden, of course, became closer to the inhabited centers of the Roman Empire. The great tyrannical jaws of that empire consumed human lives like a ravenous bear gobbling berries. In Rome, itself, non-citizens were fed to lions just for the sport of watching it. Otto knew this. So, with Marlena, Nixe, and Arn he journeyed east toward Macedonia.

It was the cursed enclosed convenience that Brunhilda had insisted upon. "I'll not continue to expose my rear end to the winter wind," she said bitterly. "It's freezing my bones."

Daga had no trouble believing something was freezing every part of Brunhilda. So, reluctantly, he set about constructing a small enclosed pavilion at the edge of the forest. There Brunhilda and his daughters regularly relieved themselves. From the first, he had considered this whole business unnatural. Had not the Celts always gone in the woods where feces disappeared in a short time? Now Daga became especially nettled when it fell his duty to remove accumulated excrement from the convenience.

But, as the months passed and brittle cold weather descended, Daga, himself, felt drawn to the shelter. Then in the spring, with foul odor on the rise, it was no wonder when a pyosis appeared in his genitals, that he should blame it on the filthy outhouse. There was no way he could link this malady with his wonderful Gretchen.

He had continued to have sexual romps with Gretchen regardless of the other associations either had. Now, he would have to squelch his desires rather than explain the exudate and pustules to her.

Daga performed certain rituals before the great god, Wodan, and after a time, he received blessed relief. His genitals seem to heal, and he avoided the outhouse with a vengeance. How could he know the dread of the disease had invaded the deeper areas of his body? He resumed his favorite pursuits: meetings with Gretchen and searching for Marlena.

Daga felt sure that Otto knew more than he was telling. Why, for instance, did he make frequent trips into the forest when, seemingly, no one knew his whereabouts. He sent people to follow Otto, but so far they had found nothing. Otto was an evasive man.

Franz and Adolph had shot one of the Greeks and had been ordered home to help their brothers defend the homeland. Correspondence to Greece required too many good men. Besides, Daga was quite sure that Marlena and Arn were not in Athens. They would have appeared in the slave market for one reason or another and spies had watched the market for over a year.

CHAPTER XII

Philo's family felt that the marriage to Theana had gone well. And, as time passed, Philo was drawn more to Theana than he had thought possible. She was indeed a classic Greek beauty with dark hair, clear, pale skin, and flawless features. The soft, ebony hair, when unbraided fell to Theana's waist. It seemed to Philo that the hair was Theana's most sensuous feature, though she certainly was not lacking in any feminine attribute.

But the union was not blessed with children. Penelope felt that somehow Philo was distracted by the memory of the lost Marlena. And to some extent perhaps she was right for no matter how hard he tried Philo couldn't forget Marlena. On the other hand, he had become very fond of Theana, and their marital relationship was good. They were simply confronted with the fact that Theana was barren.

Theana was an exceptional person in many ways. She had been an only child. Her father, frustrated over being without a son, had done an unusual thing in Greek society. He had educated his daughter. In the process, he had come to notice a deep sense of justice and righteousness in her. It was the combination of these traits that drew Philo closer to his wife as the months and years proceeded.

It didn't take months and years for Dorea to love Theana, however. Their bonding was immediate. Theana saw Dorea's potential from the beginning and convinced Alcandor and Penelope that she should teach Dorea to read. Dorea was a quick study. Soon she and Theana were spending hours hovered over works of the masters of Greek drama. Dorea's thespian retorts were to increase by multiples.

The sun had settled behind the western hills and headed itself toward Megara. The sounds of business and the worries of the household died away. Philo sat on the edge of his bed watching Theana brush her hair. For a few minutes, he drank in the scene. He let himself long to touch the hair, to feel its silken sensuality, to hold it against himself. Then he went to her.

"Let me brush," he said.

She turned to him and savored the tenderness in his deep blue eyes. Without a word, she handed him the brush. For a while then, he made long sweeping strokes with the brush, stopping occasionally to hold great locks in his hands and press them against his face.

"I'm not sure I can stand this much longer," Theana said.

"I'm sorry, dear, am I hurting some way?"

"Oh, good grief no. I love what you're doing, and I love you, you big oaf."

"Then what?"

"I'm talking about the insanity and immorality of infant exposure," she said. Solid conviction was in her voice.

Philo continued to brush. This was a subject of frequent conversation between them. Philo knew he wasn't going to tell her anything new, but he was wise enough to know that his wife was probing for something that repetition might help. "Greeks have done it for centuries. So have other people."

"I know it, but does that make it right? Do we tolerate murder in any other form?"

"It's not murder. It's custom. How else would you deal with deformed and unwanted babies?"

"I certainly wouldn't place them on the steps of the temple and blame their deaths on the gods."

"Could not the gods save them if they chose?" said Philo.

"Could not the gods have prevented their lives in the first place? Where does our responsibility begin? I think if children are living and breathing the gods expect us to care for them."

"Theana, you're wonderful. I know the gods must be speaking to you, but what can we do?" Philo continued to brush and each stroke seemed now to brighten and liven Theana's dark tresses.

"We can do what Greeks do about any social injustice. We can speak out. We can set examples."

"Set examples?"

"We can take the babies — at least some of them."

"You're serious."

"Never more serious."

She turned and took the brush from Philo's hand. Then she gave an enticing shrug, and her gown fell completely away.

Philo grinned. "Are you sure we ought to be making our own babies with those others on the way."

Theana engulfed him with her nakedness. "I'm willing to take my chances," she said and giggled.

Long before Theana's barrenness was becoming apparent, they had talked about infant exposure. For as long as any Greek could remember, unwanted babies had been placed on the steps of the temples of various gods. There they lay, at first stunned, then crying, then screaming in alternate spasms until exhaustion. Then, finally, lacking water or food, they starved or perished due to exposure to the weather. The caretakers of the temple came early each morning to dispose of the dead. They checked carefully to make sure they didn't touch any child who was still breathing. Until a child died, any adult could come and claim him. Obviously, most of the unwanted babies were girls.

At the temple of Artemis, god of the family and somehow perversely where most infant exposure occurred, a Greek could ascend to the entrance with no heed or compunction toward the screaming infants that might be present. They were, for all practical purposes, dead already.

They would have no name, no marker, no grave. They were a reality that was not a reality.

Those few Greeks who wanted to do anything about this whole scenario were interested only in removing the nuisance. They wanted the children placed in the back ways and alleys so they wouldn't have to hear them and smell them. Was not that the natural place for city garbage?

Theana was outraged. Philo came to agree with her sooner than she could have expected. Somehow their hearts began to beat as one. They thought the same. They developed plans of action.

Caleb became a stalwart ally. Though he was far from home, he had never forgotten the teachings of his childhood. When Philo had been a boy with a thousand questions, it had been Caleb who answered him, Caleb who had no doubts about his God, Caleb who spoke softly, reverently, confidently, Caleb who had deep respect for all life.

So when Philo had asked, as most children eventually do, what he should do with his life, Caleb had given him a Hebrew answer. "The most noble quest of any person is to know God. You may be physically involved in any number of tasks, but through them all you can find God if you truly seek him."

Through the years Philo had forgotten those exact words, but the deep conviction stayed within him. Find God.

Philo and Caleb sat on the portico where Philo had taken the Celtic arrow. For months the whole family had avoided the place, then gradually they had returned there. The beauty of it drew them now as it always had.

Caleb was speaking, "When any nation neglected her children, there was always tragedy to follow. Some have said the tragedy was our God's judgment. Others said we were simply the victims of our own foolishness, why blame these things on God?"

"I wish I had your conviction of one God, Caleb. Who knows, maybe you're right. I do feel certain of one thing: Whatever gods there are can't be pleased with people killing babies. I'm going to speak against it before the senate. I'm hoping that later they will let Theana speak. There's a distant chance for it."

"You must present a plan of action," said Caleb. "If you arouse opposition to exposure, that opposition must be directed."

"I suppose we should start with minor demands first," said Philo. "Some sanctions, some promotions of adoption, that sort of thing."

"No, no," said Caleb. "You don't understand politics. You have to make outrageous demands to begin with, then make it seem a compromise to the opposition when you actually get what you want."

"I don't understand," said Philo.

"You have to know what you want."

"I know I don't want to see innocent babies slaughtered."

"Let me help you to see something ... What you really want is a people who would rather die themselves than see their own child die. Am I not correct? If the hearts of the people are not changed, then babies will go on dying one way or the other. You could establish orphanages, encourage adoption, and outlaw exposure all on a legal basis, but if the hearts of the people are indifferent, another evil as bad or worse will arise."

"What, then, should I ask?" said Philo.

"Ask for monetary support for every poor mother in Athens."

"You can't be serious. They'll laugh me out of the house."

"Not if you do it right. You must round up support before you speak. Your supporters must cheer upon every salient point of your speech. They must be louder and louder. Then, in your last great flurry, you ask for the money, upon which request they bring the house down. No one will have a chance to laugh, and you'll be surprised how many people will join the throng."

"You can be devious, Caleb."

"All for a good cause," said the wily Jew.

"But that will only be one moment. What about the days of argument to follow?"

"They will not forget the voice of the people. Then after standing your ground for some days, say you are reluctant but willing to compromise."

"What will I ask for?" said Philo.

"Ask for the right of women to speak in whatever forum they choose. The true mothers can turn the hearts of the people."

"It might work. On the other hand, male pride might outweigh selfishness. You're talking about changing a way of life men have dominated for centuries."

"I'm a Jew. Don't you think I know about that. And yet, through the ages there have been exceptions to the rules."

"I know Theana would lead the way, and a great leader she would be."

They heard footsteps approaching the peristyle; and when they turned, Biocles was coming onto the portico. "And what are you two scheming today?"

"You'd be surprised, Minotaur," said Philo.

"Me? Surprised at what you dream up. You know better."

"Come to think of it, no one would be less surprised than you, and there is no one I would rather understand than you. Come. I want to take you for a walk." He put his arm around the shoulder of his friend. "How's your family?"

Biocles and Marcella had three children. They had come in rapid succession after the marriage. Marcella was a true child of the Mediterranean, dark olive skin, wide brown eyes that saw wonder in all around her, adventurous, passionate —right for Biocles. They were well, thank you.

Down the cobbled street, strode Philo and Biocles. They passed the stone and stucco walls of home after home as they descended into the great market place of Athens, the Agora. The sights, sounds, and smells there were like nothing in any other part of the world. There one could see and buy almost anything, from spices to slaves, from nuts to jewels, from tools to animals, from clothing to chariots. Then, if one knew where to look, he could purchase intangible things: influences, sensations, villainy.

Biocles liked to stand with his eyes closed in the spice market. He would tilt his head far back and sniff the air like a deer sensing danger or seeking a mate, drinking in all the fine aromas and thanking the gods for a nose. Now, as they came to that place, there was no time to stop. Philo was not headed to the Agora but through it.

"Tell me Minotaur, of all the virtues of Greek society, what do you think is the greatest?"

"Leave it to you to ask something like that. You know I don't think about things like that."

"For me, take a shot at it."

"I remember we were supposed to be the world's first civilized democracy. So I guess I would have to say: the importance of the individual. Of course, we still have a long way to go on that." Biocles then turned and pointed to a lifted platform where slaves for sale stood stripped to the waist, a common sight in the Agora.

"I have to agree," said Philo.

They walked on through the Agora until they came to the temple of Artemis. There columns of white marble reached fifty feet into the air. Below the columns, the same white marble formed the broad steps which ran completely across the front. An angular roof decorated with sculpted demigods covered the temple.

"Tell me," said Philo as they stood gazing at this Greek marvel of architecture, "do you see anything here that seems to contradict what we stand for?"

A squad of Roman guards trooped by. "The cursed Romans."

"Of course, the Romans. But supposing they hadn't happened by."

At that moment, a baby on the steps of the temple stirred and dislodged itself from its perch. It rolled roughly down banging itself on the rugged edges of stone until it hit the street. Then, the infant screamed in terror.

Forgetting Philo's question entirely, Biocles exclaimed, "This is an absolute abomination." He ran to the baby and took it into his arms. "There, there, little one," he said softly as he placed the bundled baby against his shoulder and patted its back. The child quieted and Biocles put him back on the steps. "I can't stand this," he said to the world in general. Then he turned to Philo, "You brought me here to see this again."

Philo, as he knew he would, had recruited his first ally outside the family. Still, he wasn't sure he considered Biocles to be outside his family. Could a brother have been any closer than Biocles?

"Theana and I are going to get this issue to the people. We're not a wealthy country, but there's no need for us to throw our children away."

"Sure, Phil. You know how I feel. But this is something our people have done forever. How can two or three citizens make any difference?"

"We can begin. We can try."

Greece had never become a united nation. Composed, historically, of various city states, the country had come together only occasionally to fight common enemies. They had not risen together to oppose Rome, and so had been defeated. But the Romans so respected the Greeks that they returned to them much of their own self-government. At one time they had even granted the Greeks independence with only limited restrictions.

Philo and Theana would be concerned with the area of Athens only. They still had the city-state mind set. The city council was composed of Greek aristocrats. The Romans approved this council, not wishing the added burden of foreign government. The Roman emperor demanded only two things of conquered territories: tribute (taxes) and peace.

CHAPTER XIII

Philo, Theana, Caleb, and Biocles had done their work well. Surprisingly, Theana and Caleb had composed most of the speech. Theana had inserted the passion of a childless mother, and Caleb had used Hebrew ethics with a Greek twist. They spent hours weaving their philosophy and fervor into a script of progressive logic and emotions.

Philo had helped, guided, and approved the speech while spending most of his time on the political scene. Using his family's aristocratic influence, he procured an excellent time for his speech. He also touched on his subject lightly in small groups wherever he went, probing to see where he might find support.

Biocles, one of the most popular men in all of Athens, gathered a volunteer gallery. These would be the ones to enthuse over every good statement made in support of banishing child exposure. They were then trained and cued by the cunning Jewish slave, Caleb.

Philo stood in the open <u>Metroon</u>, largest of the government buildings in the Athenian Agora, before the combined assembly of the legislative body including the rulers, the generals, the council, the committees, and the citizen assembly called the <u>ekklesia</u>. These officials seated themselves on the white marble tiers of seats that formed an arc around the open floor of the speaker's area. Beyond this arc was standing room for the gallery. Most of the time the gallery was scant because most lawmaking procedure was boring. On this day, there was a capacity crowd.

The officials drew their white tunics, chitons, about themselves and relaxed in a dubious mood. Many knew the subject Philo would broach, but few took the matter seriously. At least that was the case until, one by one, they turned and saw the crowd behind them. Then they began to whisper among themselves, "What is happening here?"

Philo grasped his scroll in his right hand but left it rolled. At the last minute he had decided not to refer to notes, after all he had read the script a hundred times. He walked three paces to the left then three paces to the right looking into the faces of those assembled, greeting them first with his eyes and the trace of a smile. Did not Aristotle pronounce his most profound teaching while walking around? Perhaps Philo could now tell why. This pacing stilled his senses and brought his mind into sharp focus. He began.

"Fellow citizens of Athens, I come today acutely aware of all it means to be a citizen of Athens: to stand in the shadow of Olympus; to be descended from the world's greatest thinkers and teachers; to be a part in democracy; to understand the combination of body and spirit; and to celebrate life as only a Greek can celebrate it."

With each of these phrases there was applause from the gallery. Then, at the last, there was a great uproar.

"I couldn't bring the words I have to say today to the people of Egypt, or Syria, or Persia, or Thrace, or even to our protectors, the Romans."

At the mention of the Romans, the gallery booed. The legislators were more discreet.

"Has not our father, Aristotle, taught us that to live ethically and morally is to live with fulfillment and satisfaction? Are not we, as Greeks, called upon to strive for the highest and best standards in our world?" And so Philo continued, not worrying about how long his speech was, but rather building point upon point, and trying to stay connected to his audience. Most of the council members were wondering where Philo was going with this.

Then Philo began to speak about the sanctity of life itself. "We Greeks, and especially we Athenians, have realized for centuries the value of all that life includes. We have endeavored to develop mind and spirit without leaving the body behind. No people anywhere have celebrated life as we have. We buffet our bodies to improve them. We train to wrestle, to lift, to swim, to run. And we train our minds and souls as well. We study, we experiment, we explore, we compose. Mathematics, drama, astronomy, literature, poetry, philosophy, medicine, biology, and yes, government have all been either begun or improved by the Greeks."

"Now I ask you, my fellow citizens, why? Is it worth all the effort?"

At this a resounding "Yes" arose from the gallery and applause came from the council in reply.

"Of course it is," returned Philo. "It is worth the effort because all the effort enables us to savor life, to get more of the precious item that the gods have given. We, as no other people, understand that life is not just a quantity but a quality."

"So now I ask you all in good conscience, is it morally right for us to take from others, without compunction, what we value so highly ourselves? Is this not stealing? Indeed, is it not murder?"

The entire audience sat stunned. Even those who were supporting Philo were not sure they would have gone this far.

Philo stood silent, motionless, head bowed. Then he looked up at his hushed audience and softly, but clearly, said, "I am speaking about infant exposure."

A murmuring swept the Metroon, and Philo raised his voice above the noise. He was now passionate, challenging, louder with each sentence. "How can we call ourselves moral? Indeed, how can we call ourselves civilized when we can take a baby and abandon it to suffering and death? I say let's stop it."

Biocles' group stood as one and came through with a roar of approval. The council members sat and looked at one another as though they were wondering what to do. Then a tittering bit of applause broke out among them.

"And if we are to stop it, we must do something to prevent it. I have considered the matter for some time and have come to the conclusion that we must financially aid the poor mothers of Athens so that there is no need for exposure."

The biggest ovation of the day erupted from the gallery. Wild shouts of approval rang across the Metroon. In awe and consternation, many of the council members now rose to their feet and stared at the gallery. Others began to applaud, and the effect of doubt was overcome by the tumult.

When this demonstration died away, Philo spoke again. "We sit here today a body of legislators whose business it is to make decisions, choices if you will. We make choices for people who made the choice to send us here. We revel in the fact that Greek society gives more choices to its citizens than any government since time began. But, should those choices include the right to rob children of any choices at all … ever? Shall liberty oppose liberty? I think not! It is tyranny that opposes liberty. And what is tyranny but the abuse of the weak by the strong. We have for centuries opposed tyranny, and I oppose this tyranny of child exposure. It doesn't make sense, it is morally wrong, and it is taking from a helpless soul what the gods have given us that we so richly cherish. I stand against it. And I pledge to you that I shall stand against it until it no longer blights our society."

Philo was finished, and the gallery once more exploded with applause and cries for justice for children. Those members of the council whom Philo had enlisted for support joined the ovation.

The campaign against child exposure was under way. But there was no way Philo, Theana, Biocles or anyone for that matter, could have anticipated all the quarters from which opposition would come.

Theana began her collection of cast-aways in the weeks following Philo's speech. Realizing they could only take so many, she and Philo had decided upon four. Theana gathered two boys and two girls. She didn't inspect the babies except for sex, feeling that she would not reject any of them for lack of comeliness. She wanted to believe that any life was worth saving.

It was difficult for Dorea to accept the new "family" at first. But when she began to see them as a prospective and captive audience, she warmed to the task of helping care for them.

The children were integrated into the life of the house of Alcandor where they were not only accepted, but loved. Soon after, Theana became pregnant.

CHAPTER XIV

When, at last, Otto's little band had come into the region of Macedonia, he began a search for a new home for Marlena, Arn, and Nixe. He had decided that, in view of Marlena's experiences, he was looking not for security, but for kind people.

Nixe was getting too large to be carried continuously, even by the red giant, Otto. So, she was left to walk on her own for periods of time. As the miles wore on, Nixe's limp became more noticeable; and the imbalance of her configuration became more of a burden. She tired as they climbed a rocky road in the warmth of early fall sunshine. .

"Ma, please, let's rest," Nixe said to Marlena.

Marlena was holding her hand. She knelt and looked into her huge blue eyes. "You are doing so well, little Nix. I think you deserve a rest. Do you think you can make it to that big shady tree?" Marlena pointed to a huge hornbeam that stood beside the road only a few dozen steps ahead. To tell the truth, she was tired too, tired and discouraged. The journey had been long; and so far, they had found nothing.

The sight of the shade encouraged Nixe. "Oh yes," she exclaimed. Then she released Marlena's hand and made for a huge boulder that was covered in shade.

Otto spoke. "The child is an inspiration to me. She has such zest for life, gets excited about such small things. In spite of all this hard journey, I see new hope in her eyes every morning."

"Otto, if it weren't for you, none of us would have hope," said Marlena. "And you know Nixe worships you. Everyday I see her watching you more and more!"

"Yes, I notice it and take heart in it. It's a great reward for what little I do."

Arn was tagging along behind the others. "Why must we stop? Somehow, I feel we are getting closer to Greece, and I want to see Athens."

Marlena turned to him. "I've told you many times; we are not going to Greece."

"You can speak for yourself. Someday I will visit Biocles and Philo. Besides, don't you ever want Nixe to see her father?"

"Arn, sometimes you can be so stubborn. Can't you see how embarrassing and unsettling such a meeting would be for everyone?" They were approaching the shade of the hornbeam and the boulder where Nixe was seated. "Enough," whispered Marlena.

So the little group rested beneath the lush green leaves of the hornbeam. Hornbeams seemed to take root and prosper quite apart from other trees either of its own ilk or any other. This one was some thirty-five feet tall, had grayish, flaky bark and serrate edged, dark green leaves so large and thick that shade beneath it was complete. The group sprawled on the grass and sat on the stones. There they remained silent for long minutes drinking in the sheer pleasure of rest from toil.

Arn, with young sharp ears, was the first to hear the tinkling of a small bell. None of them had noticed a well worn path coming around the hill and meeting the road just beyond the hornbeam. Now Arn looked up the path and said, "Listen, I hear something coming."

All four turned and stared up the path. "Baa, baa, baa," came the sound of goats. The tinkling became stronger and an insistent voice spoke clearly, "Get on with the likes of you."

Then the first goat appeared on the path, stopped abruptly, and stood staring warily at the travelers beneath the hornbeam. Behind him the other goats stopped. Soon they all began to bleat. The voice of the goatherd now spoke in mild agitation. "Well, what is it now? I'd sell the lot of you if I could afford sheep."

An old man, white hair and beard blowing in the soft breeze, came striding through the goats which did him the favor of ignoring him. One buck stood completely astraddle the path, and the old man simply kept walking pushing the goat gently aside with his knees and thighs. Then he spotted Otto's little band resting in the shade.

"Ah, weary travelers?" Without a word of introduction or explanation, he went on. "Maybe a drink of fresh spring water would brighten your spirits," he said. "Soon these obstreperous beasts will smell it and you no longer will be a hindrance to their progress. Come," he said with a gesture down the road.

He kept walking as if there weren't a chance that they would refuse his offer.

Marlena and Arn, being the only ones that understood Greek, looked quickly at one another. "Sounds like a good offer to me," said Arn. He then sprang to his feet and followed the goatherd, leaving Marlena to explain things to Otto and Nixe.

The old man went only a few paces down the road before he took a side path. It was well worn so that it became obvious to Arn that the goats had been there many times. Soon the goatherd came to the spring. It bubbled forth from between rocks. The pure, fresh water foamed over one stone then fell free some four feet into a small pond. Only ten or twelve steps away, a small brook proceeded from the pond.

The old man stepped to the falling water, stretched out both hands, washed them vigorously, cupped them for a container, and began to drink.

Arn approached him with youthful enthusiasm. "I'll say, that looks good."

"Indeed, it is sweet wine from the gods," said the goatherd. He then stepped aside and looked directly into Arn's curious eyes. "Be my guest, young man."

Arn saw in the old man's face a rare grace, a magnetic warmth that placed him completely at ease. He moved to the spring, took a long drink, then splashed the water in his face and finally over his entire head. He stood shaking out his locks of thick hair.

"Ah, a man after my own heart," said the goatherd. "Not just a thirst of tongue, but a zest for life."

Otto, Marlena, and Nixe had followed the old man shortly behind Arn. But when they were only a few steps down the road, some twenty or thirty goats came bolting past them. So when the three arrived at the spring, they found the pond surrounded by drinking goats and Arn talking to the old man while shaking a spray of water from his head. One by one, they drank from the spring.

The old goatherd watched. When they were finished, he extended his arms to his sides, staff in his right hand. "I'm Nikos, goatherd, son of a goatherd," he said. His ancient brown eyes sparkled with inexplicable merriment.

Beginning with Arn, each gave their names until it was Nixe's turn. "I'm Nixe," she said, "and I think I like your goats except that I don't like the way some of them smell."

Marlena explained to Nikos who promptly gave the child a broad smile. "That, of course, would be the bucks of the flock the little one is sniffing."

A commotion broke out among the goats. Two bucks squared off and butted heads straight on. Crack! Both were knocked backward whereupon they reared up on their hind legs, eyed the other fiercely, and butted heads again. Crack!

"Oh, my goodness," said little Nixe. Her eyes were wide as buckets, and her hands covered her mouth. "They'll kill each other."

Nikos saw her concern. He placed his hand gently on her shoulder. "Don't be concerned, little lamb," he said.

"That's just Hercules and Agamemnon. They've been doing that for years and have yet to seriously injure one another. I just stay away from them when they're like that."

Before Marlena could explain to Nixe, Nixe bounded away. She went directly to the fighting goats and placed her small body between them. The others stood astonished as Nixe pointed her finger first at Hercules, then at Agamemnon. "You stinky goats ought to know better than this. What would your mother think if she could see you doing this?"

The goats stood at first surprised, then almost amused, and finally enchanted. Nixe went to each of them, knelt down, looked them directly in the eyes, and patted them. Hercules licked her face.

"I've been messing with goats all my life," said Nikos, "and I've never seen anything like that. They must think she's a nymph or something."

Otto, Marlena, and Arn laughed uncontrollably while Nikos scratched his head. "I don't suppose you'd care to explain this riant outburst over an evening meal, would you?"

Marlena spoke briefly to Otto, then turned back to Nikos, "You are generous, but we must find a place to rest for the night."

"It would be an honor for Copella and me to offer our humble shelter for the night if you would be inclined to stay," said Nikos. "Copella would never forgive me if she knew I let this little angel pass without first bringing her home."

And so it was agreed among them that the keeper of the goats and the child with magical powers over the creatures should spend the evening together.

Copella heard the goat bells and went to the open door of her little stone house. The house was set into the side of a rocky hill. Its door and window casements were painted light blue, a little darker than the azure of the sky. To the left of the house was a corral with a fence of heaped rocks used to fold the goats. To the right a well worn path curved around the hill toward the setting sun. Large boulders and a few evergreens dotted the grassy hillside.

Copella's most striking physical feature was her naturally curly, snow white hair. She was a short woman, with a comfortable, but not fat, figure. And, though she was in her early sixties, not a wrinkle blemished her smooth bronzed skin. Her bright brown eyes betrayed a joy that sprang from deep within.

She stood at her doorway facing south toward the mountains of Greece, the savory fragrance of goat stew emanating from the fireplace behind her. When she saw Nikos and the goats coming, she walked out to meet them. Then she spotted the strangers, and quickened her steps. She went to Nikos, and after first giving the strangers a curious stare, gave her husband a warm embrace and a kiss on the cheek.

Noting her distraction caused by the strangers, Nikos took the opportunity to tease his wife. "It took you long enough to make up your mind, woman. Do you love your man or not?"

"The older you get, Nikos, the longer it takes me to figure out which old goat I should kiss," said Copella with a grin.

Snickers arose from the small group of travelers.

"I only hope the gods note how much abuse I take and still maintain my good humor," replied Nikos, doing a very poor job of feigning injury. "Come, my dear, let me show you to these people."

Then he turned to the travelers. "This is Copella, the loveliest cook in all of Southern Macedonia. She is known to have an incisive tongue, but makes up for it by being a passionate lover."

"You oaf," she said, and kicked his shin without sincerity. "Can't you keep anything to yourself. Tell me about these people."

So Nikos introduced Otto, Marlena, and Arn. When he came to Nixe, he knelt before her. "And now, little elf, I want you to meet my Copella."

Copella bent forward and looked. As she did, Nikos said, "Her name is Nixe."

Nixe had never known a grandparent, nor any older person well for that matter. Now the natural attraction of the very young for the very old overwhelmed her. She saw acceptance in the face of Copella, and when Copella stretched forth her arms, Nixe ran to her and gave her a fierce hug.

"Well now," said Copella still holding Nixe but backing her face away, "this one could certainly steal my heart." Then looking at Otto, Marlena, and Arn, "I'll bet you folks could use something to eat if it isn't already burned."

Arn and Otto helped Nikos bring the goats to the fold while Nixe and Marlena were introduced to Copella's little house. Extra places were set at the table. Nixe did not let Copella out of her sight, and when Copella paused to add a bit of water and flour to the stew, Nixe clung to one of her legs. Nixe began to call her Copie.

When seats were given at the table, Nixe insisted on one next to her Copie. Then, when all sat and began their meal, Nikos asked for an explanation of the laughter he had evoked at the spring.

Marlena explained. "You said Nixe acted to the goats as though she were a nymph with magical powers. In our native tongue, "nymph" is exactly what the word "Nixe" means."

"I suppose there is a story behind that," said Copella.

"Actually, there is a very long story behind it, so long in fact that I'm sure we don't have time for it now."

Arn could see Marlena wanted the subject changed. "I'm curious about Hercules and Agamemnon. Wouldn't most goat keepers sell one off since the two of them fight so furiously?"

"Ah," said Nikos, "those two are indeed a strange brew. They fight over does, but both of them are devoted to the flock. You should see them when a feral animal attacks. They are as brave as they are stubborn. They attack a wolf, or bear, or even a mountain lion from two directions. Neither backs away from sharp claws or ripping teeth. Somehow, they have learned to cooperate in fending off these beasts. You may not have noticed how one of Agamemnon's ears flops down more than the other. That ear was torn almost completely away by a big gray wolf. I had to sew it back with some of Copella's fine thread.

"Anyway, when Hercules saw that, in spite of the wound, Agamemnon turned again to the fray, he decided he would help. We still have the huge wolf pelt. It has two large holes where Hercules' horns went through its soft belly, but still it helps keep us warm in the winter.

"Since that time, I've seen the two of them ward off many predators. Once they fought a black bear."

Marlena was explaining to Otto and Nixe, neither of whom understood Greek, while Arn sat wide eyed. "So I can see why you respect those goats and don't need a dog for a helper."

"They wouldn't tolerate a dog," said Nikos. "And, yes, I do respect them. Of course, I scoff at them all day long, but it is only friendly teasing, and they understand. I certainly wouldn't trade my goats for sheep. Goats have a lot more character. And besides, sheep don't give decent milk."

There were gentle chuckles all around including one by Nikos who seemed to enjoy his own humor as much as anyone else. Most of his speech was punctuated with grins and chuckles as if he were intending to say, "In case you don't know it, this is funny."

That night Nikos and Copella insisted upon Marlena and Nixe sleeping in their bed, but Marlena would have no part of it. The two of them slept on a pallet before the fireplace. Otto and Arn slept in the hay shed next to the goat fold.

As they lay snuggled into the hay, Arn stared through the open walls of the shed at the bright stars. "Do you believe in angels or spiritual beings that take the form of people sometimes," he asked Otto.

"I know what you're thinking," said Otto, himself enjoying the moonless starlit night. "I don't think Nikos and Copella are angels. What gods would put their angels to guarding a bunch of smelly goats?"

"Copella has bewitched Nixe."

"All children respond well to kindness, Arn."

"Do you think there would be any chance we could stay here for a while?"

"We'll see, Arn, we'll see."

Before the dying fire, Nixe huddled close to her mother, thrust her lips through layers of soft yellow hair and into Marlena's ear, "I really do like Copie," she whispered.

"Yes, darling, I know."

CHAPTER XV

Nixe's eyes popped open shortly after daybreak. Without disturbing Marlena, she slipped on her sandals and out the door of the small house she went to greet the Macedonian sunrise. She was drawn to the goats. From their corral she heard low, contented baas. When Nixe had slipped quietly through the gate, she found Copella milking a large doe.

Copella sat on a low, three-legged stool and talked to the goat as she pulled her healthy teats. "You're a good old girl, Persephone. Maybe you aren't as beautiful as you once were, but perhaps your name sake has given you the wisdom to see your own youth perpetuated in the lives of these kids."

Then Copella laid the side of her face against Persephone's flank as she continued milking. Looking to the side, she saw Nixe standing silently watching her every move. "You are quiet as a shadow, young lady. Would you like to try milking Persephone?" Then she turned her head toward her kneading hands and the clay milk crock.

Nixe nodded and came to her side. Then Copella rose and pointed to the stool, "Sit, little Nixe, and let me show you." Copella bent and handled a teat with each hand. "There is a gentleness and yet an insistence. There is also a rhythm." Copella kneaded one teat and then the other, keeping a steady flow of milk from Persephone's udder. Then, she stepped back and put a hand on Nixe's shoulder. "Go ahead Nixe, try."

Nixe looked at Copella and then at Persephone who pulling slightly at her slack tether now had her head turned and was staring at Nixe.

"It's all right, Perse, girl. Nixe likes you," Copella said.

Nixe grasped a couple of teats and tried Copella's rhythm, but no milk flowed.

"You must pull a bit harder," said Copella motioning with her hands, a bit of grimace on her face.

Nixe jerked hard. Persephone bucked knocking Nixe aside and tipping the stool. The milk crock stood intact, but Nixe lay on the ground tears slowly coming to her huge blue eyes.

Copella picked her up and gave her a great hug. "There, there, my little one. Part of this is because we don't speak the same language. I'm going to talk to Nikos about that right away. I'll bet you are hungry. Let's go see what Copella can find to eat."

The embrace by Copella was reward enough for Nixe's efforts. She loved to be near Copella, to smell the aroma of so many good things that permeated her clothes, green grass, goat milk, cooking fire, flowers, fruit, mountain air. But there was something else about Copella that Nixe understood inherently: acceptance.

The morning meal was dried fruit, barley cakes, and fresh goat milk. Nikos and Copella had been whispering to one another during all the preparation. As the whole group sat to eat, Nikos began a short speech.

"As you can see, Copella and I are growing old. The Roman world has absorbed our children, two sons. They left together some years ago and have not returned. The last we heard they had been recruited into the emperor's army."

"The truth is that we need help keeping this farm. Even now, we don't take advantage of our possibilities. There are so many things one can do with goats besides eat meat and drink milk. For instance, we could make more cheese, spin more thread, make leather goods, and for that matter, we could weave cloth if we could learn how."

Arn and Marlena looked at one another and grinned.

"I don't know where you people are going or what you are looking for except that you seem to need work. Copella and I have talked it over, and we want you to stay here."

With the last sentence, Nikos spread his arms wide in a gesture of welcome.

Nixe understood. She jumped to her feet and grabbed Marlena. "Oh Ma, oh Ma, can we stay, please, please."

"You are generous, and we like you very much," said Marlena. "I think that when we are through eating, Otto, Arn, and I will take a walk and talk about this."

"Fair enough," said Nikos, then he turned and smiled at Copella.

Nixe stayed to help Copella clean the table. Otto, Arn, and Marlena climbed the hill behind the small house. They passed Copella's four large apple trees and found two gnarled olive trees distorted with age but still producing a good crop. Beyond the trees, a few rows of barley stood almost ready for harvest. Then the hill rose steeply, and the three began to climb over stunted limestone cliffs until they came to a flat outcropping where they could sit and look out over the valley below.

"It is a beautiful place," said Otto. "Not as striking, maybe, as the Alps, but certainly more graceful."

"Why, Otto, I think you have something of a poet in you," said Marlena with a warm smile.

Otto ignored her remark, but not her person. "I think you should stay here. I don't know a more pleasant place or more pleasant people. They do need help, too. But I think that's not the biggest thing for them. All of you, especially Nixe, make them happy. They're the kind of people to whom the happiness is more important than the farm."

Otto turned his gaze from Marlena and Arn back to the valley and the trail that led around the hill and into the trees. "I'm needing to get home," he said. "I miss Katerina and the children. I've been gone too long. Only the gods know what they think about me."

"We owe a lot to your family for lending you to us. I only hope Katerina is not the jealous type. You know I would have stolen you away from her a long time ago if I had thought I had any chance," said Marlena. She looked at Arn and winked.

"You flatter me, Marlena. I know you have a love, and it's not me. Still, I want you and Arn to know that you are like family to me. You are good people, and the world is full of the other kind. Little Nixe has become dear to me, too."

"She'll cry when you leave," said Arn.

"I suppose she will. But the gods have been good bringing Copella and Nikos into her life. She'll be fine."

They all stood and looked down the valley. They could see the road on which they had come and the brook that the spring formed. Nikos was driving the goats to pasture out toward the sun. From the little rock house with the light blue trim a narrow band of smoke rose and bent with the soft breeze. A pair of ravens circled lazily over the scene. Marlena and Arn gave Otto long affectionate embraces. Both questioned that they would be alive without him, but that was not all that set their bond with him. They were fellow travelers trying to walk away from the hypocrisy of their own religion and customs. They were rejects, but they had a kindred sense of right and truth and good. They didn't fool themselves about knowing much of what these things involved, but they had learned a little the hard way.

A couple of days later, Otto left Nikos and Copella's farm. Everyone wept including Nikos and Copella who sensed the deep friendship between these Celtic wanderers. Otto made things easier by not lingering. He had said his good-byes to Marlena and Arn two days earlier up on the flat rock above the cliff. Now, he lifted Nixe high over his head and looked into her red, swollen eyes. "I love you, little elf," he said and covered her moist cheeks with kisses.

Nixe enclosed Otto's huge head with her arms and held her cheek tight against his. Through sniffs and sobs she said, "Your whiskers always tickle."

"I leave them long just for your amusement," said Otto. He set her on her feet and turned to the road.

A few evenings later, Nixe played in the house with Copella, Nikos checked the goats, and Arn and Marlena sat on a small wooden bench in front of the little stone house with the light blue trim.

"Nikos said that it's only a week's journey to Athens," said Arn.

"It has been years since we saw Philo and Biocles, Arn. Why do you keep thinking about them?"

"Biocles took me off the death altar. Have you forgotten?"

"Of course not," said Marlena apologetically. "I'm sorry, little brother. It's just that sometimes I think I must forget or I'll go crazy. We had to leave them to protect them. They'll probably never understand that and may be less than happy to see us."

"But don't you want to take the chance, Marlena? Don't you ever think of them, wonder how they are, what they are like now?"

Marlena was already seeing Philo in her mind, picturing him that passionate day in the alpine meadow. "If you only knew," she said. Most nights that immediate cares didn't overwhelm her, she went to sleep thinking of Philo. Hundreds of times she tried to put those memories aside, then at last she decided she would just enjoy them and leave her heart to settle the virtue of her decision.

As she reached her later teens, Gretchen's taste had turned to younger lovers. And Daga, growing prematurely weak it seemed, did not have the energy to pursue her into the woods and argue with her. If the truth were known, he felt he had the upper hand toward a new conquest. And, if his plans worked out, the new experience would be sweet in more ways than one.

Otto had been absent from Kresboden for over six weeks. His wife, Katerina, was distraught, and his young son and daughter openly expressed doubt that their father would return. The natural thing for Daga to do as chief priest of Wodan was to comfort the family. He particularly enjoyed comforting Ava, the willowy red headed daughter who, at fourteen, had become the most beautiful woman in Kresboden. Her hair was not as bright as Otto's nor as curly. It hung around her shoulders in wavy locks that circled her round face and added glow to her emerald green eyes. Her mouth was a bit large so that when she smiled, her straight teeth showed all the way back to the molars.

Daga decided that she should become a priestess of Wodan. That would require many hours of intense instruction. Everything had to be just right to please the gods - the chants, the clothing, the prayers, the customs. Yes, it would take many hours each week for years. All this was explained to Katerina.

She would think about it. Somehow she had noticed Otto's bland attitude toward Daga. Otto had never said anything, but like all women, Katerina noticed little things, facial expressions, lack of interest, body language. While she was deciding, she felt it would be all right for Daga to instruct Ava in preliminary matters. This would take only a few hours a week from the active teen-ager's time.

One morning, Daga noticed a tingling in the fingers of his left hand. As the days passed, the tingling became numbness and crept up his left arm. The muscles of the arm resisted his brain's commands. He did rituals. He took special potions. He exercised the arm as vigorously as possible. Nothing helped. The numbness got worse.

CHAPTER XVI

Katerina, once a young beauty, was not growing old gracefully. Her light brown hair had not lost tone, but calluses appeared on her hands, knees and feet. Deep lines furrowed her forehead, and shadows surrounded her eyes. The life of a warrior's wife was not an easy one.

She harvested late ripening vegetables in the garden behind her log house. Her young son, Zigmond, worked beside her. Ava was cleaning the house; she was to join them later. Neither Katerina nor Zigmond heard Daga arrive. He knocked lightly at the door and called for Katerina.

Ava's voice answered, "Come in, Daga, Ma and Zig are in the garden."

Daga stepped through the door to find Ava sweeping the hearth. He went to her and placed a quick kiss on her cheek. "You are lovely this morning child, just as you always are."

This was a new experience for Ava. Daga had never greeted her like this before. His salutations had always amounted to a word or two then a wave or a pat on the shoulder. Yet, he was a more and more familiar figure in the household. She shrugged. "Thank you Daga. I never would have thought you noticed."

"Ava, I'm growing older, but I assure you I'm still very much a man." He remained only a step away and began to speak to Ava of her beauty.

Kresboden was still the most beautiful sight in Otto's memory. As he came through the forest edge into the dale that encompassed his home, he beheld once again the circle of log houses, the giant meeting lodge, the open smithy's stall, the play area where children and young mothers frolicked, the wood shop where carpenters continually fashioned their goods, and the tanner's house at the far end where animal hides stood stretched on green willow racks. Every house had antlers of various animals attached to the front doors and walls. These not only warded off evil spirits, but they lent fertility to the families within.

Otto had decided to creep into his house silently and surprise Katerina. He lifted the latch bolt gently. As he slipped into the house, he heard a muffled cry. There, against the far wall, Daga had Ava pinned. His left arm hung paralyzed at his side, but his right hand was over Ava's mouth and his body pressed hard against her semi-nude body. Her torn frock hung from her waist. Daga was speaking with low snarls. "You must accept this as submitting to the high priest of Wodan. It may hurt a little bit, but later on you will enjoy it, my love."

That was all he could say before Otto had raced across the room, seized his gray hair close to its roots and spun him around. Scowling into his face, he growled, "You filthy snake." He sank his right fist into the center of Daga's face with such force that he crumbled the bones and buried his nose in the midst of them. Blood spurted, Daga reeled across the floor and crumbled into a heap beside Otto's favorite chair, the one draped with the stag skin.

Ava shouted, "Oh Pa, oh Pa! I'm so glad you came." Then she burst into loud sobs as Otto held her in his arms.

"Come, sweet Ava," he said. "You must rest." He placed her on the bear skin before the hearth and covered her. "You are all right now. You lie here while I kill Daga."

"No Pa. Don't do it. Please don't do it, especially here in our house. I can't stand it."

"Just think of it as throwing out garbage," said Otto. Then he turned to Daga. But Daga had crawled to the door. Daga half stood, opened the door, and went out into the village green. One of the small children there saw his face and went screaming to her mother.

Otto stood at the door and seeing the repulsion of the child, looked at Daga. He had only seen one such sight in his life. When he was younger, he had known a man who had been kicked in the face by a horse. Daga's nose was buried and the nostrils of it were turned out and up. Half his forehead slanted in. One eye was protruding at an angle from its socket. His upper lip was caved in and his upper front teeth tilted forward. All of this swam in a sea of half clotted blood.

"I'll kill him later," said Otto. "Let him live with that for a while." He shut the door and turned back to Ava. "All right, sweetheart," he said. "Maybe the gods have something worse in store for Daga, anyway."

Nikos, with Copella's wholehearted assent decided to add a bedroom to the little stone house with the light blue trim. It would be behind the present house so that the back of the fireplace could give it some warmth in the winter. This bedroom would be for Arn and for Otto when he returned for visits. In keeping with the modest dimensions of the house, the new room was small. There was just enough room for two single beds and a wooden chest for personal belongings that could also double as a seat.

For weeks Nikos and Arn searched their hillside for flat stones of just the right size. They loaded these stones onto the family cart which was pulled by Electra, the only beast of burden on the farm. Electra was a brown jenny burro with huge carob eyes and hairy ears as long as the rest of her head. She had a very definite idea as to her purpose in the scheme of things at the goat farm. Her pulling force was one burro power, not one and one-half burro power, not one and one-quarter burro power.

If Nikos or Arn put too many stones on the cart and told Electra to go, she would nudge slightly then stand perfectly still. Any insistence by Nikos to make her move met with stubborn and solid resistance. But when the proper number of stones were removed, Electra proved to be a reliable helper. Nikos understood Electra. He was old enough that he had to take frequent rests himself.

So it was that when enough stones were accumulated at the back of the house that Nikos and Arn began work on the room. They knocked a hole in the back wall of the house next to the chimney and shaped this opening into a doorway. They built three walls leaving room for a window in back that would look up the hill to the apple orchard, the old olive grove, and the rock escarpment above. The plank roof and floor were placed last. All through the process Nikos was teaching Arn, and Arn's respect for the old man grew.

When the window frame was painted light blue, the room was finished leaving only the carpentry for the two beds and chest. Nixe wanted to paint the beds and chest light blue, but Arn would have no part of it. This was to be a man's room. It was Arn's first room of his own, and he took singular pride in it. He stood in the center of the room with Nikos and Copella looking out the window and up the hill.

"You have made me feel a part of this place," he said.

"You are not just a part of this place," said Nikos, "you are a part of us."

"I'll never be able to express all of my gratitude," said Arn as he gave them each a hug.

"Your being here with Marlena and Nixe is all the gratitude we want," said Copella.

Arn did have something in mind, but he wouldn't tell about it yet.

Nixe had decided to have a serious conversation with Persephone. She sat on a stump in the meadow close to where Persephone was grazing and began to call to her. "Come here, Perse. Come on, girl. I won't hurt you. I just want to talk to you so we can be friends."

Persephone lifted her head and looked toward Nixe with the kind of blank, indifferent stare that only a goat can muster.

"Can't you see I like you, Perse. I like all the goats. Of course, I have to get on to Hercules and Agamemnon once in a while, but they understand." She held out an open hand. "Come on, girl, let me pet you."

Cautiously Persephone moved toward Nixe. She stopped just out of arm's reach and looked into Nixe's eyes with added interest.

"I'm sorry I hurt you when I tried to milk you, Perse. I just didn't know how. From now on I will be careful. I know being milked must be a very personal thing. Maybe I didn't even have the right."

The goat took a couple of steps and licked Nixe's nose. Nixe reached out and rubbed her ear gently. "Does this mean we can be friends?"

"Baaaaa," answered Persephone with such force that Nixe was startled.

At her movement, Persephone stepped back. "Oh, no, girl, it's all right," said Nixe. "It's just that I didn't know you could talk so loud."

That seemed to please Persephone. She gave another loud "baaaaaa," turned, and trotted back to the flock.

Marlena saw the whole scene from the farmhouse. When Persephone licked Nixe's nose, any misgivings she had about staying at the farm were gone. A sense of warmth and belonging came over her. "Goats," she whispered. "I never would have believed it."

Arn had settled on what he wanted to do for Copella and Nikos. He busied himself making a weaving loom.

Marlena was on the hill by the olive trees helping Copella find roots and berries that made dyes for thread. Nikos had gone into the village to trade goat cheese for honey and to have some olives pressed for oil. He had loaded Electra with the cheese and olives and left at daybreak.

Most of the people in the valley said Electra was lazy. Nikos preferred to think of her as overly contented. She always seemed to prefer the status quo whatever that condition happened to be. If at rest, naturally she wished to stay at rest. She never ran and had only one pace of walking which was exactly the slowest speed that Nikos would tolerate before securing and using a sycamore switch. The strange thing, then, about Electra was that once she established the gait and was guided by Nikos, she went into some sort of trance, no doubt imagining cool shade, green grass, spring water, handsome jacks and whatever was contained in that pleasant donkey Elysium in the sky.

So it was that when Nikos wanted Electra to stop, rather than simply giving the command, it was usually necessary for him to aim her at a fence, a wall, a tree, a bush or whatever barrier might halt her progress. She walked directly into the corral gate, shook her head a bit and stood waiting for Nikos to open it.

Once Nikos had stalled Electra, he headed for the house with his load of honey, olive oil, and a bit of salt. Copella met him at the door with a hug. "What did you bring me, you sweet thing?"

"Aha, now I am no longer the oaf who talks too much. You only love me for my wealth," said Nikos.

"I'm afraid you have perceived the iniquity of my heart," said Copella with a grin. "But I still want to know what is in the basket."

"Honey for my honey, what else," proclaimed Nikos.

"Oh, you are a good man, my Nikos. We'll have honey cakes for dinner."

So when the little group gathered around the table that night, they were greeted with the fragrance of freshly baked honey cakes. There was an established order by now. Fortunately, the table was round, Nikos and Copella having found long since that more chairs would fit around this shape. It was the only shape they felt a house of hospitality should possess. Nixe sat between Copella and Nikos. On Copella's left sat Marlena, and Arn completed the circle.

They savored their honey cakes and praised Copella. "However could I have even started these if my man had not made the trip into the village," said Copella.

"I suppose if we must pass out credits, Electra must have her part. After all, she did carry the load," said Nikos.

Arn raised his glass of milk. "Here's to Electra," he toasted.

Everyone smiled and raised their glasses. "To Electra!"

"So what about the bees?" asked Nixe.

Then they all had a good laugh indeed.

"There is news from Greece," Nikos began. Marlena and Arn gave one another a curious glance. "It seems that Athens is in turmoil over the issue of child exposure."

"I'm afraid I don't know what child exposure is," said Marlena.

Nikos explained the whole process.

"No wonder there is turmoil over it," said Marlena. "I can't believe such a thing."

"It's been done for centuries," Nikos continued to explain. "It's an ancient custom of many civilizations."

"It doesn't sound very civilized to me," declared Arn.

"No, it doesn't. But, until recently, it has been accepted without question. Now word is that women have come out of their homes to speak against it, and there are near riots in the streets."

"Evidently the temple officials, who it was thought would side with those against exposure, have come out for it. They say that it gives the gods a chance to correct their mistakes."

"Those who are against exposure feel betrayed. They are claiming that the priests are only protecting their income. It seems that many people who place babies at the temple also give offerings in hopes that the gods will find homes for the children they can't support."

Later that evening Copella and Nikos played with Nixe. As old as they were, there was still much of a child in them both. They didn't deny it; they relished it.

Marlena and Arn sat in the moonlight on the little wooden bench in front of the house. Arn spoke first, "Can't you imagine Biocles and Philo in the middle of that battle to save the children? I wish I could be there and help them. Surely there would be something I could do."

Marlena, usually quick to squelch such talk let Arn go on. When he paused she spoke, "I've had bad dreams lately. I've had some strange premonitions when I've thought about Philo." A look of perplexity and foreboding came to her face. "Somehow I sense they are in danger, Arn. Somehow I feel now is the time for us to go to Athens."

Arn's eyes lit up, and he jumped to his feet. "Marlena, that's wonderful. I thought I would never hear you say it." He wrapped his arms around his sister. Together they wept.

"I only hope it turns out to be half as good an experience as you anticipate," she said.

CHAPTER XVII

Many times rumors carry only a grain of truth, and sometimes they contain no truth at all. Such was not the case in what Nikos had heard in the village. In Athens customs were being threatened, and tempers were flaring. Not only was the custom of child exposure at stake, but also being overturned was the relegation of women to the homes.

While Theana was sounding the battle cry of "Women Unite to Save the Children," others had decided that women should unite to preserve the customs. One group was fighting to preserve what they believed to be their heritage. Others were fighting for life over death. Already many had been injured in street brawls. In every tavern, gymnasium, spa, bordello, and home, the conversations were the same: what about child exposure. Theana, Philo, Biocles, Caleb and others had accomplished their first goal. They were causing their city to face the issue. They had not anticipated, however, the fury of the opposition.

Theana was six months into her pregnancy. The baby within her must surely have been a healthy one for he grew large and active. Even beneath loosely draped clothing, this baby showed that he would soon appear in the outside world.

But this would not deter Theana from her appointed speech. The time had come for her to go to the steps of the Stoa of Attalus in the Agora and speak to the people of Athens about child exposure. She felt very much that her condition would add to the impact of what she had to say. Philo and Biocles worried. There was a mob mentality there along the road to the Acropolis. But Philo knew Theana had come too far to turn aside now.

For Theana this was a day she had dreamed of and lived for. In the history of Greece, few women had this opportunity. Everything, simply everything, must be right.

Her ankle length chiton was immaculate. She wore the special cotton one, a rare garment in a world of woolen clothes. It had been bleached no less than four times. Its pristine whiteness shone as she expected it to, a light in a dark world. Because of the baby, she had abandoned the narrow belt women usually wore. Her cloak was draped over her shoulders and arms with just the correct number of folds.

Theana wove her shimmering, raven hair into two braids that she twined around her head coiling the ends into a bun at the back. Pearl barrettes held it snugly in place. Many Greek women would have used artificial face coloring, lip rouge, and eye shadow. Not Theana. The natural contrast of her jet black brows and long curling lashes plus her black eyes with the smooth white skin of her face was dramatic and beautiful.

Her mother was one of the ones who had advised her against this adventure. Protective, conservative she had pled with Theana to retreat to her home and be a good mother. Even so, on the evening before, she had brought Theana a pair of new black sandals. They were made of soft goat skin, and they were polished to a high shine so that Theana was a perfect vision of black and white. She chose only one contrasting adornment, a necklace of sparkling malachite, green, the color of life.

She had practiced her speech dozens of times. She had practiced gestures and expressions. She had gone to the temple and prayed the gods to give her the attitude that people could perceive and believe in. Somehow, her sincerity must come through what would surely be fear as she stood before the large gathering. Too much fear and years of preparation would be gone for naught. She told herself she would concentrate on the issue and try to take cues from the people.

All these things came in an unending flurry through Theana's mind until she knew she must relax. "I need some distraction," she thought. "Of course, I'll find Dorea."

She came upon her in the peristyle where Dorea was doing Clytemnestra from Agamemnon, the great play by Aeschylus. When Dorea saw her she threw her arms into the air and tossed her head back sending lose locks of fine brown hair swirling about her shoulders.

"Good news," she shouted. "As the old proverb says, may morning rise out of the womb of night. My news is this: the Greeks have taken Troy."

And Theana replied, "No, I cannot grasp it, incredible."

"And speaking of wombs, how do you fare this day, most beautiful of ladies? Has the time come that we long have foreseen?"

"Yes, Dorea, I've come so that you might wish me well."

Dorea ran to Theana and hugged her widest part. "Well, indeed, and very, very well, my dear Theana," said Dorea directly at her abdomen. "I shall remember this day and when my unborn nephew is competent enough to absorb it, I will tell him of your beauteous splendor."

"Child, you are everything my confidence needed," said Theana. She encircled Dorea's head with her arms and whispered into her ear, "I love you dearly."

By mid-afternoon the fog that had rolled in from the sea that morning had lifted, and bright sunshine bathed the Agora. Before the Stoa of Attalus a crowd of citizens and travelers gathered. They filled the space before the steps and spilled out into the street itself giving little heed to the traffic of horses, wagons, carts and such that sought to pass.

Some had come early and stood around in little cliques debating about this opposition to child exposure.

Then, Philo arrived. He walked half the way up the steps and called the crowd to attention. Both "for" and "against" were curious as to what would be said, so they all listened.

"You, my fellow citizens, have a rare opportunity this day," Philo said loudly. "You will see and hear from the heart of a woman who has a deep passion for the life of all who live here. I know this is true because this woman is my wife. No man could be more proud of his wife than I am this day of Theana. Please hear her with attention and respect."

Then, Philo turned and gestured toward her and Theana ascended the steps of the Stoa of Attalus alone, a planned gesture of strength. Cheering and booing alike rose from the throng.

Her face beamed, her voice seemed exceptionally strong. "Fellow citizens of Athens, I greet you in the name of all we hold sacred and beseech you to hear what I have to say."

Biocles had rallied supporters, but in the process of this promotion, word had spread to their opponents. It was impossible to tell which group was the most ardent. Too, there were always people in the Agora who were from other places, near and far. This occasion was no exception. These travelers were curious about such a large gathering and came to the Stoa steps asking questions. They were surprised to see a woman come forward to speak.

"Beneath my breasts a new life grows. I'm sure you've noticed." This broke some of the tension in the crowd. A chuckle rippled through the group. "To me this life is very special. I guard it with my own life as any sane mother would."

"Then what are you doing out making silly speeches," cried a heckler.

"Yeah, yeah," shouted his supporters.

"I'm here because, although my child is sacred to me, I know that he is not the only child in Athens. There are many others whose lives are not guarded. This little baby will have two brothers and two sisters taken from the steps of the temple of Artemis."

A cheer rose. Then a sneering cat call. Then the waving of arms and shouts of, "Go home."

Theana smiled. "I'm happy that I have a home to go to, would to the gods that everyone had one. Do you realize that every year hundreds of babies die on the steps of our temples and out into the Athenian hills because they don't have homes, because no one, absolutely no one, will give them one?" Theana spread her arms and looked to heaven. "Where is the great heart of Athens when it comes to child exposure?"

"You shut up," cried a loud antagonist.

Then, the derisive turned on the supportive with fists and sticks. Stones rained down all around Theana. One struck her abdomen. She bent forward in pain, and as she did another stone hit her left temple. Blood poured from her head as she fell to the steps. Her snow white tunic collapsed in a heap capped by the red and black of blood and ebony hair, innocent beauty felled by anger and ugliness. The crowd went hush.

Philo rushed to his wife, Biocles at his side. When Philo raised Theana in his arms, he could tell her breathing was shallow. She opened her eyes and mouthed, "I love you." No sound came forth. No more sound would ever come from her lips.

With her limp body still in his arms, Philo turned his tear-stained face on the crowd. "You have killed my wife and with her you have taken our child. Is this what you truly are, people of Athens? She thought you were more. She thought you were better. Apparently, you are not. Go fling your babies on the temple steps. Kill them and with them the hearts of their mothers. It's the real you. Forgive us for not seeing it." Then Philo hung his head. Biocles put an arm around the shoulder of his friend and led him away.

The entire crowd was stunned. Only a few saw a young mother with a modest hood over her head faint and fall into the street. When she fell, a few locks of yellow hair spilled from under the hood. The young man beside her bent and ministered to her. The child with them cried, "Ma, ma, did they hit you too?"

The young man lifted the woman and took her to the edge of the crowd where she could get fresh air. There she soon revived, and the three walked away. Some noticed that the little girl had a slight limp. The young man had a bow slung across his back and a small quiver of arrows.

At the edge of Athens, they sat in the shade of a mountain laurel beside the dusty road. "Are you going to be all right, big sister?" asked Arn.

"I need a drink of water," said Marlena weakly. Her face was still ashen. Nixe clung to her as though by sheer will power and physical tenacity she could keep her mother from fainting again.

Arn took the gourd water bottle from around his waist and gave Marlena a drink. She sipped slowly.

A small squad of Roman city guards approached. They stayed in step, but their pace was not hurried. They wore steel helmets a bit like a basin turned upside down, short leather skirts, brownish red tunics, and over that long shirts of knitted chain mail. They carried short swords and long daggers. Small headed spears rested on the shoulders of all but the leader whose spear swung on laces across his back. He walked with a swagger, the affectation acquired from many battles that had gone his way. They stopped directly before the three travelers and stared. The chief squadsman, a large, muscular, hairy man with a great black beard looked mostly at Arn. He spoke in acceptable Greek. "Can you use that bow, young man?"

"A bit, sir."

"We need archers in Asia Province," he said. "How would you like to be part of the emperor's army?"

"I, I have to look after my, my sister and my niece," stammered Arn.

"Are you a Roman citizen?" asked the sergeant.

"No, sir."

"No? no? ha! I can take you under Roman laws of conscription."

He grabbed Arn's arm and swung him around to look at his entire body. "Healthy enough, I think," he proclaimed with a grin.

Marlena was remembering what Copella had said about both of her sons disappearing into the Roman army. It already had been a bad day, now her whole life seemed to be falling apart. "No," she screamed. She got to her feet and went storming for the knarred, weather beaten sergeant. "You can't have my brother!" She beat on the soldier's chest with only comic effect.

The whole squad began to laugh. Then the sergeant, upon seeing Marlena in full view, said, "Well now, maybe we will just take your sister and leave you be." Releasing Arn, he grabbed both of her wrists and held tight, bending her arms away and causing her to kneel before him.

"You barbaric animal," she cried. Nixe came and began to kick his legs. The soldiers thought it was all very funny. Then, Marlena bit the sergeant's knee. When she did, he released one of her wrists and slapped her hard knocking her to the ground.

"By the gods, I think she may be fun if I can just tame her," he gloated.

Arn could see the lecherous look on the sergeant's face. He had seen the look before in the eyes of Daga, the high

138

priest of Wodan. He had been a child, unable to protect her then. Now things were different. "Leave her alone," he said, stepping in front of Marlena. "I'll go with you."

"No, Arn, no," cried Nixe.

"You can't, Arn. Please don't," cried Marlena.

Arn spoke to the squad master. "Give me a few minutes to say good bye to my family."

The sergeant nodded his approval, and Arn led Marlena and Nixe back to the shade of the laurel. They were both sobbing. Marlena's cheek was cut and bleeding.

Arn placed one arm around each of them. "Please listen to me," he whispered. "You both must be brave. Hush now. Hush." They stopped the sobbing, but tears continued to pour from their eyes. "Remember what you are made of," said Arn. "We are children of the northern warriors. We will survive." He took his arm from around Marlena and lifted her chin. "You must go back to Nikos and Copella. You must not tarry." He took the water bottle from his waist and gave it to her. "Go as far as you can as fast as you can. But don't run, especially in front of these men. Fear will stir their emotions."

Then Arn knelt before Nixe. "Promise me you will be brave, little elf."

"I don't want to be brave. I want you, Arn."

"I promise I'll come back." Nixe's head was down; tears dripped from her nose. "Now can you promise me you'll be brave until then." Arn was pleading.

Nixe raised her head, nodded, and wrapped her arms around Arn's neck. He stood with Nixe clinging to him. Gently he released her grip and placed her on the ground. He gave Marlena a short embrace and turned away.

Then once again he faced the sergeant who commanded him, "Stand at alert."

Arn stood still and straight, whereupon the sergeant laid the flat of his spearhead on Arn's shoulder and very formally announced: "I conscript you, what's your name?"

"Arn of Melz."

"I conscript you, Arn of Melz, to the service of the Emperor of Rome. Take your position behind the squad."

Marlena and Nixe stopped their retreat long enough to look back. Emotions of fear and loneliness already were upon Marlena, but through these feelings a new awareness came to her. Arn had behaved like a man, a true man, brave, gallant, and determined. Maybe he would be all right.

As Arn walked to the back of the group, one spoke. "I think you got the worst of that deal, sergeant. You should have taken the woman."

"I can't get a week's pay for a woman. Besides, there are lots of women around."

"Not like that, sarge. Not like that."

The sergeant gave them a stern look. "All right, let's straighten up this unit," he shouted and led them away. He had a slight limp. Blood trickled from his knee, but he dared not give it any attention. A Roman soldier wounded by a defenseless woman - the gods forbid.

The next day Marlena and Nixe trudged north toward Macedonia. "Why ever did we go to that place, Ma?" asked Nixe. "It was filled with evil."

She was ten years old. Marlena decided it was time to tell her about Philo. "You've never asked about your father, Nixe. Is there any reason?"

"I've always thought as long as I had Uncle Arn and Otto what did I need with a father."

"Yes, you've had the love of very good men." She paused, held out her hand to Nixe who took it readily, then she began. "I have a long story to tell you, but we have a very long walk ahead so maybe it will help us pass the time. Where shall I begin?" She paused and thought. "Many years ago, Arn and I lived in the great northern forest in a village called Kresboden …

CHAPTER XVIII

At about the same time in that same Kresboden, the people were gathered in the forest clearing where they were accustomed to worship. Daga, high priest of Wodan, stood before them speaking. His face was caved in and his left eye bulged causing him to resemble some monster the wood carvers might design. But somehow the revulsion of his appearance had become a bit fascinating to these people.

Daga had spent many days going about the village talking to people trying to turn them against Otto. Now he would bring these preparations to a proper culmination.

"These weeks while I have rested to regain my strength, I have remained silent. Many of you can not look at me. My face is the product of a man crazed with jealousy. Otto is jealous of my power with you and with Wodan. He leaves his village and his family and expects to return with all the respect he had before he deserted us. He doesn't deserve it, and he will not get it," screamed Daga.

Many of the people cheered. But Otto did have the respect of others, especially those who had fought with him. He had stayed quiet about what had happened that day he hit Daga so hard. Now, as he sat and listened to all the lies Daga spouted, fury welled up in him. He stood and pointed his finger at Daga. "He tried to rape my daughter," he shouted. "I should have given him worse."

The people gasped at the thought: their priest a rapist? Even the most skeptical had a hard time believing it.

"The deserter is also a liar," screamed Daga. "How dare he challenge the integrity of the high priest. You, yourselves, have elevated me to this position for my piety. You know me. I am not a rapist. Until recently, you have known Otto, but he has been absent so much lately how can anyone know what has happened to him and what he is like."

"Ya," cried the people. "Ya."

"I say away with him. Otto get out! Otto get out!" shouted Daga.

The people turned on Otto and Katerina who was standing at his side. "Otto get out! Otto get out! Otto get out!"

Otto grasped Katerina's arm and walked through the crowd. No individual who valued his health dare lay a hand on him. Daga's face was proof enough of that.

At his log house, he told Katerina to pack the family's things.

"Don't tell me you aren't going to stay and fight this," said Katerina. "All my married life I have waited on you to come back from battles. More often than not you have come back a winner. Now, when it's time for you to fight for our home, you're going to walk out."

Otto sat on the big bear rug before the hearth. "Come Katerina, my love, and sit with me. We need to understand one another."

Katerina knew Otto was a good man and a brave man. It was true, she did need to understand him. She relaxed on the rug and leaned against Otto. He put his arm around her and began.

"There are many things I haven't told you because I didn't want you to worry," he said. "Many years ago I caught Daga in the act of raping Marlena …" He told her, then, all the story of Daga's infamy and how he had tried to kill Arn to get him out of the way. He told how he had helped Arn and Marlena these years, and about where they were and what they were doing.

"Now here's an important thing I want you to know. You remember Karl, of course."

"Yes, Karl was a good man I always thought."

"And I agree with you. When we were following Marlena and Arn who were with the Greeks, I decided to tell Karl about Daga. Karl and I have stood beside one another in battles many times with our lives on the line and had learned to trust one another. We spent many evenings by the campfire talking about Daga and our religion."

"Now here is the thing I can't get out of my head. In all that time I could never convince Karl of what an evil person Daga is. We were the best of friends and Karl listened, but the crutch of his religion was too much for him to cast aside, and he thought Daga and his religion were the same."

"Do you see what I am trying to say, my Katerina?"

"If you couldn't convince a friend like Karl in all that time, how could you convince a whole village who is already hostile," she said. "I'll pack."

"Before you do, I want you to know something else."

"Yes."

"I know of a peaceful little valley in Macedonia where there are good people, and their religion is not such a burden."

"Where is Macedonia? I've never heard of it."

Back at the meeting, Daga wasn't through. If Otto was gone, Ava would be gone. Daga wanted more than ever to have Marlena back. It was Marlena who had given him the burning desire for pliable, shapely and youthful bodies. It was Marlena whose beauty and energy had bewitched him. He must convince the people that more men should be sent to find her.

He stood before the people in his most convincing attitude, raging. He waved his good arm and glared from diverging eyes. "We suffer tragedy upon tragedy because we have not yet recovered the sacrifice to Wodan. I pledge to you a new dedication to this task. Wodan must be appeased at all costs. We will need new and dedicated servants to go."

Franz stood, his own body was broken and he stooped badly. "I was dedicated," he said.

CHAPTER XIX

Otto was gone, and Arn was gone. The goat farm not many miles from the Macedonian village of Florina was a sadder place. But, as the days and weeks passed, joy returned. It was not in the nature of Nikos and the irrepressible Copella to remain forlorn.

Marlena swept the floor while Copella sat peeling apples. "You may mourn. It's all right," Copella said to Marlena. "But, you can not let grief consume you, not in this house. Life is too short. Too many good things remain. Nixe needs a mother."

Marlena went to her and embraced her. "You and Nikos are wise people. Of course, you're right. But, you have no idea what Arn and I have been through together. We are more than just brother and sister. We have survived taking heart from one another."

"Arn said he would come back, didn't he?"

"I suppose your sons said they would come back too." Marlena regretted it as soon as she had said it. "I'm sorry, Copella. That sounds mean. I would never be mean to you."

"It's all right; I understand. Yes, they said they would come back, and I expect them to come back some day, but not to stay. Men have a way of making their own place in the world."

"I guess I'll have to face that fact about Arn, but today I'm not ready to think of it."

"He finished the loom before he left. Did you know that? He left it in our bedroom. I think he wanted to surprise you," said Copella.

"That's Arn. I thought sometimes he would do anything to please me. When I scolded him, he never lashed back. Once I gave away a small fortune that belonged to him, and he never held it against me. Then I suppose I will never forget that the reason he went with the Romans was to defend me."

"Why don't we start something new on the loom this morning," said Copella. "We have dyed our thread."

"I'd like that. The colors will not be the same that they were in Melz, but that will only mean that our pattern will be original," said Marlena.

Nikos had decided to pick more apples the first thing that morning. It was important to get them at just the right time so that they could be sliced and dried—too early and they wouldn't be as sweet—too late and they wouldn't slice well. He hummed as he worked up behind the house filling basket after basket with ripe red fruit.

Over in the goat fold Nixe had full charge of the milking. "The child gets more milk than I do," Copella had said with a self-effacing grin, as Nixe swelled with pride. "If the truth were known, those goats would rather follow her than Nikos too," she added. Then everyone laughed.

Persephone liked to talk back to Nixe. As Nixe milked away, she asked questions. "Perse, I'll bet you have had no idea that my father is Greek. He lives in Athens and is very sad. He would have married my mother, but my mother had to leave."

"Baa."

"He married a very pretty lady in Athens. I saw those terrible people kill her. And she was going to have a baby."

"Baa, baa."

The milk flowed freely as Nixe worked her soft hands and kept a smooth rhythm. "Do you think we will ever see Arn again, Perse? I know he wants to come back, but who knows what those horrible Romans will do to him."

"Baa, baa."

"You know don't you girl? He's coming back, isn't he?"

The goat turned and looked into Nixe's pleading eyes, "Baa, baa, baa."

"You make me feel so good," Nixe told Persephone. She wrapped her arms around the goat's neck and gave her a little squeeze. Whereupon Persephone licked her ankle.

"Perse, you are a mess," chided Nixe, "but you know I love you."

Then when Nixe had released Persephone's tether, she stood and looked out over the rock fence that formed the goat fold. A small cloud of dust rose from the path that led around the hill and out into the valley. She put a hand over her brow for shade and stared into the distance. There were three figures on the path. No, there were four. Who?

Then she could make out a giant red beard. "Otto," she screamed.

She shoved the corral gate open and left it. She flew past the house screaming, "It's Otto, it's Otto."

Marlena and Copella stuck their heads out the door in time to see Nixe running down the path and out across the meadow. Was her limp gone? She was still screaming at the top of her voice, "It's Otto, it's Otto."

Otto's arms opened wide and Nixe hurled herself at him like an elfin missile.

CHAPTER XX

Philo's depression was total. He sat and stared blankly at the wall, or at the sky, or at whoever might be trying to talk to him. He couldn't sleep; he wouldn't eat; his bones ached; he suffered chills and sometimes fever.

As the weeks passed, he became frail. His complexion was sallow, and his eyes sank in their sockets. Occasionally, Penelope or Biocles could communicate with Philo. To all others he might as well have been dead.

Penelope understood, but she knew Philo must fight through the depression. She thought he would be better if he would talk about things. So, day after day as she sat with him, she would probe, being careful not to go too far. But what was too far? Her son's sanity hung in the balance. She prayed the gods would give her discretion.

Not surprisingly, Dorea was just as bad and in some ways worse than Philo. It had been Penelope who had taken her aside that afternoon and very quietly explained to her that Theana had been killed.

At first, though she had contemplated such a tragedy theatrically, Dorea couldn't grasp such a reality.

"Theana will be back in the morning," she told Penelope with a blank stare. It was just the end of Act I to her.

"No, Dorea, I'm sorry. Theana is really gone. We must cherish every memory of her, but we must not fool ourselves. Theana will never return."

And so it went for over an hour: denial and gentle insistence on reality. Then the awful truth sank into the soul of the child. Now twelve, Dorea was capable of great grief.

"No," she said. "No, it can't be, not my Theana." Then she screamed such a shrill and terrifying cry that people on the street outside stopped in amazement of what torture might be happening in the house of Alcandor. She ran from her small bedroom into the courtyard. There she circled the fountain weeping, sobbing, screaming, alternately beating her chest and pulling her hair.

Penelope was right behind her. "You can't do this child. Please, please stop. Think how you will frighten the children."

Then Caleb came and spoke to Penelope. "She has to rid herself of some of the shock, Madame. It seems terrible but this is nature's way. We must be with her so she won't harm herself, but please give her a chance to let the feelings out.

"I suppose you're right, Caleb. Bless you, you usually are," said Penelope loudly over the wails and sobs of her daughter.

Penelope and Caleb sat on the little bench beside the fountain until Dorea's frail body fell in exhaustion at their side. A soft sob continued to pass her lips but physical exertion beyond that seemed impossible. Then, Caleb scooped her up into his arms and carried her to her bed.

In the early hours of the next morning, the entire household was awakened by loud wails coming from Dorea's room. And so it was to be for many days until Penelope and Alcandor were forced to make a decision that neither of them liked. They had tried to keep Philo and Dorea apart as much as possible, but some meetings of the two were inevitable. Penelope at last decided there was a possibility that, commiserating, the two might help one another. Then, one afternoon she heard them together on the portico. As she stood beside the entrance, these words of Dorea fell on her ears.

"Sophocles, Aeschylus, Aristophanes wrote dung. Nor is there any solace in Euripides. When love is ripped away so violently the soul finds little rest in words or even self inflicted pain."

"I see you, my brother, the hapless one wasting down to death silently, keeping your body unfed as though 'twere pollution to taste of bread. Perhaps the comfort of afterlife is our sole solution. Though we know nought of the life to come perhaps there is truth in fable's shadowy stream."

Staring at Philo she said dramatically, "The care-cloud lowers on your darkened brow. There seems no hope here. I think I will not waste away but take a quicker route to the one chance of relief." Then she went to the balustrade and looked longingly over it at the street ten meters below.

Philo sat staring into space. Whether he received Dorea's message Penelope couldn't tell. But she certainly understood it. She burst onto the portico and swept Dorea into her arms. Out of Philo's sight she fled.

That afternoon Dorea was taken to the farm in Hymettus under the constant care of Caleb. At least Philo and Dorea were then separated by some distance so that depression could not feed depression. It was a hard thing for Penelope and even for Alcandor, but they could see the better of it. Caleb, even in his maturity, was no less charmed by Dorea than anyone else. He would be gentle with her and good for her. Penelope would go to the farm often.

Early one morning, just at dawn, Penelope found Philo on the portico. He stood there with a scene before him that he had cherished. But he didn't look at the scene. He did see the larch trees as they stood bare and mocking. To him, in their deceit, they were the only honest thing he saw. They were real life, looking good then suddenly barren. They spoke to him: If the love of your life isn't false, then love itself will turn on you. He stared blankly into the gray sky away from the trees.

"The cost of love," said Penelope, "is the potential for heartbreak. Some people don't think it's worth the price. Do you?"

Philo kept staring at the sky for long moments so that Penelope thought it was another of those times that he wouldn't answer. Then he turned to her.

"I suppose what you're asking is: should I have given my heart? If I had it to do over again, would I?"

"Yes, something like that."

"I don't know. Twice the gods have destroyed me. Maybe they're telling me to stay away from love."

"Or maybe they're telling you to ask for strength. And maybe they're telling you to choose the good memories over the bad."

"Oh, Mama, it's the good memories that are killing me. Why do those things have to be just memories? Memories are for old people who are ready to die—maybe I'm ready to die."

Penelope was wondering if Dorea's speech had impacted Philo's thinking, but she said nothing about it. Instead she tried to turn his thoughts around. "Good memories can strengthen people of any age, Philo. The good memories can turn rotten on us, though, if we live totally in them. We must take strength from them to go on to other things."

Did he hear her? She wondered, but she wouldn't find her answer that morning. Philo returned to his silence.

Biocles came often and sat with Philo. Most of the time that was all it amounted to. He sat. Philo sat. There were few or no words.

Then, some months after Theana had been slain, Biocles felt he must talk about her. He sat with Philo on the marble benches in the courtyard of the house of Alcandor. Caleb saw that the garden there was well kept so lilies and shrubs prospered all around the little fountain with the dryads.

"There's something I've wanted to tell you for a while now, Phil, but I've been afraid I would remind you of bad things, and you'd feel worse. Now it seems you couldn't feel worse anyway, so I have to tell you there is some good news with the bad."

"Theana hasn't died in vain. Would you believe that since her death, there have been very few babies left at the temples for child exposure? It has become a rare thing to see infants on those steps now. The council hasn't made a law. There are no more open protests. The people of Athens just refuse to do it."

Philo turned and looked directly at his friend for the first time in weeks. "You're making this up."

"Put on your cloak. I'll show you," said Biocles, unable to conceal his irritation.

Philo hung his head and mumbled, "I, I can't go today."

Biocles rose to his feet. "Sooner or later you're going to have to decide if you're going to be a person again," he said. "Do you think you honor Theana by staying here moping your life away month after month? I'll say this for Theana. She lived every minute until she died. That's more than I can say for you." He turned and walked from the house.

It was the nature of Philo's depression that any thought of good was suppressed. His mind kept telling him that something bad would eventually come of everything.

He had fought with all his might, but the Romans still ruled Greece. He had been insanely in love with Marlena, and she had been quickly taken away. He had developed a deep love and respect for Theana, and she had been killed in a most tragic way.

He couldn't see that Biocles was trying to reach deep into his heart and shake him from his depression. He only saw that here was a lifetime friend who was now turning on him. The anger in Biocles made it clear. It had been inevitable. Soon Penelope would turn on him and life would be the complete charade it was destined to be from the start.

As handsome as he was, he began to think of himself as being ugly. The small, flat, brown birthmark on his left cheek became an object of his attention. The rest of his face was not the reality. The birthmark was the reality. Now, as his skin became sallow and his eyes sank into their sockets, he felt the effect of the birthmark was taking over. It was larger and uglier. Of course, he should have expected it.

A year had passed. At Hymettus, Dorea, with youth's resilience, had passed the worst of her depression. Caleb and Penelope had loved her through it and surprisingly the animals had helped.

She stood in the pasture performing for the sheep as though they were the aristocratic elite of Athens. She poured her remorse out in long passages from tragedies of the masters, emoting to the sky and daring even the most virile of the rams to disagree. At length the sheep became fond of her strange but reassuring presence. They gave prolonged baas at the end of long passages, and Dorea rewarded them with deep bows and curtsies.

Philo had grown long hair and a long beard. Penelope refused to let either of them become unkempt. She sat beside Philo on one of the marble benches in the courtyard garden. She was brushing Philo's long locks gently, methodically. For a week she had felt that she had been given the medicine to cure or kill Philo, and she didn't have the courage to give the pill. So, she went on suffering the evil limbo of her son's depression.

As she stroked Philo's long, black tresses, she looked into his eyes and saw nothing. The time had come.

"Philo, dear son, I want you to listen to me. Are you hearing me or are you so far away that you can't hear?"

Philo continued to stare blankly.

Penelope laid the brush on the bench. She knelt before Philo, took his hands, and looked deeply into his very soul. Tears streamed down her face. "Will you hear me, Philo?"

His eyes blinked, and he saw Penelope. Then he nodded his head.

"That isn't enough, Philo. Tell me, will you hear me?" She was pleading.

"I'll listen, Mama."

"There's more than one way that we can die, my son. Mentally a person can turn and walk away from life and be just as dead as if his heart quit beating. If that happens to you, Philo, you have allowed the evil people who killed Theana to kill you too. Are you listening?"

"Yes."

"No one else can come and give you a magic potion to restore your soul, but within you there is still the strength you need. What this amounts to is a choice. Death and life stand before you. You, Philo, you must make a choice between the two. I beg you for all of us who love you, choose life."

Philo said nothing, but for a second Penelope thought she saw an answer. She prayed with all she was for two days. Then, as she sat silently again with Philo on the portico, he turned and spoke to her as naturally as if his words were a continuation of a conversation that had lasted for hours.

"I want to speak privately with Caleb," he said.

Penelope wanted to leap to her feet and go running, but she felt inclined to at least act as casually as Philo had spoken.

She stood in the doorway and watched as Philo and Caleb chatted quietly. She began to thank the gods. An answer to her prayers was unfolding before her. She didn't just sense it, she knew it—faith perhaps, a mother's intuition perhaps.

An hour later Caleb stood a half mile away at the doorway of Biocles' home talking as though he were part of the family. "Philo wants you to take him to the temple steps, not just the temple of Artemis, but the temple of Apollo, the temple of Athena, and all the rest."

Biocles sprang into the arms of Caleb and the two began to leap in happiness. "All right. It's good, it's good," they shouted.

Philo and Biocles strolled through the Agora and then from temple to temple. Biocles did most of the talking.

"Theana is becoming a legend in the hearts of Athenians," he said. "Many were there and saw her give her life. Those have told others. The fact that she was pregnant has inspired a story of double martyrdom."

"It was just that," said Philo as he stood before the empty steps of the temple of Artemis, scratching his head and marveling.

"It certainly was. The people here speak of her with the same awe they speak of Pheidippides coming from Marathon or Socrates drinking the hemlock in the name of truth and honor."

"So that's why the steps are clean."

"Come, let's see the temple of Athena," said Biocles.

They climbed the Acropolis hill from the west, looking up at the Propylaca, the gate that stood before the Temple of Athena Nike. Each stone step going up became a task for Philo. His frail body lacked the strength for this. Biocles could see it. He let Philo get near exhaustion, then, half way up the hill he said, "Let's take a break."

He didn't wait for Philo to answer. He plunked down on the step where he was and turned to see Philo beside him. A great satisfaction warmed his heart. They were together again. And they weren't just together, they were together with a mission.

Biocles summoned a subject he knew would be of interest to Philo if, indeed, Philo's interest could be stirred.

"Have you ever heard about the mystics of the great eastern mountains they call the Himalayas? News from the caravans is that those people can summon great peace through meditation and communion with their gods. They tell tales of monks sitting for days shunning food and water. Then, when they emerge from these trances, they seem to live lives of serenity."

"I've heard some of it," Philo answered. "But that place is a very long way from here."

Biocles spoke with a smirk, his dimples contracting to their deepest, "Well now, wouldn't the journey be half the fun."

CHAPTER XXI

Quintus Servillius Gavius, tribune of the fourth cohort of the Twelfth Macedonian Legion, was entrusted with keeping the peace and collecting Roman taxes in Asia Province at Pergamum. Governor of the area, he was in charge of both the military and political affairs. Unlike many Roman governors, Gavius did not choose to merely serve out his time in a remote region, counting the days when he could return to Rome. He had come to appreciate the people he governed and therefore took his responsibilities seriously.

At fifty, Gavius had served in the senate at Rome and in battles from Spain to Cappadocia. At Pergamum he had found a society much more advanced than he had anticipated. Lying up the Caicus River a few miles off the eastern coast of the Northern Aegean Sea, it was accessible to Greek travelers and so to Greek culture. Schools of medicine, astronomy, literature, and mathematics thrived there.

Gavius had brought his wife, Cornelia, and his two daughters, Servilla and Marcia, to live with him at Pergamum. Gavius was a handsome, intelligent man with dark brown hair graying at the temples. His green eyes were those of understanding but also determination. He had a large, typically Roman, nose, a round face, and a strong body gone a bit soft with age.

Cornelia, still an attractive woman, was in her early forties. Her black hair glistened and her smooth skin showed not a sign of a wrinkle. She was a modest, retiring woman, but she loved her husband and was more than happy to go with him to Pergamum.

Servilla, in spite of getting her father's name, was very much like her mother, but Marcia with the light brown hair and green eyes was an embodiment of her father's personality. At eighteen, she wanted to go everywhere Gavius went. She wanted to see the country. She wanted to meet the people. She wanted to see the soldiers train and see them fight if possible. She wanted to know about government so much that she became at first an encouragement then a pest to her father. Still, he loved her with all his heart.

Just outside the walls of the high city of Pergamum was the small village of Byra. There an encampment of Roman soldiers was stationed strategically so that they could both train and be available for military service. This was a place especially interesting to Marcia for here came military auxiliary of many nations to be indoctrinated into the Roman army.

A non-Roman citizen could not be a member of the regular army, but few Roman forces ever marched without auxiliary personnel aiding them. Many times whole centuries would be made up mostly of auxiliary with only Roman officers. These members of the auxiliary were usually permitted to wear their own native costumes and use their own armor and weapons. It was up to their own centurion to decide where and when these troops could best be used.

So it was that Marcia could go to Byra and observe all manner of exotic people and their ways of war. There were wild Scythian horsemen from across the Euxine Sea (Black Sea). There were oriental bowmen and Persians with huge curved sabers. She could see Greeks, Arabs, Egyptians, Judeans, Phoenicians, and Syrians. And there were still followers of the ancient Celtic tribes who came to this land in times of unrecorded history.

As revolts came and brigands controlled overland passages, Gavius had applied to Rome for more troops to keep the peace. The emperor, Tiberius, and Rome ignored his call for help so Gavius began to make the best of what he had. His major concern was not directed at assembling a large marching army, but in perfecting the efficiency of the contubernia, small squads of eight to ten soldiers. It was these small groups, widely distributed throughout the domain, who were actually responsible for Pax Romana.

In his ruminations, Gavius pictured a peace keeping contubernium coming upon a band of robbers twice its own size in the process of overcoming travelers on the road. As he puzzled over the predicament, which was indeed quite common, his mind hit upon the idea of archers.

Supposing, for instance, that the small band of soldiers took cover and accurate archers began to shoot the criminals one by one with no damage whatever to their own troops. This would at least delay a hand to hand sword fight, if not render it totally unnecessary.

There were some problems with this plan, however. Archery was not a vital part of Roman warfare. Indeed, the typical Roman short bows and cross bows were not capable of the cast Gavius had in mind. So, because of this, he sent word to all the realm round about that he was looking for archers who could aim well and shoot far.

Mid morning one late April day, Marcia showed up for the archery trials at Byra. She was accompanied by an entourage of four, but she walked rather than be carried in a litter. Beside her were two lady attendants. They were middle-aged Syrian women, helpful with both physical aid and matronly advice. Behind these three walked two enormous Numidian guards with bodies black as pure anthracite coal. They were dressed alike, bare chested and bare headed, they wore skirts of bronzed mail, a huge bronze belt highly polished, and large, flat necklaces of bronze. Red garnet flashed from their dangling earrings. Short Roman swords hung from their waists, but their weapons of choice were the elephant spears they carried constantly.

Marcia was strictly forbidden to have any sociable conversation with these black guards, but she had a mind of her own. It was not that she was a rebellious person for she was both proper and moral, but she was simply too gregarious to ignore her constant companions. She called them Ham and Zool, short for Hammurabi and Zulubul. Both were a head above the crowd, but Ham stood a fraction taller than Zool and wore a small beard. His nose spread over most of his face, and it flared when he smiled. Zool had pronounced cheek bones that seemed to bury his black eyes. As huge as they were, you could see neither in the dark unless they smiled. Then it would be as though detached pearly, white blocks seemed to float through the night. Marcia often inquired of their welfare or brought them little gifts. They were completely devoted to her.

This day as Marcia strode through the tented camp, she was greeted by those officials who knew her and made way for her to pass. She went straight to the target fields where she found a contest of archery finalists in full sway. She had learned to watch the practice from behind the archers who always placed the sun at their backs. There she could follow the flight of the arrows and observe each archer's form.

She took her place behind the middle of the shooting line with her attendants, Amar and Bezel, beside her. Ham and Zool took their places just behind. They stood at "alert" but not rigidly so because they were charged with being aware of all that was going on in their area. The spears in their right hands were equal to their heights. The shafts were made of acacia wood and were broad as flag poles. The heads were polished steel, big as buckets. Ham and Zool spread their stance, poked the butts of these spears into the ground beside them, and silently observed the proceedings.

As usual, the northern Orientals were the most impressive as a group. They had learned to perfect longer bows and more accurate arrows than the others. They stood and placed arrow after arrow in the circumscribed target at the side of a berme some seventy paces away.

Mixed with the Orientals were single archers of other races from around the great sea. This day Marcia caught sight of golden blond hair hanging shoulder length from beneath a simple leather hunting cap. The archer moved with such grace and accuracy that she couldn't look away from his back.

Then he was proclaimed winner of the contest and turned to face the officers' table. Whereupon, beholding his face, Marcia fell immediately in love.

She turned to Amar, her youngest attendant, "Tell the centurion in charge that I will speak to the winner this morning."

"But, my lady, do you think it wise to have such contact with the troops?"

"It appears that this is a special bowman, Amar. Perhaps I can learn something from him that will help my father."

"As you say, your ladyship."

In a matter of minutes, the young, blonde archer stood before Marcia. He knelt on one knee and removed his hat. "I'm at your service, your ladyship," he said gallantly.

"Oh get up," said Marcia, "I'm not the queen."

The young man rose. "Forgive me. I've never been in the presence of aristocracy," he said.

"You are right," said Marcia. "I am indeed aristocracy, for better or for worse. I'm Marcia, daughter of Gavius." Then she gave a smile, one that all the military called devastating for a great majority of them were smitten with her.

"I'm Arn of Melz, lately come from Macedonia, your ladyship."

"Well, Arn of Melz, I suppose you know my father, the governor, is interested in archery."

"I've heard as much."

"Then where is Melz, pray tell, and was it there that you learned to make such a bow and use it so well?"

Arn gave simple answers. "Melz is a village in the alpine mountains of Europa, and, yes, I did learn archery there."

Marcia fell more in love with every word Arn spoke. How could she see more of him? "Arn of Melz," she asked, "would you come to the governor's residence and speak to my father of archery if he so desired?"

"I'd be more than happy to," said Arn, "and it would brighten my day to get a glimpse of you again."

Marcia, holding a handkerchief, raised it to her face to hide an obvious blush. Then she turned half away. "We'll see about that," she whispered and hurried past Ham and Zool. Startled, they turned and scurried after her leaving Amar and Bezel to find their way the best they could.

The governor's palace at Pergamum reflected neither the grace of Greece nor the grandeur of Rome for it predated the influence of both. It was a stolid but obviously sturdy edifice to the credit of some anonymous Assyrian of centuries past. He had discovered the dependability of granite stones and the knowledge of how to stack them one on another and make them stay. The archways were simple, the windows and doors, except the entrance, were small. But there was more than enough space inside for the governor, his family and servants, and any diplomatic visitors who might appear. Plus, there was the advantage of a huge stable behind. Marcia loved horses and all that pertained to them.

Upon arriving in Pergamum, Cornelia had looked around the ancient halls and decided that her family would occupy the south wing. She had brightened the place with large candelabras and tiers of shimmering drapes. She then informed Gavius that larger windows should replace the cruciform apertures which had been popular with Assyrian archers.

Having sent Ham and Zool to the stables to prepare for her afternoon ride, Marcia strolled through the halls of the south wing until she found Cornelia and Servilla in the first lady's drawing room preparing for a governor's banquet. Their problem was hors'doeuvres. Whether to serve hummingbird brains or snails vexed them completely.

"Good morning to you both," chirped Marcia, breezing into the room like a puff of fresh spring air.

"And to you, my daughter," said Cornelia. Servilla only looked up then continued to study her victual list.

"Come here. I want to look at you, child," said the attentive mother. "Are you all right?"

"I'm more than all right. I'm wonderful," said Marcia coming to her mother's side and placing a kiss on her forehead.

"Then maybe that's the reason for the color in your cheeks. Tell me what has happened this morning."

"Mother, why do you always think something has happened. The sun is out. The air is fresh. Life is new all around. Why shouldn't I feel well?"

"Where have you been?"

"Mother …"

Now Servilla saw a point to take. "She likes to go to the soldiers' training camp and watch all the virile young bodies."

"Servilla, that's not fair," shot Marcia. "I take interest in the military and the government. If you want to hug the home furnishings, well fine, but don't put me down for

164

getting out and seeing the world." Then she spun around and headed for the door.

"Now girls," began Cornelia, but Marcia was gone.

Back in her own suite, Marcia questioned Amar and Bezel. "Did you ever in your life see a human male so gorgeous and so gallant?"

"I'm afraid I haven't" said Bezel, the older of the two. "But you must take no further note of it, my lady."

"Take no note! You're insane. Take no note of Vesuvius erupting! Take no note of lightning striking the Coliseum! Take no note of Pergamum changing from dismal granite to pure gold."

"You, my lady, must marry Roman aristocracy. No common outlander will do. Surely you understand this," said Bezel, her serene brown eyes pouring out sympathy upon the love-struck Marcia.

"Maybe Arn of Melz could be made a Roman citizen. Maybe he could work his way up to a position of note."

"You are dreaming, my lady," said Amar.

"Well, I can try to help," said Marcia. Her mind was racing now with "what ifs." She was a natural conniver and manipulator, but all for a good cause she thought. Then speech came again to her lips. "First, he must meet father."

Arn of Melz had been in more than a dozen scuffles and twice was beaten severely. Upon the second beating, fearful of losing his best archer, his centurion sent the sergeant (tesserarius) of his squad to talk to Arn. They discerned Arn's problem to be unique.

In his life, Arn had received little teasing and no coarse ribbing whatever. When the rough soldiers began to refer to his private parts and speak regularly of human excrement and sexual aberration, it both offended and insulted Arn. Of course, when they discovered this sensitivity they increased the harassment.

One evening Rufus sat next to Arn's cot and tried to explain. Compassion was not a widely distributed commodity in the ranks of the fighting soldiers and was not the forte of Rufus.

Rufus, had he not gained the respect of the men around him by valor in combat, might well have been arrested and placed in the asylum on looks alone. A large scar began above his right eye, crossed the bridge of his nose, and created a slanted division of his entire left cheek. He was missing two upper front teeth that were not neighbors, and the rest were chipped and ragged. His skin was pocked. His left ear lobe was missing. His left eye wandered skyward while his right eye gazed furiously ahead. Massive eyebrows shaded his sockets, but they didn't balance the effect of a pate slicker than a mirror.

His body was equally battered, but it was tight. Rufus, in his mid-thirties, was an all out, fast-charging and no-retreat fighting man's fighting man. But he did like Arn because he had found that Arn was no complainer.

"Look," he said, "the world is a rougher place than you have known, my friend."

Arn looked at him through purple, swollen eyes. "You have no idea what my life has been like," he mumbled.

"Maybe I should say the world is a coarser place than you've known. All soldiers curse and fling foul insults as though they were telling bedtime stories. Most of them mean nothing by it. It's the bloodshed, I think, the killing, that makes us like that. Why don't you try laughing it off before the fights start?"

"I'm not sure I can change that fast, Rufus."

"You can try. Think about it. The centurion values you."

"He does?"

"He does, indeed."

"I'll try, Rufus."

And so it was that Arn began to see the coarse humor of rough and barbaric men. Seldom did he laugh at their suggestions, but at least he began to shake them off. Gradually, he became one of the favorites of the century, especially when his ability as an archer came to light.

Since the governor's daughter had called him aside in plain view of everyone, Arn became the center of ridicule for the entire camp. The irony was that Arn saw envy as well as humor in it all and liked it very much. He longed to see the pretty and affable Marcia, knowing full well what effect it might have on the troops. Her face came repeatedly to his mind. Maybe the Roman army wasn't so bad after all.

He thought of Marlena and Nixe at the goat farm in Macedonia and wished they could know that some happiness was coming his way. He pictured Nikos telling Nixe about how to make the goats do what she wanted. He pictured Copella and Marlena weaving on the loom he had built. He remembered what his own room was like.

Three days after first seeing Arn of Melz, Marcia was back at the target range. She found an unusual event transpiring, a clout shoot. In this exercise targets were placed fifty paces from the archers and horizontally upon the ground.

It was a shot unfamiliar to Arn of Melz. Loft was critical. He took his time learning and concentrated intensely on what he was doing. So, he was perhaps the last on the field to recognize the presence of Marcia and her attendants.

Meanwhile, whispers of anticipation spread through the ranks. Would the charisma and abilities of their comrade once more command the attention of the governor's daughter? They were pulling for him because vicariously he represented them all.

But Arn was not called away from the exercise. The troops were dismissed for noon recess and each man went his own way for the time being. Arn sat leaned against the trunk of a juniper and saw Marcia just in time to notice her passing. As he sat regretting his misfortune in not getting to watch her, Rufus came to him.

"There's someone to see you in the grove behind the officers' tent," he said with a wink of his good eye.

"Remind me to polish your armor," said Arn. He wanted to leap to his feet and run, but he knew it wouldn't be smart to call attention to himself.

In the shade of the oak grove, he removed his hat, bowed, and spoke first to Marcia. "Good day, my lady. I'm happy to see you are well."

"And to you, Arn of Melz."

Then turning to Amar and Bezel, Arn smiled broadly, "And a good day to you, ladies."

They smiled but tucked their heads into their puffed sleeves and said nothing.

Then he surprised them all by addressing Ham and Zool. "Good day, fellas," he said. "You're looking sharp."

Ham and Zool came very close to bursting into laughter. Their lips thinned and tightened over one another and their bodies shook.

"Arn of Melz, you do not address the guards," said Marcia with a giggle.

"Pardon me, maam. If I am to converse with you often, I will have to learn manners. But believe me, I've always wanted to have some friends as big as these fellows," Arn said with a smirk.

"Arn of Melz, I believe you could be funny if you put your mind to it."

Arn straightened to an "at alert" stance and tried to look very serious, "Not at all, Maam, not at all."

"I've talked with my father, the governor, and he will speak with you about archery at noon on Tuesday the next," she said.

"The governor is gracious, but I fear I will embarrass myself, and he will not be as forgiving as my lady."

"Listen carefully, Arn of Melz. When you come into my father's quarters you will be announced. Come before him at a respectable distance, bow and bid him a good day. Then remain at alert until he bids you sit. Don't speak to anyone else present unless he introduces you to them. That will get you off to a good start, then you can follow your best instincts. My father is a kind man and is very much interested in archery. You'll like him."

"If he's anything like my lady, I'm sure that I will."

The attendants giggled.

"Arn of Melz, you must not speak such forward words in public," blurted Marcia.

"I'm sorry, maam. I intend no offense. I will try to squelch my admiration for you."

"See that you do," said Marcia in disdain so false it was quickly seen through.

"Perhaps I'll see you at the governor's palace," she said.

"As you say, my lady," said Arn with great reserve.

"You learn fast, Arn of Melz," said Marcia and walked away.

Arn was satisfied that Marcia's caution of meeting him in the seclusion of the oak grove had saved him much embarrassment. But when he rounded the large officers' tent, he found half the encampment staring at him curiously. Then, suddenly, they gave a great cheer and started what would be unrelenting harassment. He tipped his hat to them.

Young Arn of Melz had found a way into the hearts of the troops. He had taken their beatings and stood undaunted. He had out shot them all on patrols and on the target range.

Now he was winning the attention of the camp sweetheart, Marcia Gavia, no less.

How far would it go? How far could it go?

CHAPTER XXII

The fact that Gavius loved his daughter didn't necessarily mean that he trusted her judgment in military affairs. He had, himself, investigated the background of Arn of Melz and found what he heard to be interesting. In addition to his abilities as a bowman, he found that Arn could speak Greek.

They sat together, just the two of them, before a small meal with fruit and sweet red wine. The room was large, but it certainly wouldn't compare with the halls of Roman palaces. The floor of Assyrian granite had been overlaid with white Athenian marble. Sparkling draperies of wool and silk covered the walls. Oil lanterns with metal reflectors hung in profusion from the vaulted ceiling. The April warmth had not yet penetrated the granite of the palace, so a monstrous fire burned in the hearth across the room. Busts of famous Romans lined the walls and a statue of extra natural proportion stood in the center of the room. It was some eccentric Roman sculptor's idea of the likeness of Jupiter.

He stood stripped to the waist, a handsome but dispassionate creature. Chain curls formed the bulk of his long hair and beard. In his raised right hand was a thunder bolt, and hovering over his left shoulder was an eagle.

Around the statue were divans, chairs, tables, and lamps. The chairs they sat in were Ethiopian mahogany with carved relief by an Alexandrian artist enamored with date palms, asps, and crocodiles. Behind them was the elevated judgment seat of the governor. Not the most resplendent of palatial surroundings, the room was still impressive enough to bedazzle Arn. He sat wide-eyed while Gavius asked a slave to pour wine. Arn didn't greet the slave.

"My daughter tells me you are probably the best archer we have at Byra," said Gavius.

"She is more than kind," said Arn trying to keep his mind on the conversation.

Gavius had given young Arn a thorough visual inspection. "Perhaps she is," he said. "We shall see." He was thinking that most women would be "more than kind" to such a handsome fellow.

"Tell me, which do you think most important: the bow, the arrows, or the archer's skill? I must know where to place emphasis."

"What good is a bow without an arrow," said Arn now concentrating on the governor's question. "And if you have those already, then the archer's skill is most important. But what good is skill with no instrument."

"I need you in my diplomatic corps," said Gavius. "Let me put my question like this. You have seen our archers. What do they need to improve the most, the fastest?"

"There's no question in my mind about that, sire. The bow. You have here at Byra a collection of bows and bowmen of many nations. I can out shoot most of them because I've spent much of my life refining the efficiency of my bow, not because I'm stronger than they are."

"Ah," said the governor, "and what is different about your bow?"

"With your leave, sire, might I have a quill and parchment."

So Gavius ordered his slave to bring the quill and parchment, and Arn began to draw. To his surprise, Gavius found Arn to be an artist and a craftsman. Each graceful curve he drew had a purpose and each purpose was fulfilled with correct proportion. He spent an hour explaining his own theories of arrow trajectory.

"I'm going to have my chief bowyer call you out, Arn of Melz. I want you to go to his workhouse and speak of bows with him. I'll see you again. In the meantime, I want you to seek out any facet of archery that might improve our chances in a fight."

"I understand sire," said Arn. "I will try to help."

Arn would never love Rome, but he was devoted to the cause of peace, and he found in Gavius a man unusually devoted to the welfare of "his" people.

As he walked across the courtyard to the front gate of the palace grounds, Marcia stepped from behind a vine trellis and took him by the sleeve. "I have to talk to you," she said without address. "Meet me at nightfall outside the city wall just behind the palace stables." Then she disappeared as suddenly as she had come.

Arn couldn't stay still. He knew he shouldn't be too conspicuous, but his heart was pounding and his feet had to move. He paced beneath a large sycamore in the yellow moonlight. What would it be like seeing the beautiful Marcia alone? Did she like him as much as he liked her? Did she have covert business? Important people were always hatching some scheme or other.

"Arn of Melz," came a soft voice from the shadows.

"My lady," whispered Arn.

"You honor me by granting me your presence, Arn of Melz."

"It's quite the opposite, my lady," said Arn as Marcia walked into the moonlight, her eyes sparkling from the fuel of intelligence, adventure, and happiness. "Isn't it dangerous for such an important person as you to come alone into the darkness outside the city confines?"

"I'm not all that important of a person, Arn of Melz. Besides I'm not as alone as it may appear. Ham and Zool are never too far from me."

"But doesn't that make them privy to a little too much?"

"Ha," said Marcia. "Ham and Zool knew too much about me a long time ago. I'm afraid if they decided to talk I would be in very much trouble."

"You're making it sound as though you're a, a wayward woman."

"Oh, no, Arn of Melz, you're wrong. I value my good name above all else. I'm not a wayward woman, but let us say traditions and customs don't imprison me."

"So tell me why I am here tonight."

"I like you very much Arn of Melz," Marcia said, and without hesitation she continued. "I would like to see you advance in the Roman army and perhaps gain your citizenship."

"I'm not interested in becoming a citizen of Rome, my lady. Life holds other interests for me."

"I know nothing of your background, but in this world being a Roman citizen holds great advantages."

"And what must I do to gain this great advantage," said Arn coming ever closer to Marcia's side.

She reached out; took his hand and looked into his face. The moonlight turned golden on her smooth skin and there came a perceptible quiver to her chin. "First I must know you want it. Then you must make a notable contribution to the Empire. You'll probably have no trouble there if I am correctly interpreting what my father has to say. Finally, you must have a sponsor of high rank within the government."

"The last requirement rules me out, my lady. I'm only a poor goat keeper."

"Am I not here, Arn of Melz? You are of finer qualities than you think. Somewhere in your heritage there is courage, intelligence, and graciousness. That is true aristocracy and it is aristocracy missing from most of the elite in Rome." She dropped his hand.

"My lady is, herself, too gracious," said Arn. "But should this venture please you then I will try to do my part. I can think of nothing at this moment that would gladden my heart more than pleasing you."

"The darkness hides my blushing cheeks, Arn of Melz. I must go, but first I need to say this. It may go against your manly nature, but I know of no way for us to meet except that I summon you when I can. This will be our place and time. I will only send dates. I know you must go on patrols and perform other duties, please don't think me offended if you don't appear." Then she kissed him on the cheek and was gone before he could speak.

He didn't move. Standing in the moonlight, he closed his eyes and savored the finest moment of his life. He imagined again every word she said, the sound of her voice, the happiness on her face, the smell of her hair, the touch of her hand, and finally the feel of her lips. Arn of Melz was enchanted.

There followed weeks of happiness in which Marcia and Arn met as often as twice a week. Arn would have a small piece of paper pressed into his hand usually by Rufus, but sometimes by total strangers. When he opened the paper he found scrawled in feminine hand, "Tonight, M." Arn had learned only the rudiments of reading and writing but he knew very well what that message meant.

There were times when Marcia felt compelled to tell Arn governmental matters in which he had no interest. There were times when Arn told Marcia details of a patrol in which she had no interest. But each sat and enjoyed the company of the other as they became more open.

Five weeks after their first meeting, Quintus Servillius Gavius again summoned Arn to the governor's palace. He wanted a report on what Arn had learned.

Arn told him that he was making progress with the bowyers. Soon a small collection of new bows would be available for the troops. He had also discovered something in speaking with the oriental archers that he thought might be of interest to the governor.

"And what might that be?" asked Gavius.

"Whistling arrows," said Arn.

"What kind of gimmick is that?" asked the governor. "And what possible use would there be for them?"

"Just imagine," said Arn, "a group of bandits attacking a small caravan. Someone hears a strange whistling sound and one of the bandits drops dead. Everyone stops what they are doing and begins to look at one another. Another whistle is heard, and a second bandit falls to the ground with an arrow in his chest. Then, a third whistle is heard. What do you suppose would happen, sire?"

Gavius leaned across the table to Arn. "I certainly know what I would do if I were there. I'd jump to the earth to avoid any arrows."

"Exactly. Then your patrol, which has remained hidden, can rush forward and disarm the bandits before they have time to react. Eventually the bandits might be terrorized by the sound of the whistling arrows alone and take flight at the first sound of them."

"My boy, I think you may have something," said Gavius. "What would a whistling arrow look like?" Arn spent the rest of his time with the governor that afternoon drawing pictures of what the Orientals had described to him. The principle was simple: A current of air being split by the edge of a hole in the end of a sound chamber formed around the arrow shaft. Gavius grasped the idea quickly and sent immediately for his fletchers.

Arn left him scratching his chin and talking to himself. "Whistling arrows, of all things."

Lions were disappearing from the byways of Asia Province. Once a menace to defenseless travelers throughout the territory, they were now on the wane. No one knew exactly why. An occasional lone scavenger could be seen or even an occasional pair mating, but prides of lions had retreated as far south as Arabia.

So it was an unusual and fearsome thing when the roars of what seemed to be a large male lion were heard outside the city walls of Pergamum. People would rouse from a sound sleep at the loud bellowing of this rogue beast. His pug marks were found in the city streets, and mangled animals of every description were discovered almost daily. The boldness of this wanderer was punctuated one morning at Byra when it was discovered by the tracks that he had walked the main passage between the soldiers' tents. He then circled the officers quarters more than once. An order was issued to find and destroy this dangerous animal, but he proved to be more wily than his pursuers.

In light of their growing affection for one another, both Marcia and Arn chose to ignore the presence of a feral beast roaming the city, after all, he could only be in one place and Pergamum was a large metropolis. The morning Rufus slipped the note into Arn's hand he had no thoughts whatever of a bloodthirsty lion. All that was Marcia leaped into his mind, and the day flew by like a falcon in free fall.

That evening as Arn waited in the deepening shadows beside the sycamore tree, he thought of how his relationship with Marcia had grown. He had come to love her profoundly. For weeks he had longed to take her in his arms and cover her face with kisses, but he had found Marcia to be a cautious woman. It seemed to him that Marcia loved him too, but every fraction of physical contact she allowed was measured. Neither of them were experienced lovers so each touch meant something special to them.

That was only part of their relationship. Both of them fed off the other's enthusiasm and high esteem. They challenged one another's reasoning and teased with unquestionable affection.

Marcia ran breathlessly into the open space beneath the sycamore. "I have such good news," she said.

"It must be," said Arn. "I've never seen you run."

"I can run plenty, if I want to," said Marcia. "I hope you haven't thought that I'm one of those weak, retiring, sitting room socialites."

"You underestimate your image. No one would ever take <u>you</u> for that."

She didn't bother to comment. "The fletchers have found the secret of the whistling arrows, and my father is very pleased. He can hardly wait until enough of them are made to supply regular patrols."

"That is good news, my lady."

Marcia drew herself into a stance of mock authority. "I think I shall now allow you to call me 'Marcia' as long as we remain alone." She had to giggle.

Then a low, deep growl emanated from the shadows and Marcia's look changed from mirth to terror. "What's that! It sounds terrible," she said as she grabbed Arn's arm and held tight.

"It, it could be the rogue lion," said Arn obviously shaken himself.

Then the silhouette of the huge animal emerged from the bushes not twenty steps away.

"Get behind me and stay behind me," Arn told Marcia. "Don't run and don't cry out. A wild animal will always attack fearful prey. As long as he's not certain what he's getting into there's a chance he will turn away."

Marcia was behind him and now Arn was whispering. "If he attacks, let me occupy him, then run for your life."

He heard no answer. "Do you understand me, my Marcia?"

"Yes, yes, yes," she stammered. "But I don't want to leave you."

All Arn said was, "Don't argue." He was unarmed. His only weapon was to try to think like the cat. He kept facing him then spread his legs and crouched as though he himself were about to spring.

The lion crept closer, and as he did the snarls from within him grew deeper. He got closer and closer to the ground. His every muscle became so tense that Arn and Marcia could actually see him tremble with excitement.

Ten steps from them the beast stopped and hugged the earth. The moonlight caught his evil face, his lips curled away from his monstrous, sharp teeth, his red eyes were blazing, and his pointed ears were laid back into his thick mane. His long tail was extended bone stiff behind him. Arn and Marcia saw the tuft of fur on the end of it twitch. Then he sprang.

A resounding smack cracked through the little grove, and three hundred pounds of dead meat fell with a great thud at Arn's feet. Marcia screamed out in terror, tears ran down her face, but she did not run. Arn turned and took her in his arms. He crushed her to himself and covered her with the kisses he had dreamed of.

As Marcia's terror died away she realized she was responding to Arn. She did love him, and for that very reason didn't trust herself in his arms.

"I, I'll have to go," she said.

Arn held her away from himself and looked into her face. "My Marcia," he said, "in my most extreme imagination I've never thought of loving anyone as I do you." Then he placed a kiss on her lips. It was soft but long, very long.

Still only inches from his face and locked in his embrace, she gave a deep sigh. "My dearest Arn, I'll never forget this moment. I'll never forget your bravery and your tenderness." She took a step back. "I'd like to stay here forever and forget there is a world out there. If you asked me to, I surely would, so please, please don't ask. My heart can only stand so much."

She turned and walked toward the governor's palace, but she stopped and looked back. "I love you, Arn of Melz."

The next day a group of soldiers tracking the lion came upon his corpse. He had died by some mysterious calamity. There was a hole in his chest the size of a melon. No one had ever seen such a wound. Word spread and everyone was pleased but bewildered. Apparently, not a soul in all of Pergamum had stopped to consider the potential devastation of an elephant spear.

That same night that the lion had died a villager had heard a scream from the very area of the incident. He had gone there only to find what he knew to be the familiar figure of the governor's daughter wrapped in a man's arms. The man was fair with long blonde hair.

Quickly his tale spread through the community and reached the governor's ears. Two days later Arn of Melz disappeared from Asia Province.

A heartbroken Marcia searched everywhere. All she could learn was that Arn of Melz had been transferred and that he had been confined to quarters until he left. She went to her father.

Refusing to sit down, Marcia paced the floor before his desk and lashed out. "You have done this. You have sent Arn of Melz away. Where has he gone? I'll go to him."

"He has gone south, how far south I don't even know myself. I told the centurion I didn't want to know. You have to believe this is best for you."

"I don't believe any such thing."

"You know you must marry aristocracy."

"Curse aristocracy," cried Marcia. "He stood unarmed between me and a raging rogue lion and didn't flinch a muscle. I would have gone away with him to Cathay if I had to."

"He was a good man. I could see that. I don't doubt your taste, daughter, but I doubt your judgment. You'll see the wisdom of my decision as the years go by," he said.

"Now go and find some good thing to do. The sooner you occupy your mind, the sooner you will forget Arn of Melz."

Marcia turned from her father, but she did not forget Arn of Melz. Indeed, she would remember forever the night of the lion. And the gods of Asia Province were good to her, for in her reverie the sweetness of Arn's final kiss far outlasted the nightmare of the lion.

The fletchers of Pergamum were now producing whistling arrows at a rapid rate. Each arrow was finished with the cresting of Arn of Melz: circles of russet red, deep blue, and bright green just below the feathers. And below these rings was a small silver circle denoting a Roman citizen. The honor had been bestowed upon Arn of Melz in absentia for his meritorious service and upon the recommendation of Quintus Servillius Gavius, governor of Asia Province at Pergamum and tribune of the fourth cohort of the Twelfth Macedonian Legion of the army of Imperial Rome.

CHAPTER XXIII

Biocles was spending time getting the family farm in order. The old overseer there had retired after many years, and Biocles was left to see after his old age as well as choose a new person to be in charge of the farm. His immediate attention was on people, sheep, barley, fruit trees and such, but his heart was in the rehabilitation of Philo. Penelope and Caleb joined him and even Alcandor lent an occasional word of encouragement. He couldn't understand the despondency Penelope had gone through. He knew his son would come around sooner or later.

Caleb had brought Dorea back from the farm at Hymettus. Dorea's new interest in agriculture wouldn't last long, but for the moment it kept her busy explaining things to Philo. Being with the animals had helped her perfect gestures and facial expressions. The animals seemed to appreciate these things, and Dorea needed little encouragement to perform. She was more delightful than ever.

The boost to Philo's morale that Dorea now provided came at just the right time. He had given her a nickname that had proven to be an omen for him, Sunshine.

Caleb knew that exercise would increase Philo's appetite as well as his strength. He had talked him into a daily count of babies placed for child exposure. In a month they had only found two and within the previous week none at all. Now, as they climbed the Acropolis hill, Caleb was having a hard time keeping up.

"Slow down, Philo. Your youth has at last overcome your weakness. I don't feel weak, but I'm afraid I'm not young any more."

"You'll always be young to me, old man or not. Why don't we sit for a while?"

"No, no. I'm all right. Let's just walk slow enough to talk," said Caleb.

"Fine with me." Philo slacked his pace and watched the old Jewish servant. He sensed something unusual about the expression on Caleb's face.

"In all the years I've served your family, Philo, have I ever asked any favor or concession of you?"

"I've never thought about it, Caleb. You know I think more of you as a friend, a special friend, than I do as a servant. I'm willing to consider anything you ask."

"I want you and Biocles to go to Jerusalem. I hear you talking about going east. The great city of my fathers will not be far out of your way. I long to know about what it's like. Are the great holy days and feasts still held there? Do my countrymen still cling to the faith I learned as a child? Is Jehovah God honored? And what about those of my own family, do any still exist?

"Your family has been good to me. I couldn't ask for better masters. But I'm still Hebrew, a member of the house of Jacob."

Philo could see the yearning for home in the face of Caleb. It had never occurred to him how much Caleb had been denied. As he watched the old man trudging up the hill, giving all he was to help him, he was overwhelmed by his own selfishness.

"I'm going to have Biocles come tonight. I want you to tell us about Jerusalem and about Jehovah," said Philo.

Alcandor decided he too would listen to Caleb. Stilted as he was, he had, through the years, developed an affection for him. Something about Caleb had perplexed him for years: how could a servant like Caleb be more content and joyful than his master? He felt it beneath his own aristocratic station to ask a servant such a question, but certainly he could listen with the rest of his family without sacrificing his dignity.

Dorea and the children had retired. Philo, Penelope, Alcandor, Biocles, and Caleb gathered in the conversation room. Each had his own lounge except Caleb, who was also offered one. He preferred a straight back chair. Oil lanterns lit the room and reflected their yellow glow from the white stucco walls. Small tables with dried fruit and nuts sat before them, and wine was brought for those who wanted it.

Philo began, "Before we start here, I want you to know, Caleb, that I feel this time is over due. You have long since earned the right to speak freely in this family, and I'm sure you know that. Though it may seem that we don't care what you believe, that isn't so. We stay so tied up in our own problems and fantasies that we have neglected to ask. Now I want you to take your time. What exactly is a Jew?"

Caleb knew these people were not just his masters but his friends. Still he could not be completely comfortable. A slave was still a slave. He was not free, and, contrary to what Philo had just said, he could not speak completely freely. The only way he would ever be able to do that would be if the family of Alcandor set him free. But he knew he must put that thought aside and be as open as possible.

"There is no way I can tell you all about Jews in one evening, or even a lifetime I suppose. But, if I had to typify the Hebrew people, I would say they are children of hope. Here is why.

"The father of the Jews was Abraham. Thousands of years ago, he lived in the land of the Chaldeans near the Euphrates River. God appeared to him and told him if he would get up and go where He said go and do what He said do then He, God, would bless him and his descendants forever. And not only that, but that all nations of the earth would be blessed through him."

"So he obeyed," said Penelope.

184

"He did. His family was wealthy. He gathered all his flocks and herds. Then, along with his wife, his nephew's family and his servants, he headed west, not knowing where he would stop. When he came to the land of Canaan near the east end of the great sea, God directed him to settle there."

Then Caleb told them about Abraham's son, Isaac, and about Esau and Jacob. He told them how God had changed Jacob's name to Israel and renewed his blessing on him and his sons, the fathers of the twelve tribes.

Philo asked, "So when you say the Jews are children of hope, you are talking about God keeping his promise to your ancestors."

"Exactly," said Caleb.

"But the Jews have been the most over-run people on the face of the earth," protested Biocles.

"It seems that way to an outsider I'm sure," said Caleb. "But it hasn't always been that way. Am I boring anyone?"

"Oh no," said Penelope. The rest shook their heads in agreement.

"Then let me tell you about Moses and Jehovah. The people of Israel were enslaved in Egypt. In spite of their bondage, they had prospered. There were then thousands of the Hebrew children, but they were oppressed.

"God sent a deliverer named Moses who had actually grown up in the family of the Pharaoh. Then, Moses discovered he was a Jew and began to defend the Jews.

"One day he killed an Egyptian in defense of a Jew and had to flee the country. He went into Arabia as an exile. There in the Arabian desert one day, he saw God in a bush that seemed to be burning, but that was never consumed. He was told to remove his shoes because he was on holy ground."

"'What is your name,' said Moses."

"The voice replied simply, 'I am.'"

"The name of Abraham's God had been so holy that it had not been spoken. Now Yahweh, I am, came from the bush, and it was from that experience that God became known as Jehovah, which is the traditional pronunciation of Yahweh. He is the one who was, and is, and evermore will be, the perpetual 'I am.'"

"What did Jehovah tell Moses," asked Philo.

"He told him to go back to Egypt and deliver His children. He said He would help Moses, and that Moses should trust him."

"Did he go back and organize an army," asked Biocles.

"Surprisingly, Jehovah sent Moses directly to Pharaoh. Moses was instructed to tell Pharaoh that unless he released the people of Israel, great plagues would befall the land of Egypt. Pharaoh refused, and the plagues came. The Nile River turned to blood. Locusts covered the landscape; frogs filled the houses, swarms of flies were everywhere; the dust in all the land of Egypt turned to lice. Still Pharaoh refused to allow the Israelites to leave Egypt.

"At last God was to send forth the angel of death who was to claim the first born male of every household.

"Now none of the plagues had affected the Jews, and God didn't intend for this one to affect them either, but He told Moses that the Jews must do certain things so that the death angel would not enter their homes, but pass over them."

"Can you tell us what they had to do," inquired Biocles.

"They were to prepare a special feast. A lamb without blemish was slain and prepared for cooking. Certain herbs were used. Unleavened bread was baked. Every person was to return to his own home and stay indoors that night. Then last, the blood of the slain lamb was to be smeared onto the lentil and the doorposts of the house. Everyone was to be dressed ready to travel."

"They knew it was going to work," Biocles could see.

"Indeed. And it did work. There are many other stories of the miraculous deliverance, but we won't have time for them tonight. There are just two very important things I want to add now.

"First, that perfect lamb that was slain that night in Egypt became a symbol of the hope of a permanent deliverer, the Messiah, promised by God.

"Second, the feast that night in Egypt was named the Passover because of the passing of the death angel. Moses told the Hebrew people that when they came back into the land that God had promised Abraham, they must observe this feast at this time of the year forever. To this day Jews, scattered as they are throughout the earth, long to go to Jerusalem and celebrate Passover at least once in their lives."

"Is there still some hope for this Messiah," asked Penelope.

"Didn't I say we are the people of hope," said Caleb.

"And this God, this Jehovah," said Alcandor who until now had chosen to listen quietly, "what other gods assist him?"

Caleb sat up in his chair. His eyes were alert, his muscles tensed in awareness, as though he were conscious of every particle of air about him. And yet, he wasn't looking at anyone in the group. His attention was somewhere beyond them. "If a call to worship comes to a Jew, the first sound he discerns is this: Hear, Oh Israel. The Lord your God is One."

CHAPTER XXIV

Neither Philo nor Biocles could erase from his memory the image of Caleb telling about his god. The next afternoon, they sat in the canteen of the travelers inn in the Agora and drank sweet wine made of grapes from the Macedonian hills. The place opened onto the street. Broad awnings covered a tiled area not more than four steps wide. There shoppers and pilgrims alike sat at small tables taking their refreshments and enjoying the aroma of the spice market which lay just across the way.

"I'm embarrassed that I never asked Caleb to tell me about his god before," said Philo.

"The old fellow was like a young man again. I've never seen him so animated," said Biocles.

"Do you remember that he said every Jew longs to go back to Jerusalem at Passover?"

"Of course, I do."

"Was he asking us for permission?"

"What difference does it make if he asked permission, Philo. I think we ought to go and take him with us. Don't you think he deserves it?"

"I do. And not only that, I think we will enjoy seeing the happiness it brings the old man. I like it. I like it a lot," said Philo.

Biocles sniffed the air. "I hope they have a spice market in Jerusalem."

So it was decided. Their ultimate destination would be the high Himalayas, but they would go first to the land of Judea and try to see Jerusalem. Caleb would go with them as far as Jerusalem, then return. It seemed simple, but it wasn't.

This arrangement presented the problem of trusting a slave to return to his masters from a distant land where he could easily lose himself and never be heard from again. Alcandor was against it. "Caleb is my personal property, and I can't allow this to happen," he said as he paced before the little fountain on the peristyle.

Philo and Penelope sat on two of the small marble benches between the painted columns watching Alcandor pace. It had seemed such a good thing to do, now this.

"But, Father," said Philo, "you've trusted Caleb for many years. He goes to the market and out into the city as a free man. You send him to Hymettus, even trusting him with much of your business."

"That's different," said Alcandor still pacing. He was opposed by two strong willed people, but he still ruled his own house. "That's all in the confines of our community."

"Don't you think Caleb could have escaped a long time ago if he truly wanted to?" said Penelope. "Ships leave Piraeus every day. Don't you think Caleb could get money if he wanted to?"

"Of course," said Alcandor, "but that isn't the point. He would be going to his homeland and temptations would be everywhere."

It was a long night of pleading by Philo and Penelope, but when it was done Alcandor had the last word. "No."

Alcandor, feeling the matter of Caleb was settled, was in the city plotting political strategy. Philo spent the morning pacing the floor trying to think of what he could do to help Caleb. He went to Penelope and told her he intended to go to the farm to see how the grape vines were doing. Since Philo had recovered from his depression, the farm had been one of his favorite haunts so Penelope gave the matter little thought.

In all the years since his youth the farm had changed very little. Philo still enjoyed seeing things grow; the barley crop was springing up; the apple and pear trees were blooming; and the vines a little behind the other plants were putting out new green sprigs. But Philo had not gone to the farm to see any of that on this day. He crossed between the grape vine rows to the neighboring farm as he had done when he was a boy.

Biocles was in the stable checking a sore-footed mare when Philo, having been directed by the gardener, poked his head into the stable. "How's the farm, neighbor?"

Biocles dropped the mare's foot and patted her on the flank. "I'll say, there's no telling who'll show up around here. It's good to see you, Phil. Let's go over to the house and have some cider from last year's crop. I know you didn't come just to smell horse manure."

The mare whinnied. "No offense, old girl," said Biocles gently, giving her another pat.

Philo was smiling as they strolled toward the farm house. "Sometimes I think animals are as sensitive as women," Biocles said. "It makes it hard to get by with a little bit of teasing. I hope you aren't in a bad mood today."

"I was," said Philo. "We need to talk."

So they sat on the tile patio behind the farm house, enjoyed the early spring sunshine, and drank their cider. With a long face Philo told Biocles about Alcandor's decision. When he was finished, they both sat silent, looking out across the Hymettus hill and just catching a glimpse of the high city.

Biocles was reluctant to speak. Why, he thought, hadn't Philo seen the solution right away. Then, since he hadn't, maybe it wasn't as obvious as he thought. It was worth the chance of offending Philo, but he would go slowly.

"Why," he paused and began again, "Why couldn't we just make this Caleb's trip? Why can't we go to Jerusalem, see Judea and Phoenicia, and return? Who knows what gods we may find or what teachings we may uncover?"

Philo had a blank look. The lamas of the Himalayas had been on his mind since Biolces had first mentioned them. The mysteries of eastern religion had fascinated him. He loved mountains, clear clean air, bright brooks, high forests. That's where his mind had been. He had been willing to do Caleb a favor, but the truth was that he had not been willing to give Caleb a portion of his life. Now, here was Biocles asking subtle questions but, none the less, showing him how selfish he really was. He had cut right to the core of his problem.

"You're a better man than I am, Minotaur."

"What are you talking about, Phil?"

"For you, there was never a problem of giving up a trip to please an old man. You find heart in pleasing other people. Most of the time I plunge ahead with only my own agenda in mind."

"Aw, Phil, that's not it. You're just preoccupied most of the time."

"I've told you the truth, now I'm not going to say anymore about it. Of course, this must be Caleb's trip. It's the least I can do for him. We'll take him, and we'll bring him back."

As always, they traveled light. The Himalayas were set aside, but still one never knew when fast traveling might be necessary in the ancient world. Philo and Biocles wore their most durable clothing, the leather skirts, heavy sandals, and thick capes. Each had a "Y" shaped rod to which he strapped his back pack. These packs included a shaving kit, spare tunic, socks, cold weather breeches and such undergarments as they deemed necessary. This was rolled into a blanket and encased in a hide cover which was used as a wet weather garment. They shared the load of cooking utensils, cleansing compounds, and food rations, the amount of which was determined by the days ahead without help from others. Since they would be asea for a while, rations in their packs were minimum at the start.

Both had short swords, properly sheathed, hanging from their belts. Philo carried an ax on the other side of his belt, and Biocles slung his bow and a small quiver of arrows above his back pack. Caleb carried no weapon, unless one could consider his walking staff as such. He wore the traditional Greek tunic and servant's sandals. Over one shoulder was his sack of provisions.

When they stepped out onto the street, they looked back to see Penelope, Alcandor, Dorea and the four children, now nearly two, waving from the portico. They returned the wave then walked away.

Caleb led the way. Though it had been a lifetime since he came this way, he could retrace every step back to his beloved Jerusalem.

Out across Athens they went to the entrance of the road of the long walls. This protected roadway descended the plains of Attica for five miles where it came to the seaport of Piraeus, the leading seaport of Greece, that lay on the western shore of the Aegean Sea. It was open to all peaceful ships of the sea, and since Athens provided a busy market, many of them came. Here, there was always something new. Metics, legal residents, from Egypt, Syria, Pamphlia and as far away as Numidia and Sardinia built houses after their own customs here. They erected altars to their own strange gods and established their own trades in the Emporium. Here one found the new shipments of carpets from Babylon, Persian lapis, Scythian turquoise, and all nature of things from the world beyond known only to the Phoenicians. In the warehouses and on the streets were Egyptians with brass ear rings and painted eyes, wearing only skirts of stiff linen and collars with gems and beads;

black-skinned Nubians with ivory adornments dragging their ears down to their shoulders; long-haired Medes in trousers and sequined bonnets.

The air was heavy with the smell of fish, foreign bodies, spices, hemp, and tar, all embellished and carried by a mist of salt water. People were everywhere speaking in foreign languages. Drunken sailors staggered out into the wide streets, some singing, some starting fist fights. They mingled with the workers and merchants who paid little attention to their ruckus.

Philo and Biocles had stolen away from their homes as youths and come here to gawk. It was still an attraction for them, but they wasted little time with the sights this day. Their passage had already been arranged by Alcandor, so they went straight for the quay where they boarded an outboat and sailors rowed them to their ship. She was the Olympia, a wooden vessel some 120 feet bow to stern. She was powered by a single square sail and fifteen long oars on both port and starboard. Philo, Biocles, and Caleb settled into their little cabin on the deck and shortly they were underway.

In the early spring, many sudden and violent storms beset the Aegean. So the captain of the Olympia chose not to go south immediately, but to go east through the Cyclades Islands and make for the west shore of Lydia to a port called Ephesus. In this way he could seek shelter from adverse winds and, in case of an emergency, make directly for shore which would not be distant at any point.

At Ephesus, the crew took refreshment, and brought fresh drinking water aboard. Then the ship sailed south along the coast. They turned east and could have touched land on the northern tip of the island of Rhodes, but instead went straight for the harbor of Patara which lay on the southern tip of Lycia of Asia Minor.

They had found few rough waters, and the weather was improving by the day, so at Patara, the captain of the

Olympia chose to sail due southeast into the open sea and make for Phoenicia.

When they had passed safely by Paphos on the southern tip of Cyprus and had sailed smoothly for a day's journey, they were beset by dead calm. All rowers were called to their positions, and the Olympia was headed due east in the direction the captain thought landfall was nearest. The sail, being more hindrance than help, had been furled, and the rowers had complete control of the ship.

On the second day of the calm, clouds appeared in the north. A gentle breeze soon grew into a strong wind that, try as they might, the rowers could not prevail against. The course east became a course south. The sun was then obscured and waves mounted higher than the sail mast. Rain descended in blinding curtains. Thunder roared and lightning charged the seas about them with glowing electricity.

The oarsmen worked feverishly to keep the vessel running with the wind. Should she veer, the next wave could overturn the ship. Everyone on board was enlisted to relieve the oarsmen. Philo, Biocles and even Caleb drew their shifts which lasted until exhaustion. Upon the constant and dramatic heaves of the ship, even veteran seamen became nauseous. In the area below deck, the air was foul with the results of tossed stomachs and befuddled bowels. Even so, all hands were advised against going topside lest they be swept into the sea by the waves that were cascading across the deck.

Philo and Biocles lay aft sprawled on cargo sacks. For some time they had slept the unconscious repose of exhaustion. A huge wave slammed the Olympia like a mallet the size of a mountain. It knocked Philo from his perch onto the below deck. The muck he landed in was indescribably foul.

He shook off as much as he could, but he still couldn't stand himself. Drawing himself back up onto the cargo, he stuck his mouth against Biocles' ear. "I have an idea," he said. "Get Caleb; we're going outside where we can get some fresh air."

"You've lost your mind. The storm has you crazy." answered Biocles. "We may get sick to death down here, but we'll be washed away in just a few minutes up on that deck."

Philo showed him some ropes. "We'll lash ourselves to the mast. Do you want to go or not?"

By this time Biocles was awake enough to perceive that the smell was stronger and closer than it had been. He stared at the mess Philo was in and held his nose. "By the gods, you have a point," he said with a loud twang.

Caleb sat on the far side of Biocles on a long bench in the hold. His eyes were closed, and he was praying. When Biocles nudged him, his eyes popped open. "We're going up for some air. Philo has rope we can use to tie ourselves to the mast. Do you want to come with us?"

"Was Plato Greek," said Caleb with a weak smile.

With ropes around their waists and a small length between, they tied themselves together with Caleb between Philo and Biocles. Thus bound, they went to the hatch nearest the mast and waited for the Olympia to right herself in the trough of a large wave. They would be somewhat protected from the winds.

So, when what was left of their equilibrium told them the time had come, they opened the hatch and stumbled onto the rain swept deck.

The rowers gulped the fresh air, and one shouted, "You'll drown out there." Then, wham, the hatch was shut. The deck was somewhat level but slick with the rain. Caleb slipped, but his friends held onto him. Biocles opened his mouth and looked straight up at the sodden sky, drinking in the fresh air and swallowing gulps of rain. He shook himself as if to wash the foul odor of the hold from his body. "Glory," he shouted.

"You had better wait for the celebrating," Philo shouted, trying to make himself heard above the thunder, wind, rain, and waves. "To the mast," he commanded.

The Olympia rose directly to the sky as though Atlas had one hand beneath her, elevating her with the sea. The three sat at the foot of the mast, their backs placed solidly against it. Then they began to wrap themselves with rope, handing the unused ball to the person on the right until they were encircled. One round, two rounds, three rounds.

The ship hit a crest and wind pounded them. "We'd better tie," shouted Philo as he handed the rope to Biocles once more. They were all pelted with rain and surf so that they could hardly see.

Biocles began the knots.

Down the far side of the huge wave the Olympia plunged. At the base of the wave, her bow plowed beneath the surface of the water as though she were headed stem-first to the bottom of the sea. Philo, Caleb, and Biocles were as inundated as if they had jumped directly into the billows. As they held their breaths, together they were lifted up the mast. Then they were pushed sternward by a new wall of water, but the rope held.

Then, as suddenly as the water had come, it receded. The Olympia was proving the worthiness of her builders.

Philo had a good bath. Now he shook the salt water from his head and opened his mouth to get a gulp of rain. They were all jolted, but safely seated at the mast. Biocles began to laugh.

"I travel with a lunatic," Philo shouted to Caleb.

"There are times when a bit of lunacy helps," said Caleb, his mouth close to Philo's ear.

"Come on, you apes, the gods knew we needed a good bath," yelled Biocles.

"How long do you think it will take them to get us clean," asked Philo knowing full well the game they were playing was good for them all.

Shortly exhaustion overcame them again, and tempest or not, they collapsed into deep sleep. Occasionally, they coughed, sputtered and spit water as it buried the deck, but then they slipped off immediately into that removed state of semi-consciousness that provided rest.

Philo sensed something strange. Two times, then three, he shook himself. There was warmth being radiated into his body. Then he blinked and saw it. The sun was shining. The Olympia drifted quietly along on a gentle breeze, a queen smirking victoriously at a buttermilk sky.

He untied the ropes and left Caleb and Biocles to rest. No one else was on deck. He opened the hatch to the scene below. There the rowers hung limply over their oar handles, the passengers and crew, even the captain, lay crumpled in human heaps as though the soul of all had departed. However, it was not Charon who had called them, but Morpheus. They slept the sleep of those so exhausted that they could do nothing else. The smell was the same, so Philo returned to the deck.

Biocles stood at the deck rail. "How are things down there?"

"Everyone seems to be okay. They just need a rest," said Philo.

"Do you think the storm made the fish hungry?" asked Biocles smiling.

"Somehow, my mind hasn't been on fish."

` "You never would have any fun if it weren't for me. Come on now, Caleb will be hungry when he wakes up," said Biocles, then threw out a line.

"I'm already hungry," came Caleb's weak voice from near the mast.

So the three sat with their lines over the rail waiting for fish to bite and enjoyed the warm morning sun.

`"There was once a Hebrew prophet who suffered a storm like that in these very same waters," said Caleb.

"Tell us about him," Biocles said.

"I'm not sure we have that much time."

"The way the fish are biting, we'll have all day."

"All right. The prophet's name was Jonah."

"Jonah's trouble began when he disobeyed God. God told Jonah to go and preach to the sinful Assyrian city of Nineveh. But Jonah was afraid because Nineveh wasn't a Jewish city.

"He decided that, instead of going to Nineveh, he would go the opposite direction hoping that God wouldn't be able to find him and so would forget him. So he went down to the port of Joppa and boarded a ship bound for Tarshish."

"Jehovah caught up with him, I'll bet," said Biocles.

"Exactly. He sent a storm so great that the crew threw all their cargo overboard to lighten the vessel. Still everyone aboard thought they all would perish.

"Jonah was brave enough to confess that he was the one who had brought the trouble. So, the crew threw him overboard and thus calmed the storm.

"A huge fish swallowed Jonah but found him to be an unsavory morsel. Three days later, he spit Jonah out upon the shore, thus cleansing the deep of Jonah's rebellious spirit."

Then Caleb told how the repentant Jonah had gone to Nineveh, and people there had found their way to God.

It was a long story, especially with the embellishments Caleb's family had added through the years. Caleb was not certain what part was true and what part was embellishment. But he did know that the story always ended the same way. Jonah kept his rebellious nature wanting God to destroy Ninevah rather than save it, and God continued to try to speak to Jonah about his love.

The captain had originally intended to sail east from Cypress and then come to Phoenicia somewhere near Sidon.

From that point, he could hop seaport to seaport down the coast eventually coming to Judea.

When the storm was passed, he had no certainty of his location, but he was still determined to sail east. So he set a course toward the rising sun and hoped for the best.

Five days hence, a Roman ship was spotted coming almost directly at them. Excitement spread among all those aboard as the captain ordered the Olympia to within hailing distance. They read the name on the Roman vessel's bow, Cicero. The ship's steward was ordered to an inquiry. He, with most of those aboard, stood against the deck rail. He cupped his hands to his mouth.

"Ahoy aboard the Cicero."

"Ahoy aboard the Olympia," came the reply out across the water.

"Is all well aboard the Cicero?"

"All is well, and you Olympia?"

"We have sailed stormy seas. What port do we approach?"

"It is Joppa of Judea."

Philo and Biocles gave Caleb an astonished stare.

"Do you think your God is up to something?" said Philo.

The old man tilted his head and with eyebrows raised, shrugged his shoulders and gave them a sort of "see for yourselves" expression.

CHAPTER XXV

In the great northern forest at the village of Kresboden there was a problem. Daga, high priest of Wodan, after the expulsion of Otto and his family, had tried to get more men to find Marlena and Arn. To his surprise, the people of Kresboden had refused. It seemed that nothing but trouble had come in the wake of Marlena and Arn's disappearance. The death toll was five. Now Otto was gone and Franz was maimed. It was enough. Daga began to run through the dirt streets and around the edge of the forest doing chants no one could understand. Over a few weeks time, these chants became interspersed with screams. Then one morning, Daga decided that he no longer required clothing. He appeared nude on the village green; his caved in face twisted even more wildly than before, and his limp arm dangled from his shoulder like a loose rein from a horse's neck. Calmly he walked into the midst of a group of children at play under the watchful eyes of their mothers. He tilted his head back and gave a high pitched scream that sent chills through them all.

The mothers grabbed their children's arms and ran for their houses as Daga began an exhilarated dance. He threw his good arm to the sky and yelled, "Come back. I'm here to perform for you," then continued his dance.

Soon, men of the village came running from their shops and houses. They surrounded Daga and caught him. Many of them were amazed at the strength he had. It took two strong men to hold Daga as they returned him to his home.

When the door of his house was opened by Brunhilda, he took one look and gave another air splitting scream. Brunhilda fell back. Daga kicked at the men holding him and tried to jerk away. He foamed at the mouth, cursed, screamed again, and collapsed.

The strong men threw the exhausted priest into a limp pile onto the floor of his house. One of them, still holding his ears, spoke to Brunhilda.

"You have to keep this maniac indoors. He has all the children terrified."

Brunhilda, frightened and bewildered herself, gave them a look of disbelief. "What do you think I can do? I can't tie him up. The door opens the way it always has. He's strong. You tell me what to do."

The men looked at one another, then one answered for them all. "This is the first time we have actually had to manhandle him. Maybe he'll remember what's happened this morning and this will be the end of it."

But the next morning, Daga was loose in the village, nude and screaming. And this time if anyone approached him, he sped away, his madness giving him alacrity no one was able to match.

The village council met. They removed Daga as priest of Wodan and replaced him with the acting figure of Cernunnon.

Daga's raging appearances throughout the village continued. The children were having nightmares of Daga bursting in upon them. The women protested constantly. But the men, uncertain about how to approach a former holy man, delayed any decision. What they did was: nothing at all.

In the alpine village of Melz, a penitent Hans Helvet decided his life must take a turn for the better. He married a jolly midwife named Frieda who immediately became pregnant.

Hans was so elated that he doubled the pay of all workers at the cloth factory and brewery. It was said that the finest woolen garments in all Europa were the products of Hans of Melz.

Not far from the Macedonian village of Florina at the goat farm with the stone house with light blue trim, a new house was being finished. It was just around the hill from the stone house with the light blue trim. It was situated so that Copella, standing at her front door, could see its board roof and stone chimney.

Otto, Katerina, Ava and Zig stood admiring their new home. It had not been the work of their hands only. Nikos, Copella, Marlena and Nixe had pitched in at every opportunity.

Otto's family couldn't decide on the color of trim they wanted. Wanting to be a fair husband and father, he decided that each family member should get dyes from Copella and paint a stone the color of his or her preference. These stones were to be placed in a small bag of goat leather.

At the appointed time, Nikos bringing his family along, was to arrive and draw a stone. The color of trim would be designated, and then there was to be a feast with music and dancing.

CHAPTER XXVI

Joppa was not ordinarily a busy port, but on the day the Olympia put in, it was abustle. It was, after all, the closest port to Jerusalem. Jewish pilgrims from many nations filled the inns and spilled out onto the streets and into the markets. Passover was near.

That night Philo, Biocles, and Caleb chose to camp outside the city on the road that went up to Jerusalem by way of Emmaeus. Campfires lined the roadside, their yellow glows dotting the night like two columns of fireflies organized by a Roman general. Even though it was night, a broken stream of travelers continued to move between the two columns of light. It was a clear, cool evening decked with bright stars and a fine yellow half moon. The three sat staring into their fire and listening to Caleb tell tales of the Jews.

A lad not more than fourteen veered off the road and walked haltingly in their direction. He stopped and stared behind himself. Then, returning his gaze at them, he came a couple of steps closer. "Do you mind if I rest by your fire," he said just barely loud enough for them to hear.

He was a thin boy and just a bit tall for his age. As he came closer to the fire, they could see wide, trusting brown eyes set between long black lashes. Here was a youth who had yet to know cruelty or intense fear. Thick, wavy hair poked from under his yarmulke.

"Please come and sit down," said Biocles. "You aren't lost, are you?"

"Oh no, my parents are coming."

"What's your name, lad," said Caleb.

"Levi bar Noah."

"And where might you be from, Levi?"

"Alexandria in Egypt. And what about you?"

"We're from Athens in Greece. Have you heard of that place," said Philo.

"Oh, yes," said Levi. "We learn about all the world at our school in Alexandria."

Levi's parents appeared with apologies. "I hope the boy isn't bothering you," said the mother. "He's so eager to get to Jerusalem one moment, then he's doddering at the side of the road the next. I guess he is at last getting tired. We need to find a campsite."

"You're welcome to share our fire," said Caleb. "You could sleep over behind that boulder for some privacy." He pointed to his left up the road ten or fifteen steps.

"I don't know," said the woman hesitating.

"Why not?" The man spoke for the first time. "We are Noah, Leah, and Levi of Alexandria."

They could see where Levi got his height. Noah was a slightly tall man with dark features. What Philo, Biocles, and Caleb could see most was a long, square beard. His voice conveyed sincerity and intelligence.

"And we are Caleb, Philo, and Biocles of Athens," said Biocles. "Come and rest with us. What news is there from Alexandria?"

"Alexandria is Alexandria," said Noah as he sat on a stone near Caleb. "What we are excited about is what we heard in Joppa. I'm sure you, too, heard about the carpenter." Leah stood beside him and Levi stood at his other shoulder.

"What carpenter is that," asked Philo as he threw another stick on the fire. "We didn't stay the day in Joppa."

"He must be some kind of people's prophet from what people are saying," said Noah. "I'm sure the gossip is exaggerated."

"Tell us the gossip," said Biocles.

"Jesus of Nazareth is his name. He heals the sick, causes the deaf to hear, and the blind to see. He has fed thousands with a boy's lunch, walked on water, and some say even raised the dead. What is more, he teaches as no one has ever taught. The rabbis try to trap him, and he puts them to shame."

"The Jews have been suppressed too long," said Caleb with a sigh. "They're concocting fairy tales."

Noah relaxed and put an arm around Leah who seemed the size of a child beside him in the shadow of the campfire. Levi put an arm around his father.

"Some think this Jesus is the Messiah. They're waiting for him to sound the cry of battle to overthrow the Romans."

"There are a great number of reasons that they're wrong, even with just the small amount you have told us," said Caleb. "In the first place, the Messiah must arise from Bethlehem, not Nazareth."

Noah stood to his feet. "Yes," he said. "Maybe we'll see this carpenter in Jerusalem."

Leah turned her face up to Noah so that it was lit by the fire for the first time. There was weariness but peace in her lovely oval countenance. "We need to rest, my husband," she said.

The next morning the six set out together for Emmaeus and Jerusalem. They walked as almost everyone else did. There were a few carts, asses, and an occasional camel, but most of these people expected no more than their own good health to transport them.

Daylight revealed Noah's family to be an attractive one. All had raven black hair, but while Noah and Leah's was straight, Levi's was a bit curly. Leah had large brown eyes that betrayed her every emotion, all of which were tempered with tenderness.

There was a sense of adventure in all six hearts. Fulfillment in some sense seemed at hand, and yet each would have described his expectations in a different way. Levi was curious about his ancestors' way of life, his father and mother's religious origins, the sights of the great old city itself, and many other things. For Caleb, Noah, and Leah, this was an altogether religious pilgrimage. Every step of progress along the road they seemed to feel closer to God Himself. For Philo, this was another excursion toward finding whatever gods may be and hopefully demonstrating to them that he felt strongly about the seeking. Biocles didn't struggle to enjoy life. By nature, he simply did enjoy life. He enjoyed being with good friends. He enjoyed meeting new people, going new places, and perhaps more than any of the others, he was enchanted by all that surrounded him no matter where he happened to be, especially if that place and those people were out of doors.

They walked along the road observing the fertile Judean plain that rose gradually from the sea. Caleb was accepted as leader by unspoken, but mutual, consent.

"When the scriptures speak of going to Jerusalem," he said as they walked, "they speak of 'going up to Jerusalem.' We are experiencing the geographical 'up' as we walk; and the grade will get much steeper. Jerusalem is situated so that one must ascend to reach it from any direction. But this 'up' has a deeper meaning, too.

"David, it was said, was a man after God's own heart. Even as a lad he delivered Israel from its enemies. It was not only with his bravery that he won the hearts of his countrymen, however. He sang and wrote songs and poems that helped common people express faith in Jehovah.

"He was, alas, very human, a man guilty of great moral sin, including adultery and even murder. But, when he was willing to face the fact that he was as bad as the worst of men without God, he returned to God.

"In David, at his best and at his worst, God found no deceit. So God blessed him and promised him that the Messiah would be heritage of his seed.

"It was King David who chose Jerusalem as the site of his capitol. He brought the Ark of the Covenant, symbol of God's presence, to Jerusalem to be a permanent part of the great temple there.

"And so Jerusalem, to this day, is called the city of David. And the Messiah will also be called the Son of David.

"The Jews, in their long history, have had many heroes, Abraham, Jacob, Moses, Elijah, and many more. But they loved and still do love David most of all.

"Solomon, David's son, was the wealthiest and wisest of all Jewish kings. He built the temple in Jerusalem and ruled more territory than any Israelite ever.

"And so you see, to a Jew, Jerusalem is not only high geographically, but high politically, high historically, and most of all high spiritually. The land upon which we stand is the land God promised to give Abraham. It is here that the children of Israel came when God delivered them from Egypt with a great and mighty hand. And Jerusalem is its center, high, high in the minds and hearts of every man, woman, and child with Jacob's blood flowing in his veins."

Caleb paused and looked into the faces of his little audience. Then he turned around and extended both arms toward the mountain before them. "Let us go up," he whispered, tears of awe moistening the corners of his eyes.

Philo sensed some of the old man's spirit. Indeed he felt that somehow his soul was rising in spiritual perception, going "up."

They entered the City of David from the west near Herod's palace at the Jaffa Gate. Great stone walls extended to their right and left. The towers pool and Hyrcanus Monument, a four storied, tiered structure lay to their immediate left just before they passed through the gate. The famous triplet of towers, the Mariamme, the Phasael, and the Hippicus, were built into the walls on their right. Straight ahead lay the road of the old (or first) wall which traversed the city, going easterly, directly to the temple.

Roman soldiers met them and checked their weapons. No swords, bows, knives or axes would be allowed beyond the gate. These things could be acquired once more on each person's exit of Jerusalem. They were told the city would be packed with nearly two million people during the week to come, and the Romans intended to keep peace at virtually any cost.

A Roman centurion, the first one Levi had ever seen, stopped by to check the condition of his troops. Dressed in full parade uniform, he stood talking to the sergeant of the guard. Centurions were important people in the Roman army. Only battle proven and prudent men came to this office and the Emperor wanted the world to know it. He had provided these heroic leaders with equipment no other rank was allowed to wear. "Greaves" they were called, special steel shin guards strapped on behind the knees and ankles. These greaves complemented the steel helmet and curiass (chest and back protector). Contrasting this polished steel were a tunic, a short skirt, and a plume from the helmet, all a reddish brown color.

Levi stood gaping when his father tugged him forward. "I've never seen a soldier dressed so wondrously," he whispered.

"That's a centurion," said Noah. "He's the leader. Don't stare, Levi. We'll probably see others later. The Romans must keep more soldiers here than they do in Alexandria."

Once they had passed through the gate, Noah, Leah, and Levi excused themselves to search for relatives. Levi told Biocles and Philo goodbye. He gave Caleb a hug. "I hope we'll see you again," he said as he clung to Caleb. "I like to hear you talk."

"And I like to watch you listen," said Caleb. "Don't ever lose your curiosity. The Lord wants you to learn as much as you can."

He let the boy go, then turned to Noah and Leah, "Shalom."

"Shalom," they said together as they waved. They turned and disappeared into the crowd.

For a while, Caleb wanted simply to stand and behold what was before him, to get the feel of the stone street, to listen to the rumble of the crowd, and to smell the smells of Kosher. Philo and Biocles stood waiting for the old man as he was jostled by the press of people passing that way.

"Where do you want to go first?" asked Philo.

"I, too, must inquire about members of my family," said Caleb.

To the east, the roar of a throng erupted.

"Do you suppose there's a riot like the soldiers told us about?" Biocles asked.

Another roar came from the same direction.

"I have no idea," said Caleb. "I know of no celebration at this time that would create such a stir. We had better be careful. I'll meet you back here in three hours."

When Caleb had slipped away, Biocles put his hand on his friend's shoulder. His brown eyes shown, and a mischievous grin accentuated his dimples. "We didn't come here to miss the excitement, did we?"

"Absolutely not," said Philo. "Come on."

So Philo and Biocles, now up to their old mode of curiosity, turned left away from the old wall road and headed through narrow dirt streets in the direction of the clamor that they heard. They were guided solely by the noise. As they passed the houses built wall to wall, they didn't hurry. Most of the houses seemed to be two-story. Often people peeped out at them from doors, windows, and even roofs. They had heard the crowd's roar, too.

209

They found they had to veer a bit northerly where they came upon open bazaars. The place was much like the Agora with an eastern flavor. Tent pavilions ballooned along the streets' edges, their varicolored tops and swags swelling in the afternoon breeze. Tables and tripods overflowing with all manner of goods filled the tents and covered the sidewalks. A constant chatter of merchants rose to challenge the music of flutes and lyres. There were more silks for sale here than in the Agora. Glittering rolls of this cloth shone on the tables, and lively patterns, hung on lines, fluttered in the breeze.

Arabs sold dates and nuts. Syrians displayed knives and pans. Lebanese furniture sat for anyone's inspection while the Jews in the next stall bargained for leather goods. Street after street was lined with such things, and all these streets were stuffed with people of many lands, Jews on a pilgrimage. At the first canteen, Biocles sniffed the air.

"I knew there was something I've overlooked."

"What," asked Philo.

"I'm hungry."

"What about the excitement?"

"I don't hear the noise anymore."

"Maybe someone is still there who knows what happened."

"If there is, we can find out later. I've decided to eat," said Biocles. "Something here smells very good."

Philo sniffed the air. "You're right, but this place is so crowded we'll have to stand to eat."

"I can handle that. We go that way."

They followed Biocles' nose to a booth where they found hot lamb spiced with salt, pepper, garlic, and all the good spices the Jews found to cook with. Then they stood against the side of a tent chomping these morsels and watching the crowd around them. They saw the apparel and heard the languages of many nations. Yet, regardless of the difference in these people, one thing was universal among them — anticipation.

A lanky Jew sat at a small wayside table. He gave the Greeks a friendly smile. "If you would like to rest," he said, "you may sit here with me."

They looked at one another then shrugged their shoulders simultaneously, "Why not."

They sat on small wooden stools across the table and looked at the Jew. He was a middle-aged man with a big, straight nose, blunt on the end, short black hair and beard, a square jaw and a pleasant smile. His dark brown eyes were reflective but fearless. They couldn't understand his friendliness to strangers, but at the moment that didn't need to be explained. They needed the rest. "I'm Philo of Athens in Greece and this is my friend, Biocles."

"I'm Lazarus of Bethany. Are you here for the festival?"

"Yes, we have a Jewish friend. And, as a matter of fact, we came wanting to find out more about Jehovah," said Philo.

"You have come at the right time," said Lazarus. "It is one thing to study history in a foreign land. It is quite another to experience the difference in people's lives because of the God they worship."

"We've noticed the excitement," said Biocles. "I don't suppose you would know what all the noise was about earlier."

"Perhaps the coming of the Lord. I should have been there, but I've come ahead to secure a place for him and his disciples at the Passover meal."

"And what Lord would that be?" asked Philo.

"Jesus of Nazareth, beyond question the Messiah of God," said Lazarus as he gave an unblinking stare at Philo and Biocles in turn.

"That is an incredible statement," said Philo. "Our Jewish friend has told us a little about this Messiah, the ruler of all Jews, God incarnate so to speak. Surely this Jesus of Nazareth doesn't meet the standards of all those prophecies."

"Prophecies can be misunderstood," said Lazarus, Philo's doubt not affecting him, "but personal experience cannot."

"You seem certain," said the startled Philo.

"Who could be more certain than one dead and now alive."

"You mean that spiritually, figuratively I'm sure," said Philo. Biocles was sitting wide eyed, on the edge of his seat.

"That too, of course," said Lazarus. "But no, that's not my main meaning. I know that it's hard to believe, but I was in the grave, the physical, earthly grave, and he called me forth."

Biocles bent toward Philo, put his hand to Philo's right ear, and whispered, "This fellow has been in the sun too long."

"You doubt me, of course," said Lazarus. "You haven't been here long; that is obvious. You see, there were many witnesses. You'll understand better once you have seen the Lord."

"So, he is here. Where might we see him?"

"Probably at the temple, a little later on," said Lazarus. "I must find him now and tell him my news. I hope you enjoy your time in Jerusalem. I also hope you'll find more than you might have expected."

With that he rose and left.

"Do you think Lazarus left his brain packed on his camel?" asked Biocles.

"He seemed intelligent," said Philo, "and so serene. But I have to admit what he said was incredible. Still, didn't Noah tell us this Jesus of Nazareth was reported to have raised some from the dead?"

"Come to think of it, I believe he did, but surely you aren't going along with that."

"Not yet anyway. Isn't it time for us to meet Caleb?"

They spotted Caleb near the Jaffa Gate.

"Have you found us a place to stay, old man?" said Philo.

"How about a roof top?" said Caleb. "I've been talking with a cousin who lives in the southern part of the city near the rose gardens and the pool of Siloam. All accommodations are taken, but many find roof tops comfortable enough in the spring."

"I like it," said Biocles. "We'll have more of a sense of the city around us. We came prepared to camp anyway."

"What about your family?" said Philo as they meandered through the dirt streets toward the south.

"It seems that, except for a few distant cousins, I have none. The Romans saw to that."

"Wait until you hear what happened to us," said Biocles.

"I'll wager you've seen Jesus of Nazareth."

"Not quite," said Philo, "but in the end we might have done better than that. One thing is sure. If we do see this Jesus, we will certainly listen to him carefully."

Then Philo and Biocles told Caleb about Lazarus of Bethany.

"That's a strange story," said Caleb as they walked. "It seems as though the city is full of strange stories, but I think that tops them all, especially in view of the fact that this fellow said what happened was to him. All the other stories are hearsay."

They passed by the theater where it was evident that the Jews relished gardens. Cedars and low shrubs surrounded the theater entrance. To the left of this entrance they passed through the old south wall. Then, looking east down a side street, they could see the Hippodrome, and just beyond that, the towering walls of the temple.

They proceeded to what proved to be the southeast corner of the city. There they entered an L-shaped house with walls of stone and small slit windows. It was just across a wider street from the rose garden where, row on row, budding plants grew eager to bloom forth.

When they had met Caleb's cousin and his family and had been fed, they retired to the roof in time to see the sunset. They looked to the west and saw a spire rising over the old south wall. "What structure is that?" asked Biocles.

"One of the most sacred places in the city," said Caleb. "It's the tomb of King David."

"Will we go there tomorrow?" asked Biocles.

"No, we'll go to the temple."

CHAPTER XXVII

The next morning as Philo, Biocles, and Caleb approached the temple courts, they could see beyond the massive walls to the dome of the temple itself. It shone such a brilliant white reflection of the sun that it could have been mistaken for the sun itself. Caleb insisted that they skirt the south wall and enter from the east.

It was not before they stood in front of the gates, now swung open, that Philo and Biocles understood Caleb's insistence. No wonder this was called the "Gate Beautiful." The gates, made of Corinthian brass, stood fifty cubits (75 feet) high and forty cubits (60 feet) wide. Precious metals were imbedded into these gates forming the likeness of a thriving grape vine, symbol of the Jewish nation. They stood and gawked like school boys. Nothing in the beauty of Athens had prepared them for this.

The walls of the temple and its courts ran five hundred cubits corner to corner, and within these walls, except on the west where the temple proper stood, ran porticoes with roofs of cedar supported by marble pillars twenty-five cubits high. These porches were paved with mosaic work. The inner side of the open courts was surrounded by a broad stone parapet. Flights of fourteen steps ascended this parapet to the inner court where Jews alone were allowed. Rising again from the inner court was the temple proper, the holiest place on earth to a child of Jacob.

Throngs crowded most of the outer courts, but the most excitement was to their left where they could barely see a lean, muscular man with dark beard and hair speaking in informal and relaxed tones. As they grew near, he asked the people surrounding him to sit down in the shade of the porch.

As they sat, many tried to restrain children from pressing in upon him. The first words they heard Jesus of

Nazareth say were, "Let the little children come to me. The kingdom of God is composed of such. Unless you're able to have the kind of faith a child does, you'll never fully know your heavenly father."

"This place is full of lunatics," said Biocles under his breath.

"Be quiet. I want to hear what he says," said Philo.

"I think I understand what he is talking about," whispered Caleb.

So they sat with the crowd.

After he had blessed the children, Jesus remained standing and walked among them. He didn't raise his voice, but he spoke distinctly as though every syllable were important. His baritone resonated from the stone walls and seemed to amplify from the marble pillars.

"You see official religion going on all around you. I advise you to steer clear of the officials. Listen to them as long as they stay with the law of Moses, but don't do the things they do, because they steal from the poor and rob widows. They claim to know God, but their hearts are far from him."

The three from Athens could see hundreds of people crossing the courtyard with sacrifices. Some were leading sheep or cattle. Others were bringing small cages with doves in them. The priests were inspecting these animals, accepting some, rejecting others. Meanwhile, the crowd around Jesus of Nazareth grew.

"What is God's measure of our worship?" asked one of the crowd.

"Men look on the outside. God looks on the inside. What a person truly is in his heart is what God sees. The Pharisees and Scribes, religious officials that they are, like to pray in public for all to see. When they fast, they put on rumpled clothes and try to get sad looks on their faces so people can see they are suffering. But I advise you to pray in secret and be happy when you fast so that no one knows your sacrifice. Then God, who sees in every place, will know your worship and reward you openly."

A commotion rose at the back of the crowd where two men seemed to be leading a third.

"Please let us through," one of the men said. "We must get our blind friend to Jesus."

The crowds parted and shortly the blind man, led by his friends, stood before Jesus.

"What would you ask of me?" said Jesus.

"My sight, Master. I've been blind since birth."

Jesus looked at the friends, and they nodded in agreement.

"And why do you come to me?" asked Jesus.

"Because you're not only the master of the words of life, but also the substance of life," said the blind man. His head was tilted back as though in such a posture he could hear better, his eyes lacking ability to see anything at all, even in the brightest light.

"Do you truly believe that?" asked Jesus.

"I do, Lord."

"Then I say to you, open your eyes, your faith has made you whole."

The man's eyes blinked. Then they blinked again. Now he straightened his head and looked directly into the face of Jesus. "My Lord and my God," he shouted and fell on his knees before Jesus.

Jesus took him by the hand and raised him up. "You must also thank your friends," he said. "Faith also was in their hearts."

This scene started a flood. Soon people with all manner of disease and deformity were coming to Jesus. As Philo, Biocles, and Caleb watched, Jesus healed them all. Some he touched. Some he reasoned with. Some he merely spoke to. Then, turning, he left their midst.

"That is one incredible person," announced Philo.

"You don't know how incredible," said Caleb. "How he could so criticize the scribes, Pharisees, and priests with such impunity is a mystery. You could never know the improbability of it without being a Jew."

"Look, there's our friend Lazarus," said Biocles. "Lazarus, Lazarus," he called through the throng. Then, as Lazarus turned his head, he cupped one hand over his mouth and headed their way.

"What does he mean by that?" asked Biocles.

"He wants you to be quiet," said Caleb.

As Lazarus reached them, he drew Philo and Biocles to his side. In low tones he explained, "I'm afraid I didn't tell you everything yesterday. You see, the leaders of the temple have a price on my head."

They were all startled, but especially Caleb.

"I'm Caleb, friend of these two. May I ask why these leaders would want to kill you?"

"You must be the Jew they told me about yesterday." Caleb nodded. "You see, Caleb, as long as I'm around, I'm living testimony that the power of Jesus is greater than any power those people have."

"I see," said Caleb. "Can we go somewhere and talk?"

"I suppose we could go out the Gate Beautiful. To the east are the olive gardens," said Lazarus

The stony slopes east of the city wall did, indeed, support a large olive grove. Row on row of trees shed ample shade. The trunks of the trees were short and gnarled. The branches spread much as an apple or peach tree, but they were thicker, bushier. Both bark and willow-shaped leaves were soft gray-green. The leaves were new and fresh, evidence of the vitality of spring.

As the four found privacy and rest among these friendly trees, Philo posed a question. "What is dying like, Lazarus?"

Lazarus sat on the grass and leaned back on one elbow. "Do you mean, does it hurt?"

"I mean that, but more than that. What is the passage like from life to death? What is the other side like?"

They were all seated on the grass now, admiring the olive trees. No one was quite sure how old they were, but it was evident some were very old, indeed.

"Your questions are good ones. Most people seem to be interested in other aspects of my experience. I'll tell you what I remember, but I must say at the beginning that I think God has clouded some of my memory for His own reasons, whatever they may be."

"Were you killed in an accident or by some disease?" asked Biocles.

"I fell ill of a fever. I remember being nauseated often and very weak. Then, it were as though I went to sleep, but what came next was not like any dream."

"But you do remember," said Philo.

"I passed very quickly through what seemed to be a dark valley. Then, on the other side of the valley, there was a bright light, not an earthly light but a heavenly light."

"What do you mean 'heavenly'?"

"It was an even light, everywhere brilliant, but nowhere glaring. In that light souls communicated thought to thought with no language necessary."

"Were you frightened?" asked Caleb.

"Not in the least. As a matter of fact, I don't remember much more, but I do remember an incredible serenity, a peace far beyond anything I've ever known. And I know this; I'll never be afraid of death again." In turn he looked directly at each of them, just a friendly gaze. He wasn't trying to convince, only stating facts.

"You said there were witnesses to your resurrection. Where did it happen and why were there witnesses?"

"It happened in Bethany, only a couple of hours walk from here. That's where my sisters and I live. Many people of the village had gathered to mourn my passing. When Jesus asked to be taken to my grave, many were curious and went along."

"And how was all this for you, I mean what happened?" said Philo.

"In whatever state I was I heard the master call, 'Lazarus, come forth.' I didn't want to go because it was a call from complete freedom and peace back to the cares of the world, but I knew the voice of the Lord, and my love for Him constrained me. Suddenly, I could hardly move. With great effort, I got up and went toward the voice of the master. Then, I heard him say, 'Loose him and let him go.' Only then did I realize I hadn't been able to move because of grave wrappings. When the people freed me of these, I saw them all rejoicing and there in the midst was Jesus."

"By Zeus, I've never heard anything like that," said Biocles.

"Nor would I have concocted such a story in my wildest imagination," said Lazarus. "My friends, you're privileged to be witnessing Jesus, the Christ, God with us."

Caleb immediately recognized the term from scriptures and began to discuss the idea of Messiah with Lazarus.

Philo and Biocles could only listen and try to learn what they might. They sat there for hours, unhurried, undisturbed. The bright spring sun warmed their bodies, and the presence of Lazarus warmed their souls.

That evening they sat on the roof top watching the sun descend over King David's tomb. Biocles threw himself down on his bed roll, put his hands behind his head, and stared at the coming moon, still white it was. He was thinking about things that didn't usually occupy his mind: How strong is a man's spirit? Does it go on after death as Lazarus had said? Can it still respond to those living such as Jesus? And what about Jesus? Maybe the spiritual power was all his. There was no question in Biocles' mind that he possessed unusual powers, but to what end?

Philo's eyes went from the sunset to Biocles' face. He read the questions written there.

"What do you think about this Jesus?" he asked Caleb.

"At the very least, he is an astounding person. At the most, perhaps he is the son of God. He was born in Bethlehem Lazarus told me. He is of the lineage of David. He has performed all the miracles we have heard about and more. He has a regal bearing, yet he is approachable even for children."

"You seem almost persuaded," said Biocles.

"The problem is that the scriptures leave no doubt that the Messiah will lead his people, Israel, in glorious triumph. This carpenter seems to use godly powers only to help the weak and poor."

"Then, he can't be the one," said Philo.

"Lazarus points to other prophecies, such as those in the book of Isaiah, which tell about a suffering Messiah who gives his all for his people, the slain lamb of Passover. He says Jesus is in the process of the first of two comings."

"Does that make sense to you?" said Biocles.

"Perhaps. We will see."

The next day found the three back at the temple listening to Jesus. The scribes and Pharisees had taken heat too long to remain silent. They were openly challenging Jesus.

Before the gathered throng, a tall Pharisee dressed in a blue trimmed robe stood and asked, "Is it lawful for us to pay taxes to Caesar?"

Caleb whispered to Philo and Biocles, "The Jews hate the Roman overlords. If he says it is lawful, he will have trouble with the Jews; if he says it isn't, he will be teaching sedition."

Jesus was saying, "Show me the coin used for the tax."

Then they brought him the coin.

"Who's likeness is this and whose title?" he said.

"The emperor's," they said.

Then he looked at the Pharisees with a mixture of scorn and pity and said, "Give, therefore, to Caesar the things that are Caesar's and unto God the things that are God's."

Everyone around stood astounded. "Do you realize how amazing that simple teaching is?" said Caleb to his friends.

Then, when Philo started to answer, someone else came, "Let's listen," said Caleb.

There came a Sadducee, one who did not believe in life after death, Caleb explained. He was a portly man, wealthy, aristocratic, from the high society of priesthood. He stood before Jesus with a relaxed smugness. "The law of Moses tells us that if a husband dies, his brother must be given to the wife as husband. Suppose a family of many brothers is given to the same woman, whose wife would she be in the resurrection?"

Jesus answered, "You know neither the scriptures nor the power of God. There'll be no marriage in heaven, but all shall be as the angels. As for the resurrection, haven't you read that God has said to you, 'I am the God of Abraham, Isaac, and Jacob.' I say to you, God isn't the God of the dead but of the living."

When the crowd heard it, they were all once again astonished at his teaching.

"He's making these fellows look very bad," said Biocles.

A man stood to be recognized. He professed to be a lawyer and, as Caleb later explained, was probably a follower of Rabbi Hillel, the liberal. He seemed more sincere than the others. "Teacher," he said, "which commandment in the law is the greatest?"

Now it seemed Jesus was facing both a test and an honest question. He didn't hesitate, "You shall love the Lord your God with all your heart, and with all your soul, and with all your mind. This is the greatest, and second to it, and like it, you shall love your neighbor as yourself."

This seemed the most lovely statement of theology Philo had ever heard. It was more than theology; it was the correct placement of all life's relationships. His spirit overcame the restraints of his body, and he blurted, "I have to talk to him."

"You mean out here in the open like the others," said Biocles.

"No, privately, when he starts to leave."

"I'm not sure I'm ready for that," said Caleb.

"What are you going to ask him?" said Biocles.

"What I must do to find God, what else?"

"All right, I'll go with you."

It was a decision Biocles made with his heart pounding loudly. It seemed almost too much to do. It was such a simple thing, yet he felt himself on the edge of a precipice. What held Caleb back? Suddenly it didn't matter. He had always been with Philo and he was going to be now. Still he sensed that somehow he was on his own. Yes, if it were he alone, he would go. The search was his, too.

So when Jesus started to leave the outer courts, Philo and Biocles came to his disciples and asked if they might talk with him. They explained their journey and their quest.

Disciples named Philip and Andrew, the ones with the Greek names, said, "Come with us."

So, together, they worked their way through the crowd until Andrew stood beside Jesus.

"Master, there are Greeks here who would like to speak to you."

"Andrew, you know we must spend our energy on the house of Jacob."

"I know, Lord, but these men have come a long and perilous journey seeking to know Jehovah."

"Let me see them," said the carpenter.

Andrew turned to Philo and Biocles, took them by the hand, and stood them directly before Jesus.

Now, only arm's length away, they looked directly into the eyes of Jesus, and he returned their gaze. Philo felt warmth penetrate his entire being. Something was happening to him.

"What are your names?" said Jesus.

"I'm Philo of Athens."

"I'm Biocles of Athens."

Once they had given their names, the two stood struck dumb. But words seemed unnecessary. Jesus looked into their souls and said to them, "I'm telling you the truth, unless a seed of wheat falls to the ground and dies, it remains one grain alone; but if it falls and dies, it bears much fruit. It is possible to love too much what this world calls life and to miss the quality of life that is eternal."

Then Jesus turned to go, but he looked back and spoke a final word. "Whoever serves and follows me, the Father will honor." Then he was gone.

For several minutes, Philo and Biocles stood frozen, trying to assimilate not just what had been said, but what had happened. At last Philo spoke, "I suppose we should go."

They looked around and didn't see Caleb. It was clear that their paths and Caleb's would have to fork from time to time. The man saw through different eyes and had to go his own way. They understood. "Why don't we go sit in the olive garden?" said Biocles. "Somehow my mind seems to get clearer there."

When they were out of the Gate Beautiful, Biocles put a hand on Philo's shoulder. "What did you feel when He looked at us?"

"I was going to ask you that. I don't guess I could get you to answer first."

"What will you give me?"

"Are you ever completely serious?"

"You go first," demanded Biocles.

"I felt as if I was looking into the face of purity and I didn't measure up. That was at first. Then, it were as if He realized that and reached out to me in love anyway. I stood there warm all over as though something of what He was was becoming part of me."

"Right. At first I was thinking I shouldn't be here. I'm in over my head. Then I felt an acceptance I didn't deserve, but still it was a complete acceptance."

They had come to the olive grove where they found a shady spot and relaxed.

"What do you make of it?" Biocles asked.

"I was ready to declare him deity like all those others."

"What about now?"

"I'll have to reflect on it. What happened is too close," said Philo.

"What do you think he meant by that 'seed falling to the ground' thing?"

"Didn't he explain it in a way? He talked about dying and making fruit."

"So, do you think he doesn't expect anything from people until after they die?"

"That doesn't seem likely, does it?"

They found Caleb back on the rooftop leaning on the parapet, staring at the rose garden across the street and scratching his head.

As Biocles topped the rustic ladder, he spoke to Caleb. "Hey, old friend, where have you been keeping yourself?"

Caleb turned to see the cherubic face of Biocles rising above the wall of the house. Biocles was a man he was always happy to see. He was the most open and cheerful person Caleb had known in his long life. "I saw the effect that Jesus had on you two, and I had to think. I've spent most of the afternoon discussing Jesus with my countrymen."

"What did you decide?"

Philo came up behind Biocles, and they all went to the parapet to watch the sun set.

"I didn't decide anything," said Caleb. "I only gained more knowledge. You have to understand something of what Messiah means to a Jew. The foundation of our nation by God's promise to Abraham pointed to God's anointed. Our godly character, our institutions, our rituals, and even our history center in the idea of Messianic rule. Here is a typical quote by the prophet, Daniel: "I saw one like a human being coming with the clouds of heaven. And to him was given dominion and glory and kingship, that all peoples, nations, and languages should serve him. His dominion is an everlasting dominion that shall not pass away, and his kingship is one that shall never be destroyed.""

"That's strong stuff," said Biocles. "Sounds like Caesar or somebody."

"You didn't see the eyes of this man as we saw them," said Philo. "What actual fault do your people find in him?"

"That's just the thing," said Caleb. "Except for his inference toward Messiahship, no fault can be found in him at all, and, believe me, our rabbis have tried."

That night, far into Philo's sleep, he dreamed, not of Theana, but of Marlena. A truth he never spoke of was that not many days of his life passed that he did not dream of Marlena. How this could be when he loved Theana so deeply, he didn't understand. But Marlena forever walked in his reverie.

In the reverie, he implored her to tell him what he had done to displease her, why she had gone away. She kissed him with tender passion, then slipped from his arms like ice melting into water and running out onto the ground and into the vast sea. There she remained, part of a great, mysterious, and inseparable mass that stretched far beyond sight or even imagination. Marlena.

He awoke and whispered her name aloud, "Marlena."

Then he began to whisper a prayer in a manner he found almost beyond himself, yet expressing the depths of his heart. "Jesus, if you are God, you know my prayer. Since you are the closest to God that I have found, I say this prayer to you. Could I see Marlena again, just see her, and talk to her, and know that she is well and happy, and know that she doesn't hate me?"

CHAPTER XXVIII

For two days Philo, Biocles, and Caleb searched for Jesus of Nazareth only to learn that he had been arrested. Then, on Friday, they heard a tumult and went in the direction of the governor's quarters. The tiled plaza before the building was packed with people in a frenzy. Roman soldiers lined the building walls and the steps leading into the governor's palace. They stood like stone, as though they could neither see nor hear the tumult. Many church officials worked their way through the crowd, encouraging the uproar.

On a second floor balcony stood the governor himself, Pontius Pilate, washing his hands. What thin hair he had strung down from the edges of a wide bald pate, a common condition of Romans in their fifties. A gold necklace and a medal befitting his authority hung across the white folds of his toga, and his bracelets dragged in the water as he washed. At a distance his huge nose seemed to be his only facial feature. Beside him stood Jesus, disheveled, pale, with huge bruises and cuts on his face.

The mob was shouting, "Crucify him, crucify him, crucify him."

"We've just arrived, what has happened?" Philo asked an onlooker.

"The Jews, at last, have Jesus where they want him," the man screamed above the din.

"Yes," said Philo, "Virtue should never go unpunished."

"You are an idiot," said the man, then he melted into the throng.

Jesus, along with Pilate, disappeared into the house. "God in heaven, he didn't deserve this," said Caleb.

They stood bewildered, listening to the maddened mob and watching for what might happen.

Almost an hour later, a huge iron gate on the pavement level swung open. Two Roman soldiers appeared marching in step. Behind them Jesus came bearing the beam of a cross. His clothing was soaked with blood. Streams of blood poured down his face and neck. His hair and beard were matted with blood. Profuse sweat mixed with the blood. As he exited the gate, he stumbled; and two more Roman soldiers appeared behind him. "Get along there," they commanded.

Jesus staggered to his feet and continued down the narrow street, now lined on both sides with people both for and against him. Mourning and curses filled the air. Fists were shaken in anger, and prayers for mercy were chanted. Flowers offered were knocked away by rotten vegetable missiles.

Philo, Biocles, and Caleb followed. They saw Jesus fall. One of the soldiers prodded him with a spear, and he failed to move. "Get up," the soldier commanded and prodded Jesus again. Still he lay motionless.

The soldier turned to the press of the crowd. He saw a strong looking, swarthy man and, as was the custom of the Romans, laid the flat of his spear on his shoulder. "I enlist you in the service of the emperor," he said. "Come, carry this cross."

Dutifully, almost reverently, the man lifted the cross beam. The soldier grabbed Jesus and pulled him to his feet. "Now you walk," he ordered. So Jesus stood and stumbled along the winding streets until they came to a hill called Golgotha. There were erected there three upright beams.

The man carrying Jesus' cross beam laid it on the ground. Jesus was stripped and spread upon it. Spikes were driven into his hands, and he was hoisted onto the upright. His ankles were bound to the upright just above a slanting block that offered little support because of its downward tilt. A soldier climbed a ladder and nailed a board above Jesus' head. Inscribed on this board in Latin, Greek, and Aramaic was the crime for which Jesus was being punished. It read simply: King of the Jews. Two thieves were crucified beside him. It was the third hour, the middle of the morning.

Jesus moaned and said he was thirsty. Some caring women raised to his lips a pole with a wet sponge on the end.

The crowd that gathered before the crosses still consisted of both sympathizers and mockers. The scribes, priests, and Pharisees forsook their dignity and jeered loudly. At the back of the crowd, followers of Jesus wept.

Philo, Biocles, and Caleb looked on in disbelief.

"Why," said Biocles, "Why? I thought he was the son of God. Why does he have to leave us and die like this?"

Tears streamed down Philo's face. "I have the feeling he has told us why. Did he not say, 'A seed must fall to the ground and die'?"

Biocles and Caleb began to weep, too. The hours passed slowly, agonizingly. Then, Caleb looked up at the cross and began to quote scripture. "Surely he has borne our infirmities and carried our diseases; yet we accounted him stricken, struck down by God, and afflicted. But he was wounded for our transgressions; crushed for our iniquities; upon him was the punishment that made us whole, and by his bruises we are healed."

"It was the will of the Lord to crush him so that when we make his life an offering for sin, he shall see his own seed, and through him the will of the Lord shall prosper. So, out of his anguish, he shall see light."

"The lamb," Philo said.

"The lamb indeed," said Caleb.

Suddenly, the earth beneath their feet began to tremble. People at first looked stunned then began to scream in terror and try to cling to something stable, but nothing was stable. Darkness came at high noon. The mockers fell dumb. Strange noises of surprise and agony erupted all around them. No one could tell exactly what was happening.

"The whole cosmos is reacting to this injustice," said Philo. "Truly this is the son of God."

"Truly," echoed Caleb and Biocles.

CHAPTER XXIX

Nikos drew a stone from the little leather bag. He kept it clinched in his fist and extended the fist before him, prolonging the suspense of his little audience.

In the pleasant afternoon sun, they stood in the open meadow facing the new farm house while Nikos looked out over the pastoral valley. His goats grazed contentedly at the edge of the woods. Slowly he unfolded his fingers to reveal a bright yellow stone. The house trim would be yellow. "It's mine, it's mine," shouted Ava.

"Hooray," they all shouted as they began to clap.

While they were still clapping, Copella started to play her ancient flute. It was an instrument handed down to her by her grandmother. Its tones were pure and sweet, and the melody Copella chose was full of life and happiness.

They began to dance. At first they formed a circle, twisting, swaying, kicking, and tossing their heads each in his own way. Then Nikos put his hand on Ava's shoulder and she returned the gesture. All around the circle an unbroken chain was formed. Copella played while all the others, Nikos, Ava, Marlena, Nixe, Otto, Katerina, and Ziggie spread their arms as though they were wings and clasped the shoulder nearest them on both sides. The individual dancers became one. There were steps this way, then that, then forward, then back. When anyone missed a step, there was laughter.

They danced until they were exhausted, and then sat down in the grass for their refreshments. There were fresh baked lamb, sweet wine, dried fruit, and honey cakes made by Copella and Katerina.

Marlena sat beside Otto. "I'm glad you and your family are so happy," she said.

"For some reason there seems to be more peace here than there ever was at Kresboden," said Otto. "Of course,

I'm not sure how much peace I can stand. I've always been a man of action. As long as we've been building this house I've had a goal and life has had meaning. I'm not sure what I will be like now, restless I'm afraid."

At the edge of the woods the goats began to bleat and thrash about wildly. Loud grunts and growls erupted and dust began to fly. Everyone leaped to their feet and started down the sloped meadow toward the herd.

As they grew closer, they could see a huge black bear standing at the edge of the woods. He growled and pawed at the dirt. Blood was on his face. It dribbled over his jaw and down onto the thick fur of his neck. Agamemnon, head lowered, horns bristling, charged straight at him. Hercules circled and came in from the side. They both landed direct hits, but paid a price. The bear bellowed in pain and swung his long, sharp claws. His right paw lacerated Agamemnon and sent him rolling. Then he swung his left and hit Hercules in the face ripping out the goat's right eye.

But the bear had been gored and was pouring blood from his belly. Agamemnon rolled to his feet and charged again while Hercules staggered about, disoriented.

"Quick, Zig, run to the house and get my spear," Otto ordered.

"Your sword, too?" yelled Zig as he ran.

"Yes."

No one dared go unarmed into the middle of this animal fight. While Zig fetched Otto's weapons, they all watched in horror.

Agamemnon struck the bear in the flank with such force that his horns lodged into his flesh. The momentum of Agamemnon's body then caused him to go flying over the bear's back in a somersault that dislodged his horns.

Incredibly, Hercules righted himself and stared at the bear with his remaining eye. A true warrior, he was more dangerous wounded than well.

The bear reared up and stood on his hind legs. He showed all of his jagged, sharp teeth, spread his front paws to show his razor claws, and roared in defiance. He was a monster seldom challenged in the world he knew. The affront to his body aggravated him, but the defiance of his authority infuriated him.

At that moment Zig handed Otto his spear. Down the hillside Otto charged directly into the bear sinking the spear deep into his chest. At the same instant Hercules pounded the beast from the side and he went down, his heaviness breaking the shaft of Otto's spear.

Writhing and kicking in pain, the bear threw up a terrible cloud of dust. Agamemnon delivered another telling blast. The bear got slowly to his feet. He stared at the goats, at the people. They stared back, knowing that the battle was over. It was that pungent moment for the bear when he stood on the precipice of existence. A creature of reaction, having fought to the end, he could see the end. Shaking, wobbly, he took a few short steps toward the woods and fell dead.

Nixe flew down the hillside. "Oh, my poor Herky," she screamed.

Hercules had given everything in him. He lay totally still in the meadow grass. Nixe put her arms around him, blood, dirt, and all. "Please, someone, get me some water," she shouted. She took her long hair and began to clean Hercules' wounds.

They hitched Electra to the cart and brought Hercules and Agamemnon to the corral stall where they laid them in the soft hay. Nikos, Nixe, and Copella tended their wounds while the rest of the group rounded up the frightened and scattered flock.

In tall grass near the scene of the battle with the bear, Marlena found the reason for the rage of Hercules and Agamemnon. There, in a pool of blood, lay a mutilated young kid.

"Otto," she called, "come here."

Otto was in good hailing distance herding a goat from the edge of the woods.

"What is it?" he asked as he approached Marlena.

"We need to bury this little fellow before Nixe knows what has happened," she said.

Otto stared at the carnage. "You're right. The scent of this would attract other feral animals, too. I'll take care of it. You help get the goats into the corral."

"Thank you, Otto," she said. "It was a brave thing you did, going after the bear like that."

Otto smiled, "I couldn't be outdone by a couple of goats, now could I?"

Nixe lay close to her mother that night. Nikos had built them a bed and placed it against the wall between the fireplace and the eating table. They were accustomed to watching the flames in the hearth die into red coals.

Nixe pulled the new colored blanket up to her neck and put her nose against Marlena's cheek. "I've never seen creatures fighting to the death like that. It was terrible."

"It was, little elf. You'll have to remember how brave Hercules, Agamemnon, and Otto were. Do you think the goats will live?"

"Nikos says we'll have to wait until morning before we know. I wanted to stay out there with them, but Nikos said it wouldn't do any good. We've done everything we can for them."

Nixe rolled over on her back, still close to Marlena, stroking her long, silken hair. "I wonder if Arn is having to fight like that."

Marlena turned her face and looked into Nixe's eyes. The coals of the fire were mirrored there in tears.

"You mustn't think of that, Nixe."

"I have to think of it. He's my uncle. I want him back so much."

"You couldn't want him back anymore than I do."

They were leaving Jerusalem certain they had known the son of God, and just as certain that he was too good for man's society to tolerate. They had found what they had searched for so long. A trip to the great eastern mountains now seemed superfluous. Philo, Biocles, and Caleb would return to Athens to tell the story of Jesus and teach his ethics.

It was early Sunday morning when they set out, trailing down the winding, rocky road to Emmaus. Most of the pilgrims who had come for Passover were still in the city. They were either asleep following a special Sabbath, or sitting in small groups of family or friends before the work day discussing the strange events of Jesus' crucifixion.

Of the three, Caleb was most convinced of the deity of Jesus. It was partly, he said, because of a conversation he had in the temple with a godly lawyer named Nicodemus. Nicodemus said he had spent much time with Jesus, and that he was convinced there was more to knowing God than the keeping of the law. There must be a uniting of man's spirit with God's spirit. This was a condition to be grasped by faith, simple trust in the words of Jesus and in the person of Jesus.

As they walked down the dusty road, Caleb was explaining this the best he could. "But in truth," he said, "I never fully believed until I saw him on the cross and experienced that awful day."

They came to a turn in the road where there protruded to their left an escarpment of great boulders. When they had rounded the blind turn, they came face to face with a band of robbers with drawn swords. They were a scraggly but determined group. Their cloaks were torn and dirty, their skin rough and browned, their hair and beards unkempt. They held a motley assortment of weapons: Roman swords, Greek swords, Persian sabers, Hebrew spears. Their faces were pitted and scarred, and their eyes glistened with savagery. As Philo, Biocles, and Caleb turned to flee back up the road, more brigands appeared to block their way.

The roughest looking villain of them all stuck his chin into the air with arrogance and shouted, "Your bags and your weapons or you die."

Caleb was frightened beyond speech, but Philo and Biocles had been in this situation before. They drew their swords instinctively. "If we die, you die with us," Biocles proclaimed and charged into the nearest robber knocking his weapon aside and running him through. The man gave a terrible scream and shouts arose from all sides.

Philo stood with his back directly to that of Biocles and dueled the two robbers who assaulted him. As they fought, they began to work their way to the trees across the road from the boulders. The trees would offer some shelter.

Philo and Biocles, defending themselves as they would in any battle, forgot Caleb. Another brigand fell, then another, as the flashing swords of the Greeks found no match. They heard a terrible groan, and looking toward the small grove of trees saw defenseless Caleb lying in the dust, his life's blood flowing away.

"No, no," screamed Philo as he fought through the robbers to Caleb's side. "Hang on old friend," he yelled. "These cowards will soon flee."

He lunged at the nearest bandit with such furry that his sword went through the man to its hilt. Before he could withdraw the sword, he was jumped upon from every direction and wrestled to the ground.

Biocles stood with his back to a tree trunk thrusting this way, then that. One of the brigands sat on Philo's chest, pulled a dagger, and raised it to stab. As he stretched his arm high, he screamed a violent curse that quickly turned to a gurgle.

An arrow slipped quietly through his throat, and he fell dead on top of Philo. His companions stood startled. Suddenly quiet, they looked all around. Another arrow zipped through the air and hitting with a dull thud, buried into the chief brigand's chest. He sank to the ground and closed his eyes without a word.

From atop the boulders came the strong voice of a young man. "The next man to raise a sword is the next man to die."

"I can't see him. The sun is with him," said one of the robbers.

"What difference does it make," said another. "Two arrows have flown and we have two dead men. That jackal can shoot our eyeballs out if he wants to."

"I'll not give in to a single bow," said one of the robbers and drove his sword toward Biocles.

An arrow penetrated his neck and impaled him onto a cedar tree. There he hung until his dead weight sank against the arrow and broke its shaft. Then slowly his body slid down the cedar trunk to the ground. By the time this body came to full rest, the brigands had vanished leaving a cloud of dust hovering to mark their departure. Seven of their band would never rob again.

Philo pushed the warm, stinking corpse from his chest and stood in the midst of the carnage. He spoke haltingly, "Are you alive, Minotaur?"

"Neither of us would be alive if it weren't for that archer," said Biocles as he rose from beside the tree where the last bandit had fallen.

"My old friend is gone, Minotaur." Philo was kneeling on one knee beside Caleb's body, tears in the corners of his eyes. "We never should have fought," he said. "Poor Caleb had no weapon."

Biocles came to his side and put a hand on his shoulder.

"They would have killed us all, Philo. This was our only chance."

"How do we know?" said Philo.

Down the road toward them came a man in his early twenties. The sun seemed to catch his every feature as bright light beams on every facet of a cut diamond. He was built and colored like Apollo, himself, blond hair that reached his shoulders, sharp blue eyes, flawless face, light skin tanned by hours in the sun. Over his back a long bow was slung and with it a half empty quiver of arrows.

Philo looked past Biocles and saw him.

"The source of our salvation is coming," he said as he rose from Caleb's side.

Biocles turned. "Are you an angel from God?" he asked.

"Hardly," said the young blonde with an obvious military bearing. He allowed a faint smile.

"At any rate you rescued us, and we are grateful," said Philo.

The young man saw Philo's tears and noticed the white haired old man at his feet. "That must have been a friend," he said.

"A dear friend since I was born, he has been like a father to me."

"I'm sorry. What should we do?" said the young man as though he fully intended to continue his help.

"I have to think," said Philo. He hung his head and wiped his brow.

Biocles tried to explain. "We heard about bandits like this, but we weren't ready for them. Maybe we shouldn't have fought. Maybe they would have left us alone."

"Maybe, maybe not. I've dealt with brigands like this for two years. They kill a lot of people."

Philo broke in, "We'll bury Caleb here. This is his country, the ground from which he sprang. I think he would like it. Come," he said.

They found a nice cedar and used sticks to dig a shallow grave beside it. There they placed Caleb's body, covered it, and piled up stones above it to mark the spot. They shook and pounded the dust from themselves, then, stood silently until Philo spoke.

"I'm glad I've known you old friend. I'm sorry you had to be a slave. I've never known a more noble man."

"Now you are back, here in the land of Abraham. Perhaps you've seen what few Jews have seen, the incarnation of God. I hope that has made life worth while for you."

"You'll be sorely missed."

"May I speak?" asked Biocles.

"Of course."

"You spoke of men's spirits before you left us," said Biocles into the sky. "Maybe your spirit is still close enough to hear. I hope so because I want to say something men don't often say to men, and I pray you can hear me. We have loved you. You gave a life of total service, and yet you were as happy as anyone we have ever known. Maybe now we are just beginning to understand what you saw in life."

They stood in silence for several minutes. Then Philo nodded toward the road. "I suppose we should go," he said.

"What about all these robbers," said Biocles.

"Soldiers will be by. They'll take care of them," said the young man.

Suddenly a thought struck Biocles, "Good grief," he said. "We've been so overcome here we haven't thought to introduce ourselves. I'm Biocles of Athens, and this is my friend, Philo."

"I perceived as much," said the young man.

"You, you perceived as much?" Both Biocles and Philo gave the young man startled looks. "What does that mean?" continued Biocles.

"I've seen you since you've seen me," said the young man. "Look at me closely."

Biocles stepped to within arm's length of the young man and stared. He took in the whole form of the man, then his gaze returned to his face. At last he was looking directly into his crystalline blue eyes. Slowly a vision came into his mind: He was standing before a lad of eleven who was eager to learn how to use a bow. "Arn?" The inflection of the word was high, questioning.

A broad smile spread across the handsome face, and the blue eyes sparkled with delight. Arn held out his arms.

"Arn! It's Arn! Philo, it's Arn!" Biocles yelled as he hurled himself at the young man and encircled him with both arms and legs, knocking him down. "It's Arn, it's Arn!" he kept repeating, as they both rolled joyously in the dusty road.

Philo stood amazed. Unable to communicate with either of the jubilant two celebrating in the middle of the road, he talked to himself. "It has to be Arn. That explains the way he shot the arrows. But the last we saw of him was ten years ago in the center of Europa. Can it be?"

Biocles had Arn by the head and was mussing his golden hair. Arn was laughing hysterically. "It could be," he said, and tossed himself on top of them.

When they were totally exhausted, they lay on their backs, still in the middle of the road, and looked at the sky. They stayed like that, remaining silent, for several minutes. They were too tired to speak, but they were also trying to drink in the emotion of the moment.

At last Philo rose slowly to his feet. He looked down into Arn's face. "We have a lot to talk about, young man."

"I'd say about ten years worth," said Arn.

"Yes, it's been a long time," said Philo. He began to dust off his clothes, then he picked up his pack. "There's so much to tell and yet I'm not sure I can even do a good job of telling about the last five days."

Biocles and Arn began to restore themselves to a traveling state. They looked at Philo. Blood trickled from the corner of his swollen right eye and from his right wrist. His face was abraded and dirty.

"Am I as big a mess as you are?" said Biocles.

It was obvious to Arn that he was. "You both need a bit of looking after," he said. "Do you think you can make it to Emmaus?"

"Of course," said Biocles. "A few scratches won't slow us down."

Philo felt dizzy, but he headed down the road.

"You all right, Phil," said Biocles.

Philo straightened up and kept walking without saying a word.

"We're going to have to watch him," said Arn.

Philo trudged ahead into the bright sunshine. The chatter of Arn and Biocles were only mumbles to him. He saw the blur of the road, but his mind departed into a world of its own. From the moment he knew Arn had come, he thought of his prayer on the roof top in Jerusalem, and he thought of Marlena. At the first recognizable second he had wanted to shout. Where is Marlena? How is Marlena?

But it wouldn't have been proper. It would have taken away from their reunion with Arn. It would have betrayed his long standing preoccupation with Marlena, a preoccupation that itself seemed inappropriate. And if there had been bad news of Marlena, he would not have been able to bear it.

His mind raced back to his boyhood. Caleb bent over him showing him how to hold a quill and write his name. Then Caleb was standing beside him pointing to a tree or flower and naming it. Caleb was escorting him into the Agora showing him how to examine fruit for the table.

A flash of light shone down the dusty road ahead and suddenly he was with Marlena in the alpine meadow. It was the time when they both were able to express the depths of their love for one another. Everything around them was perfect. Then, just as fast, there was the stark terror of absence, separation.

Caleb was in the peristyle talking to him about ethics, right from wrong in Greek society, yes, but more than that, right from wrong in the eyes of his own conscience. Dozens of these images of his childhood haunted him. He remembered things he hadn't thought of in years. Back, back his thoughts flew until he saw himself frightened by a screaming Alcandor. He ran through the house and threw himself into Caleb's lap. He hugged Caleb and prayed his father wouldn't follow him. They clung to one another waiting, and mercifully Alcandor didn't appear.

Caleb whispered in his ear, "It'll be all right, lad. You have to be strong. And, lad, you must try to understand your father."

Marlena stood at the edge of the forest, the ray of light from the huge fire penetrating only the spot where she was—Athena.

Jesus of Nazareth hung dying on the Roman cross, innocence and truth crushed.

Darkness, earthquakes, screaming.

Marlena sat in the boat pointing out the boulders, springs, cliffs.

Caleb standing with awe on his face: Surely this was the son of God, was, was.

Despair and hope took their turns battering Philo's soul until he bordered on insanity. All he had to do was give a little, and he would be over the edge into the dark abyss.

He would fight it. There could be no insanity as long as there remained the possibility of seeing Marlena again. Marlena. Marlena with the golden hair and violet eyes so intense, so full of love. It had been ten years but the vision in his mind had not faded one whit—Marlena.

CHAPTER XXX

Both Philo and Biocles had cuts, bruises, and gashes over much of their bodies. They had smeared blood onto Arn in their dusty celebration, so when the three appeared at the inn in Emmaus, they were received as though they had just escaped the Assyrian hordes.

The servants of the inn took their clothes for cleaning and brought many basins of fresh bathing water. Philo and Biocles sat in little wooden tubs and soaked their aching bodies. Arn poured water over their heads and laughed at their moans and groans.

"Don't laugh," said Biocles with mock irritation. "You weren't down there slugging it out with those animals. You were up in the rocks shooting arrows."

"I'll admit you fellows were giving a fair account of yourselves for old men," he said grinning.

"Old?" Biocles and Philo shouted.

"Why, either one of us could mop this floor with you, you young pup," said Biocles with mock disdain. "Growing up has made him impertinent, Philo."

"Maybe he's entitled to a bit of impertinence. After all, we probably wouldn't be here if he hadn't happened along," said Philo. The rest had restored his presence of mind.

"That has nothing to do with it. We can't let him get out of line. We could soon have a monster on our hands."

They all laughed and sank onto their beds. They were clad only in toweling. Rays of sun slanted in from the slatted doors that opened to their balcony. The warmth of spring and the exhaustion of their bodies became sedatives. They did a thing rare for themselves: sleep in the afternoon.

Philo, in a half daze, thought of Marlena. It had been right for them to talk about Caleb on the last of their walk to Emmaus. It had seemed as though Caleb's story was bursting to be told. Looking back, it was a poetic thing that he would never leave his homeland again. No conquering army would beat him into unconsciousness and haul him into further slavery. He slept with his fathers.

But what of Marlena? How did Arn come to Judea? How did he happen along just when he did? What did he say about dealing with other robbers? What about Marlena? Sleep came.

Before he was aware of the sleep, Biocles shook him. "They're going to close the kitchen. We'd better get down there and eat something."

"I'm glad you woke me. I was dreaming that I was on the rack and daggers were cutting me."

"Ah, the wicked have no rest."

Arn spoke up, "I don't doubt that being true, but I suspect he was only reacting to the pain of his wounds. I should know." He pulled back the blanket that covered him revealing two huge scars, one on his side and one across the front of his left thigh. Neither was completely healed. "I had nightmares with these for weeks."

"Great stinking Spartans," said Biocles, "I guess you did. What have you been into, boy?"

"We'll talk about it at supper," said Arn

And we'll talk about Marlena or I'll go insane, thought Philo.

The inn seemed to be an ageless place. It was built of such massive logs and was provided with such heavy wooden furnishings, beaten with use, that they could have been there ten years or two-hundred years. The canteen seemed relatively subdued, perhaps because of the post holiday season, perhaps because it was near closing time.

The low ceiling kept conversations close. It was crisscrossed with flat oaken beams from which hung oil-burning lanterns. The lanterns emitted a faint smoke, the smell of which blended with roasting meat, baking bread, freshly poured wine, and weary travelers.

They sat at a corner table and ordered lamb.

"So tell us about the scars, my boy," said Biocles. Somehow he would always think of Arn, not only as his own son, but also as a youth. Now both Biocles and Arn had risked his own life to save that of the other. The bond was so complete they could have called one another anything and laughed about it. Biocles knew this "boy" was now much more of a man than most, but he also felt this term, my boy, to be one of endearment. Arn understood.

"I was forced into the Roman army." Arn paused and rejected any words about Pergamum. Then he went on. "They brought me to the southern part of this country for policing duty. Three months ago, a patrol squad I was with came upon a band of brigands much like the one that attacked you. There must have been fifty of them and only ten of us. We would have gone for help except that they held hostages and were about to put them to the stake."

"Burn them?" asked Philo.

"Exactly. That leaves no trace. We decided to fight fire with fire. We formed an arc upwind of the criminals' camp and set ten fires all at the same time."

"Wouldn't that burn the hostages?" asked Biocles.

"We thought the brigands would panic and leave in a rush. Then we would go in and release the hostages before the fire actually burned them."

"It didn't work?"

"Partially, most of the band did panic and run away. Then about the time we had the hostages untied, some of the gang jumped us. Unfortunately, I'm still not too good at close quarters with a sword."

"Two bad wounds," said Biocles.

"Yeah, and that is a crazy thing."

"What do you mean?"

"The Romans have a regulation: One wound and you are to be treated on the field until you recover to fight again; two, and you must be relieved of active duty."

A commotion arose across the room. One man was trying to speak, and others were hooting him down. "I don't care what you think," the man was saying.

Biocles got up and walked over to see what was happening.

"It seems as if there's always some kind of disagreement among these Jews," Philo said to Arn.

"You don't need to tell me," said Arn. "I've just come from Jerusalem. On Friday, they crucified a man who was better than any I have ever known, with apologies to the present company."

"You were there, then?"

"Yes."

"So were we. We were convinced that Jesus was the son of God. We couldn't believe his own people wanted to kill him."

Biocles returned from the other table. "You aren't going to believe this," he said as he sat down. "There's a man over there named Cleopas. He claims he has seen Jesus."

"We've all seen Jesus," said Philo.

"An hour ago?" said Biocles.

"An hour ago? You can't be serious."

"That's what everybody over there is saying. He says he spent the afternoon with him. He has a friend with him who swears it's true. They had supper together then Jesus disappeared before their eyes," explained Biocles.

"Let's go talk with him," said Philo

"It's too late. He left, going back to Jerusalem to tell Jesus' disciples."

"Oh, to have Caleb here, rest his soul. I'll bet he could tell us something about this. I wonder if Jewish prophecy said anything about a resurrection. I have to tell you, Arn, we met a man who said Jesus raised him from the dead.

Doesn't seem likely, but you should have seen him and heard him," said Philo.

"I've heard Jesus speak in Jerusalem," said Arn. "As you know, Marlena and I have abhorred the thought of any God, but this man spoke as though God is as real as a baby, or the mountains, or the sky. He addressed God as Father and did many miraculous things."

He had said it, the name, Marlena. It was music. Philo tried to act casual.

"Marlena. By the way, how is Marlena, or at least how was she the last time you saw her?"

Arn had let it slip, that name. He was going to force Philo to say it first in order to see what was on Philo's face. He knew Marlena would always love Philo, but if Philo was indifferent toward her, then he wanted to protect his sister from a presence that might prove disastrous for her. A good memory, nebulous as it may be, is far better than a painful reality.

He gave Philo a long, interested stare. There was much he shouldn't say. "Marlena was fine the last I saw of her. Of course, that was over two years ago."

The waiter came with their food. It smelled delicious. Biocles took a long sniffing breath and dove in. "We want to hear what has happened to you and Marlena these past ten years," he said with a mouthful.

"We do, indeed," echoed Philo.

"And I want to hear what has happened to you two, but it has been a long evening. We must eat and rest. Tomorrow we set out for Joppa and sail for - - where are you going, back to Athens?" asked Arn.

"Yes, we must see our families," said Biocles. "And what about you?"

"I'm going that direction, Macedonia actually. We can sail together."

"Hooray!" yelled Biocles. He raised both arms into the air and waved them around his head.

249

"That <u>is</u> good news," said Philo. In weeks of sailing he wouldn't tire of hearing about Marlena.

At Joppa, they had the good fortune to find that they could make the return trip to Athens aboard the Olympia if they would wait a day or two. Biocles and Philo explained to Arn why this privilege was well worth the wait. The story of the storm, the courageous crew, and the sturdy ship herself convinced Arn. So the three spent a day finding small gifts for their families and friends. Philo's thoughts went to Dorea. He felt he hadn't expressed his gratitude to her for the help she had been in getting him past his depression. He wanted to find something special for her.

In an Egyptian's kiosk near the docks of Joppa, he found the perfect gift, an actress's mask. It was the likeness of a dark African queen with jeweled tiara and dangling earrings.

The Olympia was underway and headed northwesterly. So it was that Philo, Biocles, and Arn spent many happy days basking on the sun drenched deck and telling stories about the last ten years. Arn preferred to listen if possible. He would weigh what to tell and what to be silent about. Certainly he would explain why he and Marlena had stolen away with Otto that night in the Alps. Certainly, he wouldn't say a word about Nixe. Nor would he reveal Marlena's marital status until he was asked about it directly. He would prefer that Philo dig for this information so he could measure his true interest. Aside from these things, there was still much to tell.

They sprawled on the rigging, a soothing breeze gently mussing their hair, and warm sunshine bathing their half naked bodies.

"I can almost see these wounds healing," said a satisfied Biocles.

"The Roman doctors said this would do me good," said Arn.

"After a few days, Biocles and I decided you and Marlena had left of your own will," said Philo, as though he could jump into the middle of a thought and still be understood. He was right.

With a hand on his chin, Arn studied to answer. "You two had no way of understanding what the rage of a Celt is like. Otto reminded us. It wasn't hard to see that Daga would spare no means to locate and kill us all."

"But wouldn't you have been safer under our protection? Hadn't we shown that we could protect you?" asked Philo.

"You surely had," responded Arn. "That was one of the things that helped us make the decision. We owed our lives to you. We felt that Daga would primarily be looking for us. If we separated ourselves from you, then you would have a better chance of escape."

"So, you left us to save us?" said Philo.

"Yes, as hard as it was for us, we felt it was the only thing to do."

"I suppose you realized that what you did would break our hearts," said Philo.

This was one of the things Arn wanted to hear. "We had to take the chance you would survive emotionally, otherwise, you might not have survived at all. Don't you think we felt the same way you did?"

"We had thought so, but when you were gone we began to doubt," said Philo. "Did - - did Marlena love Otto?"

Arn smiled. "Yes, indeed," he said, and watched Philo's expression droop. "But not the way you may be thinking.

251

When we were orphans, Otto was our only protector. He saved Marlena from being raped one afternoon. It has been Otto who has looked after us all these years, but he has a family of his own."

"A wife?"

"Of course, a wife."

"There has been no way for you to know that your strategy didn't work, at least, not altogether," said Philo.

"What does that mean?" asked Arn.

Philo leaned back on the rigging. He put both of his hands behind his head and looked up into the blue sky.

"Some months after Biocles and I returned to Athens, I was shot with a Celtic arrow. No one was able to find who had done it, but Biocles and I knew. Eventually, Biocles was assaulted by two Celts, only one of whom escaped with his life. They were probably sent from Kresboden."

"That's amazing. I'm sorry. Still it only shows what would have happened if we all had stayed together." said Arn.

"What do you mean?"

"Were you ever shot again? Was Biocles ever shot?"

"Well, no."

"Do you suppose the answer would still be no if they had found Marlena and me with you?" asked Arn.

"I've never thought of that," said Philo. He slumped over a coil of ropes and rubbed his forehead.

Arn had learned to reason like a man, and he was right.

"Have you and Marlena been harassed?" asked Biocles.

"We've had Otto on our side. He's known most of Daga's plans and has shielded us from him."

"So where were you living when you were put into the emperor's army?" asked Biocles.

"You're going to have a hard time believing this," said Arn, "a goat farm in Macedonia."

Day after day Arn told of Melz, Herr Helvet, his learning archery, of Copella and Nikos, and the goats, and many other things, but not of Nixe and not of Pergamum. Philo and Biocles told of their marriages and families, the campaign against child exposure, the death of Theana, and finally their dramatic encounter with Jesus of Nazareth.

In all of this Philo had not asked if Marlena were married and Arn had not revealed it. Philo had to know, but he was afraid to know. The potential for heartbreaking news constantly gave him pause. Day after day he delayed asking. Some mornings he would awaken with firm resolve that this would be the day. Then it seemed that a proper moment would never present itself. The day was gone, and he lay himself down again for the sleep of a frustrated soul.

Other times it seemed the moment would be perfect, but he felt awkward, unprepared. It had to be just right, this moment of truth.

It seemed to Philo that Jesus was obviously answering the prayer he had breathed on the roof top in Jerusalem. Surely Arn would lead him to Marlena. So now he had begun a conversation with Jesus. Part of this one sided conversation seemed like prayer. Part didn't. The part that didn't was just friend visiting friend. One evening as he lay on his bed and the Olympia sailed smoothly along the gentle waves of the great sea, he tried to reason with his new God: Lord, I know I only asked to see Marlena and to know that she is well and happy. But now that Arn is here, I find myself wanting much more. You know me as you know all people. You know the greatest desire of my heart is to see Marlena and to have her. But I can't ask you for this seeing that even you can't change the past, and if Marlena is married, then she is married. I've gone all these nights trying to know what to ask of you. Now I feel I know. I ask you simply to steel my heart for whatever news awaits me.

Give me the peace that all will be well regardless of the news. And so he slept.

Biocles had sensed the tension that Philo felt each time the three had spoken of Marlena. Time and again he had shied from the subject. Time and again he had left openings for Philo to speak to Arn, hoping this tension would be resolved.

The next evening after Philo's prayer for peace, Biocles retired early. Philo and Arn stood at the deck rail studying the stars. Philo could wait no longer. He had to ask. "I suppose Marlena has a husband and family of her own by now," he said with a gulp.

Arn stood silent for a moment as though he wasn't sure what to say. Then he spoke. "She hasn't had time for that," he said. "We've had so many problems, and we've had to move around."

Philo's heart leapt for joy. He wanted to dance and jump and shout and scream for joy. But a man had to be a man. He had to be reserved, not revealing his whole heart until the proper time. Nevertheless, he could not suppress a huge smile.

"You are a man now, Arn," he said slowly. "Can I confide in you as man to man, no other person being privileged to hear what I tell you?"

"I count it an honor," said Arn.

"I've had a wife so honorable, so wise, so courageous, so beautiful and so loving that no woman could be her better. I've loved her deeply. But I have to confess to you that hardly a day of my life has gone by that I haven't thought of Marlena. I've tried every mental trick I could devise to put away thoughts of her. I've tried to hate her for leaving me, I've told myself: what difference does she make, I'll never see her again. Then I'll see a blonde child, or hear a love song, or find flowers in the meadow, or a hundred other things and memories will come flooding back, a deluge I can't resist. I am back on that alpine mountain watching you and Biocles shoot arrows and making love to Marlena amid the deep, green grass and the radiant colors of the crocus, gentians, and roses."

A relaxed silence fell between them. Arn studied the reflection of the stars in the gentle ocean waves and his thoughts retreated to Pergamum and Marcia Gavia. He was standing in the moonlight with her and holding her hands. He was seeing love in her every expression and he was awkwardly trying to express himself to her. The words didn't seem to make any difference.

He shook his head and turned to face Philo. "It may be that I understand you better than you think. Do you still love my sister?" asked Arn.

"If I were to find her old, fat, wrinkled, and totally disillusioned about life, I would still love her, now, this minute," said Philo.

"Then, you must see her."

That night as Philo began to doze into a peaceful, joyous sleep, he remembered the prayer he had said to Jesus and he began to pray again: Jesus, I can see you are taking me back to Marlena. Thank you for sending Arn. Now I want to know more about you. How will I know the way to follow and serve you?

By the time the Olympia put in at Piraeus harbor, a meeting had been arranged. Philo and Biocles would spend two or three weeks visiting their families and Arn would do the same. Then, Philo and Biocles would travel to the Macedonian village of Florina. There they would locate the shop of a merchant called Tullos who dealt in cloth. Tullos would know the way to the goat farm owned by Nikos and Copella.

It seemed such a good plan that farewells were brief and light hearted. As Arn turned up the road to Florina, however, he remembered the day he had met the Romans in almost the very spot on which he stood. He remembered the agony on the faces of Nixe and Marlena, and he knew any plans could go wrong in an instant.

CHAPTER XXXI

Early summer in Macedonia was what the earth had been created for. The sun was warm and invigorating, the shade cool and refreshing. The brooks flowed brightly with fresh spring water from the mountains. New green leaves adorned the cork oaks, the beech trees, chestnuts, and hornbeams. Places almost barren in winter and even the later part of summer now glowed with grass and shrubs of maqui and garigue. Spring flowers still bloomed. Hyacinths and anemones grew in a profusion of colors, red, yellow, purple, blue, and white. Wild animals were intent on protecting their newborn. Occasionally one would be fortunate enough to see these babes of the woodland: a spotted, wobbly hart barely able to walk, a hawk chick blundering from its nest, a ball of rabbit, mostly fur, hopping in one place, going nowhere.

Macedonia was full of newness and hope. It was the right time to come home.

Arn enjoyed the walk, but he was again troubled with the question of what he must tell and what he must not. He had learned that people saw some things and heard some things that were for themselves only, never to be retold to anyone. Then, there were other things that required correct timing in the retelling. That had been the case of telling Philo about Marlena. His restraint had proven to be wise. Now he must restrain himself in the other direction. How much should he tell Marlena about Philo and Biocles before they came. Maybe nothing, just let it happen.

Dusk settled upon the low Macedonian hills when Arn came through the woods into the meadow and caught his first glimpse of the little stone farmhouse with the light blue trim. He thought of how surprising it was that he truly took this place for home. His time living here had been short, yet he had felt accepted and secure here. He had seen Marlena content here for the first time since he had been a small child and both their parents were alive. It did, in fact, seem to him that Copella and Nikos had become their parents.

He walked casually across the pasture and eased quietly to the corral. There he spoke softly to the animals. Electra gave a contented neigh when he patted her soft nose and cuffed her long ears.

"You do remember me don't you, old girl," whispered Arn. "Don't worry, I'm not here to make you move rocks," he added with a chuckle. Electra gave him a baleful look and a whinny.

From inside the farmhouse sounds of happy people taking supper came through the open window beside the door.

"I heard Electra," said Nixe, "something's going on out there."

"You think every time those animals make a sound you should see after them," said Marlena. "They're all right. Just enjoy your supper."

Nixe looked anxious.

"Your mother is right," said Nikos. "I've heard that animal for years. She's just railing at a horsefly."

Arn stole to the window and peeked in. "Is there enough for a stranger at this table?" he said in clear and abrupt tones.

They all jumped from their seats, "Arn," they cried. Marlena, Nikos, and Copella ran to the door. Nixe plunged straight through the open window and encircled Arn's head with a ferocious hug. Then the others reached him and surrounded him with hugs and kisses.

Through his grin, he was barely able to speak. "Nothing like feeling welcome," he proclaimed.

"Come in, come in, my boy," said Nikos. "We surely do have enough to feed you and more."

When Arn had crossed the threshold, he stood looking at the inside of the house, Nixe clinging to him on one side and Marlena on the other. He dragged them to the door beside the fireplace and looked into the room he and Nikos had built. "It hasn't fallen in yet," he said.

"Nor will it," chortled Nikos. "It was made by expert workmen."

"Yes, indeed it was," said Arn with a laugh. He was sure that no one believed a word of it. He looked around. Everything was the same except for the new bed Nikos had made for Marlena and Nixe. Spread over the bed was the new blanket.

"Do I perceive that weavers have been at work here?" said Arn. "And very good weavers too, I might add."

"Marlena taught me," said Copella proudly. "We couldn't have done it without the loom you built."

"You women let the lad sit down," said Nikos. "He's tired and hungry."

"He'll have to eat with me on his lap," said Nixe.

"He'll do no such thing," said Marlena. "Nikos is right. Arn needs food and rest. We can smother him with love tomorrow. Where have you come from Arn?"

"Would you believe Judea?"

They talked about Judea and Jews and Romans for an hour. Then Nixe, in spite of the previous rebuke, climbed into Arn's lap and took his face into her hands. "I've decided something," she said.

"And what have you decided, little elf," said Arn.

"I'm going to hug and kiss you more than before."

"There's nothing I would like better," said Arn, "but what brought on such a decision? Do you appreciate me more now that I've been gone for so long?"

"Well," said Nixe reluctantly, "that too."

"And what else, may I ask?"

"You're the greatest looking man I've ever seen," she said with a burst of excitement.

Everyone had a good laugh. When the hilarity began to die away, Copella spoke. "This little girl is no dummy," she said. "Suppose you give Arn one of those kisses right now and let's let him rest."

Several days after Philo arrived home, he was still telling Penelope and Alcandor about Caleb's death and about all that had happened in Jerusalem. Meeting the Carpenter was a life-changing experience and yet it had left some enigmas for him. He told Penelope and Alcandor that he had felt in the presence of God, himself, when he was with Jesus. But Jesus had said puzzling things.

For one, he seemed to demand a life of the highest morals, a requirement Philo felt no man could obtain. "Then, there was the thing he had said to Biocles and me: A seed must fall to the ground and die, or it remains alone; but dying, it bears much fruit."

"We know that is true about a seed of wheat," said Penelope. "What we must figure out is how that applies to people."

They were in the courtyard admiring once again the plants Caleb had nourished and were longing for his presence. Philo looked mostly at the grape vine. He was remembering the time before the Gate Beautiful when Caleb had said the vine was a symbol of the Jewish nation. It were as though Caleb's presence was with them.

"Of course, Jesus died. Many said that at his trial he offered no defense whatever. His crime was that he was king of the Jews, yet anyone with half a brain could see he wasn't any kind of king that was a threat to anybody, except maybe the religious leaders. I just have a feeling he meant that saying for us all, the living I mean."

"What did Caleb say about it?"

"Caleb said it had to be a secret of the spirit. You see, Jesus said the spirit of man is his most important part. He said things like, 'God looks on the heart of man,' and 'What does it profit a man to gain the whole world and lose his soul,' and 'God is spirit and those who worship him must worship in spirit and truth'"

Alcandor, listening mostly as always, looked up, "Greeks have always sought truth. We've found truth in all that is about us."

"Jesus said the most important truths are spiritual truths, and that nature is an allegory of those truths if we can but understand it."

Dorea traipsed into the peristyle half tripping over Penelope's borrowed chiton which hung loosely over her petite frame. Her hair stood rolled high on her head, and she wore every cheap necklace and bracelet to which her mother had allowed her access. But the centerpiece of her costume was the queen's mask Philo had found at Joppa. She was Clytemnestra incarnate.

Placing herself properly before her family, she stretched her neck and drew erect. "I shall soon hear all from the king himself, my honored lord," she quoted from Aeschylus. "I shall prepare a welcome home as fair may be. What light could be sweeter in a woman's eyes than to fling wide the gates for her beloved whom God has saved from war."

They all clapped with delight. It was no secret that Alcandor, the stiff diplomat and disciplinarian was completely taken with his daughter. Now, he stood and gave the child an ovation. Abruptly he sat down, grasped his chest and leaned forward. "I, I had better lie down," he said weakly. His face turned ashen and he collapsed to the floor.

Dorea threw off the mask and bent to her father. "Pa Pa, what is it?" she cried.

Philo could see there was a real problem. "Back off, Sunshine," he said gently to Dorea. "Pa is sick." Then he turned to Penelope.

"Hurry, mother, let's get him to bed," he said, and together they carried him away and laid him in his bed.

For many days the physicians told Philo and Penelope that Alcandor couldn't last more than a day or two, and yet he clung to life.

By the end of the third week, Philo began to have other worries. He and Biocles had not made it to Florina. Would Arn give up on them? Would he lose Marlena after being so close to finding her?

On the other hand, would Alcandor die? Would he rather lose Alcandor than Marlena? He prayed he would never have to make that choice. Maybe he should go to Marlena. No, he couldn't leave his father when he was at the point of death. The vigil continued.

As the days passed, Philo thought more and more of Marlena. One morning it occurred to him that there was something special he could do for her while his vigil over his father continued. From that hour he spent all his spare time in the Agora searching for one single item until at last he felt peace about what he should buy.

Biocles sat with Philo at his father's bedside. Alcandor was sleeping. "He looks as though he has aged twenty years in just this short time," he said.

"It's hard to believe, isn't it?" said Philo. "We never know what will happen the next minute in this life."

"Don't you wish Jesus could be here?" said Biocles.

"Did I tell you about my prayer to Jesus that I said in Jerusalem?"

"What kind of prayer?"

"I know this may seem wrong to you because you liked Theana so much, and you have to believe I loved Theana deeply."

"Of course, I know that," said Biocles.

"I prayed to Jesus and asked him if I could see Marlena again, once more, just long enough to know that she is well and happy. The next day, after all these years, Arn showed up."

"That's awesome. Do you suppose Jesus can still make things happen even though he is dead."

"It truly does seem that way," said Philo.

"Have you thought about the fact that we are two months late for our meeting with Arn?"

"It's the only thing I have thought about except my father's health. Do you think he and Marlena will get discouraged and leave Florina? He said they had moved around so much."

"Why don't I go and tell them about Alcandor?"

"I don't know, Minotaur. I've thought about it. Something about it doesn't seem right. I'm so torn. Marlena seems so close and yet so unreachable."

"I'll go," said Biocles with certainty and finality.

"Give me three days," said Philo.

"Why?"

"Just give me three days."

Arn spent three happy weeks on the goat farm. It was a pleasant surprise to find Otto and his family close by. Otto had told him about Daga's insanity. That seemed to settle the threat from Kresboden that had hung over them for so many years. He was a man now and no longer afraid of Daga's men, but the insidious nature of the situation would have bothered him. Where might an assassin appear with a dagger ready for him and Marlena? How long had he lived with that question hanging over him? It seemed like forever. Otto, too, seemed at peace for the first time.

Arn told them all about Judea and nothing about Pergamum. He told them about the mysterious and powerful carpenter, Jesus of Nazareth. All of life seemed to be taking a new turn, and somehow he felt that the effect of Jesus would be a part of it.

In the fourth week, Arn began to wonder what had happened to Philo and Biocles. Their plan had seemed so simple. What could have gone wrong? He was glad he hadn't told Marlena that they would come.

In the fifth week, Arn went to Florina to the shop of Tullos, the cloth merchant. No one resembling Philo and Biocles had been to Florina. There was no question that the happiness of Marlena's future was in the balance. Through the years she had made it very clear that there was but one love for her life. Some people were like that. They came along about as often as three-horned bulls.

For weeks Arn wrestled with the problem. He found himself walking alone in the meadow or sitting on a rock talking to himself. Marlena found him in that deep thought one day. He was up behind Copella's apple orchard at the spot where they had made the decision to stay with Copella and Nikos. He sat on the huge boulder and looked out over the peaceful valley below. This was the place for decisions. Marlena arrived quietly and surprised him.

"We all know something is troubling you, Arn. Why don't you tell me about it?"

He turned to her with a startled look, "I'm going to have to leave for a while."

"You, you aren't serious," now it was Marlena who was startled.

"It won't be for long. I'll leave in the morning."

"What on earth for, Arn? You just got here. We've waited so long for you, not knowing anything about you."

"You'll have to trust me, Marlena. I can't tell you why I'm going or where I'm going."

"No, no. Please Arn, don't do it." Marlena went to him and hugged him to her as tight as she could and held him. "I can't lose you again. You are my one rock in all of life's shifting sand," she said directly into his ear.

"You're not going to lose me, sister. Trust me. I have to do this."

Marlena was becoming desperate. "The Romans will get you again. They will haul you away and we won't hear from you again. Oh, Arn, don't you see. Don't go away. Please don't go away." She began to weep as she pushed herself away from him.

"Marlena, you've been a mother to me as well as a sister. We've been through things that would have killed weaker people. Please be strong for me one more time."

"I, I can't do it. When you came back I told myself that at last I would know peace in as much as the world could afford. A tension in me went limp and I've been able to relax for the first time since our mother and father were alive. A person's emotions wear out, Arn. Don't ask me to be strong again. Not now, anyway. I can't do it."

"I don't have any choice. If things go well, I'll only be gone a few days."

Suddenly Marlena was infuriated, "You will not go! I order you to stay here! I've known what's best for you for years, and I know now. You'll stay and that's the last of it."

Arn went to her. "Don't touch me until you say you'll do as I demand," said Marlena.

"This is what has been troubling me. I knew this would be hard for you. My sister, you're looking at a man who has faced death many times since I left your side. But none of that was as frightening as this. With all my heart I want to please you, and though you don't understand, it's because of that that I must go. I'll say no more. At dawn I'll be going."

265

It was a somber meal that evening in the little stone house with the light blue trim. Once Nixe, Nikos, and Copella knew Arn would be leaving they sat and stared blankly into space. Tears trickled down Nixe's face. She ate very little, and when she was done, she went to Arn and pulled herself up into his lap. Then she put her arms around his neck and kissed his cheek.

"Come, little elf," said Arn, "we need to take a walk."

He rose from the table and took Nixe's hand. Out of the house and into the meadow they went, saying nothing. When they saw the sun touch the tops of the low hills to the west, they sat down on a large boulder. Arn pulled Nixe to his side.

"I want you to do two things for me, little lamb. They may be hard to do."

"I'll try," said Nixe, holding back her tears.

"First, I want you to keep telling yourself that I love you and that I'll be back."

"And then ..." she said.

"And then, I want you to keep telling that to your mother. Encourage her. Be happy with her. I've told her I won't be long, but it seems to make no difference to her. It is as though her strength has gone out. For a little while <u>you</u> must be her strength. You are eleven now, and you understand so many things about love; do you understand what I'm trying to say?"

"I think so," she said. "The way I was with Hercules and Agamemnon that day after they fought the bear, talking to them, petting them, and watching them get well."

"That's it," said Arn.

Arn felt as though he had said goodbye all the afternoon before; he wanted no more of it. He was gone before light came in the morning. He took the path around the hill to

Otto's house where he saw the light of a candle through cracks in the window shutters. He tapped lightly on the door and whispered.

"Otto, are you there?"

"Hold on a minute," came Otto's deep voice. Then momentarily he came through the door and shut it behind him. "They're still asleep in there," he whispered. "Let's walk down the path a bit."

So they stood in the path as gray dawn crept upon the Macedonian hills.

"I can't take long to explain," said Arn, "but I have to go away for a few days on personal business."

"What kind of business?" asked Otto.

Arn came very close to telling Otto. In a way it would have been a comfort for him knowing someone close to Marlena understood. But what if, in an unguarded moment, Otto should speak of his mission? Then what if it didn't work out? Marlena would be far more crushed than she was already. No, he couldn't tell Otto.

"Trust me, Otto, it's personal, but believe me I must go."

"All right. You've earned my trust," said Otto.

"I want you to encourage Marlena. I've never seen her so low, even when we left Philo and Biocles on that mountainside or the day in Athens when I marched away with the Romans."

"You've just come back," said Otto. "Sometimes knowing happiness and having it ripped away is worse than never knowing it at all."

Arn hung his head, "I understand. Believe me, I didn't plan things this way."

Otto gave him an embrace. Just before he crushed his ribs, he pushed away. "I'll try to help. You be careful, young Arn."

As Arn found the path through the woods to the road he thought of what a rock Otto had been in his life. He remembered how he had protected Marlena from Daga, how he had found the place for Marlena and him in Melz, and how he had eventually brought them here. And all that time he was risking his relationships with his own family and his friends in Kresboden. He owed a lot to Otto, no question.

That evening Philo had asked Biocles for three more days. When Biocles had gone, Philo fell on his knees beside Alcandor's bed. "Dear Jesus," he said, "I'm not sure how you want me to pray. I only know that I saw you give healing to many people. You didn't invoke any other spirits. You simply asked for belief and spoke simple commands: Rise up and walk; receive your sight; be still; be whole. So I have to believe <u>you</u> had the power. And since you seem to be answering my prayers about Marlena, and since it is possible that you have risen, I believe you still have power. Now I ask you to touch my father and heal him." He felt a hand on his shoulder and when he turned he found Dorea standing silently in her night gown, tears welling in her eyes.

Arn, knowing Marlena was dying a little bit with every hour that he was away, tried to stretch his days. He walked on into the night until he fell with exhaustion. Then, he rose before dawn and was on the road to Athens again.

The fourth day, his body demanded more rest. He lay only a few steps off the road, but behind a clump of trees so he wouldn't attract the attention of roadway robbers. Dawn came, and he slept on. The sun appeared and was climbing slowly above the low bushes and into the morning sky. Still he slept.

At the same time, two horsemen approached Arn's spot. They were Greeks of some means. The horses had fine saddles, and behind the saddles were slung heavily loaded bags. The horsemen exchanged happy banter and proceeded deliberately, but not hurriedly. As they passed Arn's place behind the clump of trees, one of the horses smelled something unusual and whinnied.

The rider, a husky Greek with dark curly hair, reached out to the horse's neck and patted him gently. "Easy, boy," he said softly. "It's probably just a rabbit." The stallion responded with an uninterrupted and steady gait, and the horseman continued his conversation. "You're right," he said. "I've never known anyone as sick as your father to recover so rapidly."

Arn stirred, then rolled over and started to doze again. But the sunlight now struck him directly in the eyes. He blinked awake and looked around. The sun was far advanced. He had overslept. In the back of his mind, as though in a dream, but not in a dream, he heard a horse whinny.

The Greeks continued their banter and enjoyed their morning ride. They came to the crest of the hill just past Arn's spot on the road. Then, from behind them came a blast from strong, young lungs, "Minotaur!"

For over a week Marlena had said very few words. Nixe had tried to cheer her with stories of the goats and even a few songs and dances. Otto, Copella, and Nikos had encouraged her, but her emotions had taken such a plunge that even those she loved the most didn't seem to touch her.

Riding horses, a luxury beyond what any farmer could afford, were a rare sight in the Macedonian hills. So when

Copella, standing at the cottage door, saw them emerge from the woods, she called Marlena to her side.

Marlena sat at the loom letting her detached hands make something happen when she didn't care if anything happened or not. Slowly, she lifted herself and went to the door.

"There are horses out there," said Copella. "What on earth could be happening?"

For a moment they stared into the distance. One horse had two riders. The back rider on the second horse turned his head to one side and the sunlight caught a huge lock of blonde hair. In a flash Marlena recognized all three riders. She leaped from the doorway and bolted down the hillside. It seemed that her feet never touched the ground. All her body weight was gone. Her lissome, slender form floated. The wind of exhilaration carried her like a leaf in a gale. Her golden locks unfurled behind her like the yellow sails of a ship at sea. She waved her arms and shouted as she ran. "It's you, it's you, it's you."

She had thought she would never see this sight. Now the waiting, the frustration, the pain of the days and months and years fell away so suddenly that her heart could scarcely take it in.

Copella watched. She knew Marlena would be happy to see Arn again, but she never expected her to react quite like this. As Marlena neared the horsemen, they all dismounted. Marlena threw herself into Arn's arms and through gasps for air, whispered in his ear as she embraced him.

Then she turned to the other two men. Biocles stood aside knowing that this moment belonged to Philo and Marlena. They stood facing each other, speechless. Marlena was still gasping for breath from her run, from excitement, from joy, from expectation. Her beautiful breasts sank and rose beneath her frock. Tears filled her eyes and streamed down her flushed cheeks causing her flashing violet eyes to shine brighter than polished amethysts and her cheeks to blossom like roses with morning dew.

Philo drank her in. She was more beautiful than ever. Time, hardship, heartbreak, and yet courage had produced in Marlena a beauty of soul that showed in her eyes.

Marlena allowed her senses to be filled with the one before her. He was more handsome than ever. There were the scars of battle to be sure, but they only added character to his chiseled countenance. He was still a stone slab with muscular arms and legs and strong, yet gentle hands. His heavy black brows were raised in astonishment at the sight of her, and his dark blue eyes were open wide as though the lids had been propped with small sticks.

They ached to hold one another, but so much time had passed. Neither could be certain of the other's feelings.

From the corral, Nixe had seen Marlena's dash down the hill. Now she stood, for the first time in her life, seeing her father and mother eye to eye. She saw the love. The confusion that inhibited her parents didn't trouble her a whit.

"Well, are you going to kiss her?" she blurted.

Philo reached out to Marlena, and she fell into his arms. In this embrace they stared into one another's eyes, only inches away. There was the unspoken but clear message that went both ways: I've waited a very long time for this. Now the waiting is over.

Then they kissed, at first lightly. Then, as the moments passed, more deeply. This pleased Nixe beyond her expectations. Copella and Nikos joined the party as Nixe jumped with excitement, and the others clapped and gave a loud shout of joy.

When Philo at last paused for a breath, he put his mouth through the silken hair he loved so much and into Marlena's ear. "Who's the child with the good ideas?" he asked.

Marlena backed away and took Philo's hand. Still staring deep into his eyes she said, "That is the child of the bravest man I've ever known. When my world was being swept away by a storm of terror, he took me by the hand and led me to safety. He risked his life for me many times. I loved him from the first moment I saw him, and I swore to love no other man."

The truth about the child began to saturate Philo's mind. Slowly he turned his gaze from Marlena and looked at Nixe. The blood drained from his face. His heart, already speeding, began to skip beats. He saw his own features looking at him with a broad grin.

Marlena knelt before Nixe. "Nixe," she said, "this is your father."

"Yes, I know," said Nixe.

"You know," burst Philo.

"It's a long story," said Marlena. "I hope we'll have the time to share all of it."

"We'll have all the time it takes," said Philo. He released Marlena's hand and extended his arms to Nixe. "I've always wanted a daughter," he said. "And all this time I've had one."

All the admiration Nixe had accumulated through Marlena's stories came flowing into her heart. She plunged into Philo's arms.

The party included Otto and his family. It lasted long into the night. There was much singing and dancing. Marlena and Philo never took their eyes from one another, and Nixe never quit watching the two of them. "Are you going to have more children like me now?" she blurted, and broke up the group for the evening.

CHAPTER XXXII

There were days of happiness. Marlena and Philo walked in the meadow and along the edge of the woods. They talked about pieces of their lives that the other didn't know. Marlena went back to her childhood and told of her dreadful experiences with Daga. She told about Melz and Hans Helvet and how Arn had won the archery contest and she refused the prize money. Then she told what a protector Otto had been and how he had brought them to this wonderful place. At last she told the whole truth about Nixe.

Philo was overwhelmed. "I saw her limp a bit," he said of Nixe as they walked hand in hand along the edge of the woods. "So that's the reason?"

"Yes, no one gave her much of a chance, but she has proven all of them wrong."

"She's a remarkable child, Marlena, you've taught her your courage and honesty. It won't take any effort on my part to love her."

"Sometimes she's too honest, that child."

"Her questions don't embarrass me. I wouldn't have her any other way," said Philo.

Eventually Marlena told Philo about her trip to Athens with Arn and Nixe. She explained that she had been there the day that Theana was killed.

"Did she know then that I was her father?" asked Philo.

"No. I explained all of that to her on the way back here," said Marlena.

"It must have been terrible for her anyway. It was horrible for me. I have to tell you that I had great love for Theana. I felt that you had left me voluntarily and I didn't know if you were alive or dead."

"It was obvious that you loved her, and, yes, it was bad for Nixe and all of us. My emotions were so mixed, seeing you that way."

"You were alive and healthy, yet you loved someone else, and you were crushed. I fainted right there in the back of the crowd."

"Do you know, I remember a commotion. So that was your fainting. How close we came."

"We couldn't and shouldn't have come any closer," said Marlena. "This is the time and place. In some ways fate has been good to us."

They came to a log lying in the edge of the trees and sat there watching the goats graze in the hillside meadow.

"I suppose this is the right time and place for us," said Philo, "but you have no idea how long I was hurt and angry and still so much in love with you that I wasn't able to function like a normal human being."

Marlena looked at him pleading, "You do understand why I had to leave you, don't you?"

"I suppose I can honestly say that I understand the way you thought. Maybe someday I will be able to believe it was absolutely necessary."

Marlena thought of all the years she had longed to be with Philo. All that time she had felt he would instantly see the necessity of their separation once they were together again. But now she saw something more than misunderstanding in Philo. She saw that through all his love there was still hurt in him, hurt that would take time for healing.

One thing the hurt showed her was how deeply he loved her. She would show him her trust now. She would love him and never leave him. She took his face in her hands and looked into his dark blue eyes.

"My dearest, Philo," she said, "I'm so sorry for all those years." She overlooked his love for Theana and tried to bridge the gap of time. "I want you to know that I never would have had it like that if I hadn't been convinced your life was in grave danger. Can't you see my life has been incomplete. I've waited all this time and would have waited longer."

He could see she was telling the truth. What kind of man was he not to see her pain, her sacrifice, her fidelity. Then, he told himself, now is the time to shed your wounds not coddle them.

"I'm sorry, Marlena," he said. "I thought all that old hurt had ended a long time ago, but here I show it again. I promise you, you will never see it any more, ever."

"On our way from Judea Arn told me you've been too busy to think about marriage," he said. "I don't know when I've ever been so glad to hear anything, but now I want you to take time to think about it. Before I left Athens, when my father was so ill, I shopped for many days until I found a ring for you. It's a special ring that I want you to wear to show that you're my wife. So much time has been taken from us, let's not let anymore slip through our fingers. Let's be married this week."

Marlena put her lips to his in a long, soft kiss then drew away. "With all my heart I want to marry you," she said, "but can you give me long enough to get a dress?"

Philo laughed, "Oh, you are very much the woman," he whispered. "I couldn't love you so much if you weren't. Yes, I want our wedding to be all you desire."

Then he kissed her again and this time the kiss was not only long but passionate.

They spent evenings with Otto's family sitting around an open fire in front of the stone house with the yellow trim. Ziggy and Ava enjoyed collecting firewood before dark, then setting the blaze just as the sun set.

The group, now eleven strong, sat around the fire and sang familiar songs while Copella played her flute. Later, they began to talk of love and family and things that last.

Eventually Philo, Biocles, and Arn were telling once again about Jesus. They told of his teachings, and about the miracles they had seen him perform. Then, they told about how some of the Jews thought he was part God or maybe all God, what they called the Messiah or Christ.

At last, Philo and Biocles told about the enigmatic thing he had said to them when they had talked to him personally: "A seed of wheat must fall to the ground and die or else it remains alone; but if it falls and dies, it produces much fruit." What must this mean?

They all sat quietly thinking about it.

Nixe found Arn's lap and whispered into his ear, "My daddy is handsome too, but not as much as you."

"I love you, little elf," he whispered back.

Copella was the one who broke the silence in the circle around the fire.

"Have you ever been so occupied with someone else's happiness that you forgot about yourself?" she said. "Maybe Jesus meant that we are at our best when someone else's happiness is more important to us than our own."

They thought awhile. "So the death would be to your own happiness and the fruit would be other people's happiness," said Nikos.

"Well, yes, except in the long run the happiness comes right back to you," said Copella.

Otto spoke next, "I know that, in battle, a warrior who considers himself already dead is the most fearless warrior of all."

Philo, moving his eyes from Marlena for the first time all evening, looked across the circle at Biocles sitting with his arms around Ava and Ziggy. For the last few days Biocles had remained almost silent. He had moved quietly about soaking up the love he felt from every direction.

"And what about a friend," Philo said, "who is willing to give anything for the happiness of his friend, completely denying himself."

He left Marlena's side and walked by the fire and across the circle. Facing Biocles he said, "Stand up, Minotaur."

Biocles stood. Philo gave him a long hug, then returned to his seat beside Marlena.

The truth of those words and that act then began to affect them all. One by one they became aware of the selfless sacrifices everyone in the circle had made. Otto had risked his life for Marlena, Arn, and Nixe. Katarina had often faced life alone with her children because of Otto's absence. Copella and Nikos had opened their entire lives to strangers. Marlena, alone, had raised Arn and Nixe, not asking anything for herself. Arn had risked his life for Philo and Biocles. On into the night they found themselves seeing in one another some of the truth spoken by Jesus. It was part of what had brought them together. It was part of what held them together uniquely.

When they were back at the stone house with the light blue trim, Philo sat before the fireplace and drew Nixe into his lap. They were alone while the rest of the family retired. Nixie snuggled as much of her body as she could get against Philo.

"I have a young sister that I love very much. You remind me of her in many ways," said Philo.

"What's her name?" asked Nixe.

"Her name is Dorea. She is three or four years older than you, a beautiful young lady bent on being the actress."

"Is she what you want to talk about?"

"I could very well talk a long time about her, but no. I only mentioned her because she is so young, so active, and so intelligent like yourself. I see you and think of her. I've brought you a special gift, and she was very close to the former owner of this gift," Philo said softly. "When I left

Athens I didn't know why I was compelled to pack this, but now I know it has to be for you, my daughter."

"Oh, that's wonderful," said Nixe, turning her head to face him, anticipation in her eyes.

"You must allow me to explain," said Philo.

"Do you have to explain now," said Nixe. "Can't I just see the gift?"

"No, not yet. Now listen."

"All right."

"You must understand that ever since I first saw her, I have loved your mother. Nothing will ever change that."

"But she had to leave you and you didn't know you would ever see her again," joined Nixe.

"Exactly. So I met and married a very wonderful lady— no less wonderful than your mother, very much different, but no less wonderful. Do you understand?"

"There will never be anyone as wonderful as my mother," said Nixe.

"It's good for you to feel that way, and I hope you never change, but you do know there are other wonderful women, don't you?"

"Yes, of course, like Copie," said Nixe.

"The lady's name was Theana. She died standing for what she believed was true and good."

"I saw her die," said Nixe, head bowed. "It was horrible. She was a beautiful lady."

"That's right. Your mother told me," said Philo. "And I have asked Marlena for permission to give you this."

"Why?"

"Because there should never be any secrets or jealousy between any of us, and this gift I give you belonged to Theana. I give it to you because Theana was a part of me I'll never forget, and because her memory will always stand for bravery and goodness. Someday you will learn more about her, but for now, I simply want you to know that I give you a gift that means much to me and someday, hopefully, will mean more to you."

Then, Philo reached into his pouch and produced a beautiful green malachite necklace. Nixe's mouth hung open wide, and she gasped.

"I've never seen anything so beautiful. Wherever would I wear it?"

"You must keep it in a safe place and cherish it. Maybe you will have an occasion to wear it soon. We'll see."

The next morning Nixe came running from her milking. The others were gathered at the table when she came through the door. "Electra's gone," she exclaimed.

"Surely not," said Nikos, the only one in the group who understood that crazy, amiable animal as Nixe did. "Isn't she in the meadow?"

"No, no," cried Nixe. It was almost as if Nixe didn't need to look anywhere. She sensed within herself that Electra was gone.

Copella rose from her seat and went to Nixe. "Don't you fret, child," she said. "We'll find that demented animal."

"She's not demented, Copie. She, she's just different."

"I know you love her, and we'll find her," said Nikos rising from the table. "Arn, why don't you and Biocles go by Otto's house and tell him to look after the goats today. Then just continue in that direction looking for Electra. Philo, you and Marlena take Nixe and go into the woods. Copella and I will go toward the village."

When all the searchers returned that evening, there was no word of Electra. The same was true of the days following. It was a minor problem for most of them but a disaster for Nixe.

Somewhere in Eastern Macedonia, two evangelists walked the road coming west. One was a bit short, but had an aristocratic bearing. He had a round face with black hair and beard and heavy eyebrows. His conversation gave evidence of intelligence and education.

His partner was older, taller, more relaxed. His hair, originally dark also, was now sprinkled with gray.

Their conversation was lively; their pace crisp. They hardly noticed a black burro with no driver, rider, or burden come round the bend ahead and down the center of the road straight for them.

The burro stopped only a few steps away and faced them with baleful, sad eyes. Then the older man spoke. "Someone has lost this animal. What should we do?"

"His home is probably near," said the younger man. "What can we do? We don't know where to take her."

"I suppose you're right," said the older man. "Still she has an unusual lostness about her."

"What do you suggest?"

The older man went to the burro, patted her soft nose, and cuffed her ear. She gave a neigh of contentment.

The evangelists then stepped aside and continued down the road. The burrow followed them giving a low whinny now and again.

The younger man turned and tried to shoo her away. "Go on now. You can't follow us. You'll be too far from home. Shoo, shoo," he said waving his arms.

The donkey turned from the road and walked into the nearby trees.

"You never should have patted her," said the younger man to the older.

Two hours later, when the travelers were deep in conversation, the older man felt a soft bump against his behind. He turned to behold the stubborn burro.

Through the rest of the day, that night, and on into the next day, the two evangelists couldn't dissuade the donkey from following them. They had shouted at her, railed against her, and even thrown pebbles at her all to no avail. She would disappear for a while then reappear as determined to be with them as ever.

"We might as well get some good from her," said the resigned older man. "Why don't we ride her?"

"We have no rope with which to lead her," said the younger man.

"Well, she doesn't want to leave us, and she doesn't walk fast. Why don't I just try without any rein?" With that, the older man took the burro's mane and mounted her. She seemed satisfied and continued her journey down the road.

So it was that the two travelers took turns riding the donkey, letting her rest from time to time. They found water for her and watched her graze in the lush meadows of late summer.

A day later they could see a small village ahead. People along the way said the village was Florina, a peaceful town where they could find food and rest. So they agreed that it was time to stop for a while.

As they came to the inn at Florina, the younger man was riding the burro as the older walked along beside them. He grasped her mane and ordered her to stop. But the burro did not stop. Instead, she quickened her pace. "Stop, stop," cried the younger man pulling the animal's mane insistently.

"Stop, stop," cried the older man running along behind, barely able to keep up.

"You crazy beast, you've poked along for two days. Why are you rushing now?" said the younger man.

The burro pranced insolently ahead disregarding all admonitions to do otherwise.

An unspoken voice seemed to resound through the disgruntled rider's head. "Let the donkey go. Don't hold her back."

The rider spoke as if to the sky. "Who's holding her back, Lord?"

The older man had seen the younger man talk to an invisible God before. "Go ahead," he said. "I'll keep up the best I can."

Out of town the donkey went and on into the country side.

Nixe sat atop the stone corral fence looking out onto the goat-filled meadow and mourning Electra's disappearance when from amidst the goats emerged the strangest sight she had ever seen.

A small man came riding Electra. Electra was running faster than she had ever run, which was still not too fast. The man held Electra's mane with one hand while the other waved wildly in the air. Then, behind them came an older man, disheveled, hair blown, dust on his face and panting for breath as though he would soon die.

Electra came straight for the corral gate, slammed to a stop, and sent her rider flying to the ground. Lying there in the dirt, he shook himself and began laughing. "Lord," he said seemingly to no one, "that was fun, but I'm glad it's over with."

He stood, dusted himself off, then spotted Nixe. "Young lady, does this insane animal belong to you?" he asked.

Nixe had not stopped laughing. Now she came running to hug Electra's neck. "Oh, Electra, I've missed you so," she said, as Electra gave a loud bray of happiness.

"Sir, thank you so much for bringing my Electra back," she said.

"There's some question as to who brought whom," said the traveler. "May I ask who resides here?"

"This is the farm of Nikos and Copella," she replied. "We would love for you to visit us."

"We just might do that," the man said. Then he strode to the door of the farmhouse and knocked, his older partner having caught up by then stood at his side. The door swung open to reveal a white-haired couple.

"And you must be Nikos and Copella," the man said.

"We are," said the surprised Copella. "And who might you be?"

"I'm Paul of Tarsus, an apostle of Jesus the Christ lately come from Antioch on the Orontes, and this is my partner, Barnabas, an evangelist of like persuasion."

"And you have brought Electra," said Nikos seeing Nixe making over her in the corral.

"That is an unusual beast," said Paul. "I'll tell you about it, but first I must know one thing."

"Yes?" said Nikos.

"Has anyone here heard yet of the wonderful news of Jesus of Nazareth?"

CHAPTER XXXIII

Paul and Barnabas had supper with the group in the little stone house with the light blue trim that night. The table was barely large enough, but they all squeezed in. Philo explained to the visitors about the fireside meetings at Otto's house and told how, indeed, Jesus had been the subject of many conversations.

"I'm anxious to know how you happened to be in Jerusalem and what your encounter with the Lord was like," said Paul.

"We've come a long way to tell people the good news they've never heard, and here we find people who already know about Jesus," said a smiling Barnabas.

"It would be incredible if we hadn't seen the Lord already do greater things," said Paul.

Nixe liked Barnabas. She went to his side and placed her hand on his shoulder. "Do you think Jesus liked children?" she said.

Barnabas took Nixe's hand with both of his own. He looked into her curious, affable face. "I'm absolutely certain of it," he said.

Nixe hugged his neck and so captured his heart. It was stored in the already packed trophy room of her own spirit, another trapped prize of which she was totally unaware.

That evening the group around the fire had grown from eleven to thirteen. Nikos introduced Paul and Barnabas. He told how Electra had delivered them and that, therefore, they must be received with appropriate dignity.

Paul rose amid the chuckles. "I greet you all in the name of our Lord Jesus Christ," he began. "It is He who has sent us into this land. We have come knowing only that all people everywhere deserve to know of the righteousness in Jesus and the power of his resurrection."

"His resurrection?" many of them said.

"Yes," said Paul. "I, myself, have seen Him more than once, and He has called me to bring word of Him to the gentiles."

Nixe sat on Philo's lap. She whispered in his ear, "What's a gentile?"

Philo whispered back, "Anyone not a Jew, I think."

"But … ," she started, then Philo placed a finger over her lips.

"Let's listen," he said.

Paul continued, "I want to tell you many things about Jesus, but first I want to hear what you already know."

Philo, Biocles, and Arn told of their experiences in Judea. They told about all the things Caleb had said and how at the crucifixion he had come to believe that Jesus was the Christ, how they all had. Finally, they heard a story about Jesus being resurrected, but they were hardly able to believe it.

Paul rose again, "You have believed ahead of me," he said. "I persecuted the Christians, even consented that they be killed. Then, one day as I traveled about seeking more Christians to persecute, Jesus appeared to me. He told me I was not going God's way, but against God. He struck me blind so that I staggered about and people had to lead me."

"How did you get your sight back?" asked Nikos.

"A man of God came and asked Jesus to restore my sight. I promised him I would serve Jesus as He empowered me."

"That seems strange," said Philo. "How could he empower you? Even if He is resurrected, He is still far from most people. Surely He is over in Judea, not here."

"That's the best part of the good news," said Paul. "Do you remember that Jesus said: 'God is spirit'?"

"Yes," said Biocles. "I remember that."

"Now Jesus is become spirit and His Spirit is everywhere. It is, in fact, his promise that His Spirit will dwell with all who believe."

A hush fell over the entire group. For days they had heard Philo, Biocles, and Arn tell of the gentle, loving, powerful things that Jesus had done. Could this spirit, this power be theirs?

Paul stood still, sensing a movement of God. He dared not speak, he dared not move.

Philo didn't rise to his feet, but he spoke deliberately, distinctly: "Some of you know that since I was barely more than a lad, I've had a longing to know the true god or gods. It didn't matter to me what language he spoke or what country he was from. I felt that the true god could transcend such things. In that I think I was correct.

When I met Jesus of Nazareth and saw how he lived, I began to understand more of what life is about, and I saw myself more clearly. He was a Jew and I a Greek, but I sensed infinite love coming from him. Since I saw Him on the cross at Jerusalem, I have believed that he was the Son of God, and that, by some mysterious power, he was dying there for me, the lamb of God as Caleb explained. Now, because of Paul's words and because of my own answered prayers, I believe that Jesus lives and that his spirit will inhabit my own."

"I, too, believe," said Arn.

"I believe," said Marlena.

"I believe," said Biocles.

And on this belief spread until the circle about the fire was complete.

The next day Marlena, at last, agreed to let Philo out of her sight. He, Paul, and Barnabas walked the hill above the stone houses. They spoke of many things about Jesus and about what a Christ-life, a Christian life, should be.

"There are two things I want to ask you about," said Philo. "First of all, Jesus left Biocles and me with an

286

enigma. He said to us, 'A seed of wheat must fall to the ground and die, or it remains alone. But if it dies, it bears much fruit.' We've talked a lot about that here, and we aren't sure we know exactly what He meant." Then he told Paul and Barnabas about the different things Copella, Otto, and others had said that night by the fire.

"I can see how our Lord would say that," said Paul. "And your group has put much of the sense to it. But let's look at the situation and the desire of your heart as you approached Jesus. He always addressed himself, not just to the words of people, but to the questions in their hearts.

"You came with the stated desire to see Jesus, but you came with the question in your heart as to how you might find the one true God. Then when you saw him, he told you about the death of the wheat grain and subsequently the production of more wheat."

"That's right," said Philo. "Are you telling me now that Jesus gave us answers to both our desires and our questions in that simple but puzzling proverb?"

"I think so," said Paul.

"Let's sit a while," said Barnabas as they came to the large boulder atop the stone escarpment.

They found the smooth, flat place where Arn and Marlena enjoyed sitting. There they rested, looking out over the valley below. As he seated himself, Paul continued. "Let's look first at your stated desire: We would see Jesus. He obviously saw your sincerity because he was telling you something that he didn't reveal to many people: that you couldn't truly know him by simply looking on his face.

"Take a grain of wheat in your hand and look at it. You feel that you see it, a plain small seed, smooth and hard. It would take many such to amount to anything at all. But you take that seed and place it in fertile soil. Presently a green shoot appears."

Paul talked with his hands and arms as well as his mouth. He held his right hand over the rock as though it had become the fertile soil. Then he began to raise it slowly. "Soon the green shoot becomes a stalk, and the stalk puts forth branches and leaves."

Now Paul used both hands, spread out well above the rock to indicate a large, growing plant. "Then new wheat appears in great numbers. You no longer see the original grain, but you see its life propagated and its likeness multiplied. Last night we saw that principle lived out in the lives of new believers.

"By the parable he was saying, 'You are looking at my face, the seed. You won't know the essence of my being, however, until I have experienced the crucifixion and resurrection, just as you can't know the power of the seed until you witness its death and reemergence.'"

Paul dropped his hands and looked at Philo. "He knew you wouldn't be able to understand all of this at the time, but he trusted you to stay with your searching. It was actually quite a compliment."

"Perhaps," said Philo. "It seems to me that every word I hear about Jesus causes me to stand more in awe of him."

"Now let's look at what he was telling you about your search for God. In essence it was this, Philo: In order for a person to know God, he must be willing to let God be God of his own life."

"Spiritual insight is not God's reward for intellectual curiosity. He honors the falling to the ground, the death, of that part of us that would be our own god. He honors the faith that says to him: I trust you more than I trust myself. He honors our seeking his will, his direction. Then as we walk with him, live in his instruction, he reveals himself to us more and more as time goes by."

"And how would a person know the will, the direction of this God," asked Philo.

"I find that, if I wake up in the morning trusting him, he will break into my thoughts if he has to. Sometimes I will actually hear his voice, but most of the time he simply impresses my mind."

"I talk to Jesus a lot, call it prayer, whatever. I worship him in songs and praises. Then he breaks through the cares of the day and reveals himself to me."

"It's a hard thing, to give up on yourself," said Philo.

"Jesus meant for it to be hard," answered Paul. "That's the reason he spoke of it in terms of death. The seed dies. From now on men will have to answer the question: Is God's peace, power, joy, and love worth the sacrifice?"

For a while they all sat silently. Then Philo stood and began to pace the space of the boulder top. He began to remember so many times he had thought only of himself: All the time he spent in self pity after Theana's death, the devastating effect that had on his family and friends; the times he had abused his friendship with Biocles by imposing his own desires upon him; on and on his mind raced back over the years and he saw selfishness. At last he remembered only a few days before when he had tried to make Marlena feel guilty when, indeed, she had sacrificed much of her life for him.

Philo could easily see his own failure, but he felt himself standing on a burning bridge. He had a chance to go back to the old way or to go forward to the new, but this might very well be his last chance.

At last he spoke, "It sounds as if God wants to take away all that I am, my entire personality."

Paul and Barnabas were still sitting on the boulder. Paul didn't look at him, but instead spoke to the space before him. "Quite the contrary," he said. "When you allow God to control your life, he will enhance every good quality of your personality. After all, he made you and loves you."

Then he stood and went to Philo. He put an arm around his shoulder and walked with him. "I like to think of it this way: I reckon my own choices dead as with Jesus, just as he relished doing, not his own will, but the Father's. Still I live more gloriously than ever because Jesus lives in and through me. The way he lived and died showed me what love is. Now I trust him, in that love, to be my life."

He paused and looked at Philo.

"It's our will that must die," said Philo.

"Exactly."

"Then, our will being dead allows His will to live in us and His power to flow through us. That's the fruit."

"Exactly, Philo, exactly," said Paul. "Faith allows us to see through the sacrifice to the joy. I've talked to Christian disciples many times. They've told me that Jesus hardly ever spoke of his death that he didn't speak also of his resurrection. This saying of the seed does exactly the same thing. Jesus saw through the pain to the glory. Now he is allowing you to see through the death to the fruit."

A glow came upon Philo's face, and a warmth spread throughout his body. He was crossing the bridge in God's direction. Then he said something that startled Paul and Barnabas. "We must have faith that God will make love work."

Paul scratched his beard.

Barnabas had listened intently. "Yes," he said, "in spite of all those times it looks like it isn't working, love is still His will."

They started back to the farmhouse, three abreast. For a time they were quiet. Then Paul remembered. "What was the second thing?" he asked.

Philo looked at him blankly, his mind was far away.

"You said there were two things you wanted to ask us about."

"There certainly were," said Philo.

"Then what's the other?" asked Barnabas.

` "What would a Christian wedding be like?" asked Philo.

This amused Paul and Barnabas greatly. When their laughing died, Paul said, "You know the joke may be on us.

I'm not sure of details, but I feel certain we can work it out."

That late summer morning the sun came quickly, no clouds impeding its progress. The meadow before the little stone house with the light blue trim was, by mid morning, filled with decorated goats. They had bells and wild flower garlands of all colors. Some even had striped and spotted coats. Persephone had a coat of light blue, matching the trim on the house. She also sported a field lily necklace of white blooms with small russet spots. She would bleat loudly with pride through the whole ceremony. The one-eyed Hercules and lop-eared Agamemnon wore regal crowns of daisies. Electra stood amid the goats clad in a huge yellow ribbon that encircled her body and came to a bow at her mane. Everyone wore their best. Nixe had found a time to wear the beautiful malachite necklace. It was the center piece of her outfit, a frilly white dress with a bright green sash. But Marlena stood out like a clean pearl in a coal field. Copella and Katerina had bleached pure, white goat thread in the sun and woven a beautiful wedding gown for Marlena. Marlena's hair, golden and silken, was cut short at her forehead and hung in luxurious locks to her waist behind. Across the crown of her head, a tiara of white arbutus rested. All of this paled in comparison to the glow on her face.

She stood in the meadow, holding Arn with her right arm and Nixe with her left hand. Beside them stood Philo, Biocles at his side.

Before them stood Paul and Nikos. Copella was playing the flute as everyone talked happily. Persephone was bleating so that she inspired the other goats to bleat too. Electra brayed occasionally to add to the tumult.

Then Copella laid down the flute, and all except the animals was quiet.

Paul began, "From the beginning," he said, "God placed man and woman together to be part of a perfect world. And God said that the two would become as one flesh, each deferring to the other."

"And Jesus, our Lord, blessed marriage. He has compared His own relationship to His people as a marriage.

"So we come today to join Marlena and Philo in marriage. Their hearts have been knit. We all see that. We have only come to bless and sanctify that knitting."

Nikos now spoke. "Our wishes today are that this marriage will be a long and happy one. Everyone here pledges you both our support."

Everyone lifted a hand into the air, "We do, we do," they cried.

Paul then looked at Philo. "I understand that there is a ring," he said.

Biocles reached into his pocket, extracted a band of gold, and handed it to Paul. Paul held it up for all to see. The sun caught facets of its sculpture so that it sparkled as though it were aflame. Then he lowered it before his own eyes.

"There's something very special about this ring," he said. "First, it's an unbroken circle of pure gold. The purity of the gold represents the purity of the love these two have for each other. The circle represents a love that is unending.

"There is another thing about this ring. It is the likeness of two grape vine branches inseparably intertwined. We now have before us two people who are bound, not only to one another, but also to Jesus Christ. When Philo bought this ring, he was both remembering and hoping. He was remembering the words Jesus spoke: I am the vine and you are the branches. He was hoping that one day soon Marlena would have the blessing of Christ's spirit in her life. Now this has come to pass so that the ring has all of its intended significance: two Christian people joined inseparably in the love of Christ and in love for one another."

The women gave audible sighs as their hearts were warmed with the memory of their own wedding day.

Paul handed the ring to Philo who slipped it onto Marlena's finger. She blushed like a school girl as she looked at the ring, and then she raised her eyes to Philo. The love between them was electric.

"Do you promise to love and protect one another as long as you live?" Paul asked Philo and Marlena.

Together they said, "We do."

Paul lifted both arms to the sky and looked into the heavens. "We all pray God's blessing on this union," he said.

Then again the meadow rang with "We do, we do!"

Philo took Marlena in his arms and gave her a long, passionate kiss. Everyone began to shout for joy, Copella played the flute again. The animals brayed and bleated.

Nixe went around giving out bags of flower petals. They waited until everyone had the petals, then Otto hoisted Nixe to his shoulders. "Now," she cried.

Everyone threw the flower petals up into the summer breeze. The warm zephyrs caught them and lifted them above the meadow and out over the treetops.

EPILOGUE

Philo, Marlena, Nixe, and Biocles returned to Athens. From time to time, Otto returned to Kresboden. Arn went to Melz and many other places. Wherever they went, they told the good things about Jesus.

They promised to return every four years to the little goat farm in Macedonia. There they would marvel at the growth of Nixe, Ava, and Ziggie. They would relish the hospitality of Nikos, Copella, Otto, and Katarina. They would tell stories of their hardships and triumphs.

And they would once again acknowledge the truth they had learned: There is no greater mission than seeking God; there is no greater peace than knowing God; and there is no greater joy than serving God. And somewhere in the midst of this seeking, knowing, and serving, all we like seeds must fall.

About the Author

Roy Melton has spent most of his seventy-two years living in Little Rock, Arkansas. He was educated in Little Rock Public Schools, the University of Arkansas, and Washington University in St. Louis. After two years in the U.S. Air Force, he returned home where he practiced dentistry for over thirty years.

Dr. Melton is a lifelong Christian and student of the Bible. He has been a Baptist deacon for nearly forty years and an interdenominational speaker for thirty.

He has been author of many published magazine and newspaper articles. In 1992, he won the *Guidepost* Writers' Workshop award. This is his first novel.

Available wherever books are sold
or call 1-800-839-8640